W9-CZW-593

Letter from Home

Also by Carolyn Hart
in Large Print:

April Fool Dead
Engaged to Die
Death in Paradise
Resort to Murder
Sugarplum Dead
White Elephant Dead

Letter from Home

Carolyn Hart

Thorndike Press • Waterville, Maine

Published in 2004 by arrangement with The Berkley Publishing Group, a member of Penguin Group (USA) Inc.

Thorndike Press® Large Print Mystery.

The tree indicium is a trademark of Thorndike Press.

The text of this Large Print edition is unabridged.
Other aspects of the book may vary from the original edition.

Set in 16 pt. Plantin by Christina S. Huff.

Printed in the United States on permanent paper.

Library of Congress Cataloging-in-Publication Data

Hart, Carolyn G.
  Letter from home / Carolyn Hart.
    p. cm.
  ISBN 0-7862-6201-X (lg. print : hc : alk. paper)
  1. Women journalists — Fiction. 2. Women —
Oklahoma — Fiction. 3. Women — Crimes against —
Fiction. 4. Oklahoma — Fiction. 5. Large type books.
I. Title.
PS3558.A676L48 2004
813'.54—dc22   2003064551

To my writing friends who encouraged me:
Mary Daheim, Jean Hager,
Teresa Miller, and Eve Sandstrom.
And to Natalee Rosenstein,
with heartfelt thanks.

As the Founder/CEO of NAVH, the only national health agency solely devoted to those who, although not totally blind, have an eye disease which could lead to serious visual impairment, I am pleased to recognize Thorndike Press★ as one of the leading publishers in the large print field.

Founded in 1954 in San Francisco to prepare large print textbooks for partially seeing children, NAVH became the pioneer and standard setting agency in the preparation of large type.

Today, those publishers who meet our standards carry the prestigious "Seal of Approval" indicating high quality large print. We are delighted that Thorndike Press is one of the publishers whose titles meet these standards. We are also pleased to recognize the significant contribution Thorndike Press is making in this important and growing field.

Lorraine H. Marchi, L.H.D.
Founder/CEO
NAVH

★ Thorndike Press encompasses the following imprints: Thorndike, Wheeler, Walker and Large Print Press.

Dear Gretchen,

You're rich and famous now. You've been all over the world, seen things I'll never see, met people I'll never know. I saw you once on TV going to a big night at the Kennedy Center. You had on a white satin gown and it looked like a diamond necklace around your throat. That was a handsome man with you. . . .

Chapter

1

The rusted iron gate sagged from the stone pillar. A winter-brown vine clung to the stones. Pale March sunlight filtered through the bare branches of sycamores and oaks, throwing thin black shadows as distinct as stylized brushwork in a Japanese painting. My cane poked through a mound of tawny leaves, some wizened and wrinkled as old faces, some damp and soggy, smelling of must and rot and decay. The rutted road looked much narrower than I remembered.

When I'd last been in the cemetery, most of the headstones, even those dating back to Indian Territory days, had stood straight. Now many were tilted and some had tumbled to the ground, half hidden by leaves. Remnants of a late snow spangled shaded spots.

I walked slowly, stabbing my cane at the uneven ground. Nothing looked familiar. Our graves were surely this way. . . . Oh, of course. The weeping willow was gone. I'd always marked our family plot by a huge willow, its dangling fronds shiny green in summer, bare and brown in winter. A stump leaned crookedly near the plot.

I paused to rest for a moment. The sharp wind rustled the bare branches of the sycamores and oaks. I shivered, grateful for the warmth of my cashmere coat and leather gloves. I plunged my left hand into a pocket of my coat. My gloved fingers closed around the letter. The name on the return address had not been familiar, but I had recognized the postmark. My first thought when I received the square cream envelope had been as instinctive as breathing: Why, it's a letter from home. Second came a quiver of utter surprise. Home? I'd not been back to the little town in northeastern Oklahoma since I was a girl. Home . . .

When I opened the envelope and lifted

out three pages — cheap paper with violently colored roses twining down one side, the writing a dense, almost indecipherable scrawl — I almost threw the sheets away unread. The salutation stopped me: *Dear Gretchen.* No one had called me Gretchen for well over a half century. Gretchen . . . Across a span of time, I remembered a girl, dark-haired, blue-eyed, slim and eager, who seemed quite separate and distinct from the old woman walking determinedly toward the graves.

I remembered that long-ago girl. . . .

Gretchen clutched the folded sheaf of yellow copy paper and a thick dark-leaded pencil, sharp enough for writing but the point too blunt to break. That was just how Mr. Dennis did it when he covered the city council. Her first day at the *Gazette*, he'd waggled a thick handful of copy paper. "This is all you need, Gretchen. Take some paper and a couple of pencils, listen hard, make notes you can read, write your story fast."

It still seemed strange to walk toward Victory Café and not hurry inside, welcoming the familiar smells of cinnamon rolls and coffee and bacon. Victory Café — she was almost used to the name now. It used to be

9

Pfizer Café but after Pearl Harbor when people began to talk about Nazis and Krauts as well as the Japs, Grandmother hired Elwyn Haskins to paint a new name in bright red and blue against a white background: Victory Café. There was a small American flag near the cash register and the mirror behind the counter held pictures of men in the service. Anyone could bring a photo and Grandmother would tape it up. Now people were beginning to believe in victory, especially since the invasion, though it seemed that the convoys rolling through on Highway 66 were longer than ever and the trains clacking past day and night pulled more and more flatcars carrying tanks and trucks and jeeps. Sometimes soldiers leaned from open windows and waved.

Gretchen stopped for the red light at Broadway and Main. She waited impatiently. The light was new and lots of people honked their horns at it when they had to stop. There'd been a big fight in city council about putting in a stoplight. Mayor Burkett got his way, insisting their town needed the light. After all, he'd pointed out, everything was different because of the war and they had plenty of traffic, people stopping off from Highway 66 and soldiers coming over the Missouri line from Camp Crowder and local folks streaming into town to buy whatever shopkeepers had to offer. There were lots of people in town every day, but most of them were old or middle-aged. The young men in uniform were never there for long, off for three-day passes and sometimes ten-day furloughs before their units were set to ship out. There wasn't much to buy, but people had money from war work. Lots of townspeople like Gretchen's mom had gone to Tulsa to work in the Douglas plant. Mom was making good money, more than they'd ever seen, thirty-five dollars a week. The Billup Shoe Store had closed. Mr. Billup couldn't get enough shoes. Most everybody had to depend upon friends or family to find shoes at Froug's or Brown-Dunkin in Tulsa and rationing only allowed two pairs a year anyway. Mr. Pinkley's gas station went out of business, but there was a motel — Sweet Dreams — on the edge of town, and some new little houses built from lumber salvaged from old barns and the abandoned Morris house. Mr. McCrory's gas station was going great guns despite rationing. He specialized in repairs and everybody needed to keep their old cars running for the duration.

When the light changed, Gretchen hurried across the street. She wanted to run, but she held herself to a fast walk. She, Gretchen Grace Gilman, was on her way to the court-house, the big red sandstone building that looked like a castle with bays and turrets. When she was little, she'd made up a story in her mind about a princess held captive in a turret and a handsome swashbuckler like Errol Flynn leaping ledge to ledge, sword in hand, coming to the rescue of the fair maiden. That had been exciting but nothing to compare to the excitement she felt now. The courthouse was her beat and so was city hall on Cimarron Street. Of course, Mr. Dennis or Mr. Cooley covered the big sto-ries, but there was plenty for Gretchen to write about. She'd been to both the court-house and city hall first thing this morning, checked the sheriff's office for any overnight calls, asked the court clerk about lawsuits, dropped by the county records office to see about deeds registered, and scanned the po-lice blotter at the police station. This was her last run to the courthouse and city hall for the day. She'd already turned in her stories for today's paper. Last deadline was one o'clock, but that was for late-breaking news, wire stories from the war front, especially the fighting in Normandy. Ever since D-Day, they'd had a map on page 1 showing the progress of the fighting. Most of her stories were turned in by ten. The press run was at two. She glanced across Main at the café. The windows needed a wash. Mrs. Perkins did a pretty good job. But she couldn't — or wouldn't — move as fast as Gretchen and she didn't help Grandmother the way Gretchen did when she worked there. That's how Gretchen had expected to spend the summer until the miracle happened: Mrs. Jacobs, the junior high English teacher, telling Mr. Dennis that Gretchen wanted to grow up and be a reporter and that she'd make a good hand while the *Gazette* was so short-staffed because of the war. Mrs. Jacobs told Gretchen to go ask for a job when Joe Bob Terrell was drafted. Gretchen had put on her favorite dress — a yellow-and-white-checked dirndl with starfish appliqués at the shoulder and near the hem and white ricrac as an accent at the neck, waist, and skirt — and pulled on short white gloves and a yellow straw hat. She didn't have any good summer shoes, but she'd taken her white sandals and polished them and hoped Mr. Dennis wouldn't notice that the straps were frayed. She'd never forget, never in a thousand million years, that May afternoon. School was almost out and Mrs. Jacobs got her excused from last hour. It was only May but it was hot, the temperature nudging toward ninety.

Everybody said it was going to be a hot summer, the summer of 1944. But Gretchen didn't remember any summers when it hadn't been hot and dry and sometimes the wind blew dust through town, coating the buildings, turning the sky a smudgy orange. At the café, they'd wipe everything with a damp cloth, but it was hard to keep the dust out of the booths and off the tables and chairs and they'd come home to a house with a fine layer of dust on everything. It wasn't dusty that May afternoon. The sky glittered a sharp, bright, clear blue and she'd held tight to her hat as the Oklahoma wind gusted, bending the trees, skittering trash down the street. When she got to the *Gazette* office, she'd stared at the door and been so scared she'd almost turned and run away. Could she do it? She was editor of the *Wolf Cry*, the junior high newspaper. Mrs. Jacobs liked her stories, had given her bylines all this past year. One story, the one about Millard, Mrs. Jacobs sent in to the interscholastic contest. When Gretchen won first prize, she'd felt funny, happy, and sad at the same time. But Millard would have been proud for her. Mrs. Jacobs had told Gretchen to cut out all her stories and take them to show Mr. Dennis. Mrs. Jacobs called them "clips." Somehow, her hand sweaty, her stomach a hard tight knot, Gretchen opened the door and walked inside. To her left was a door marked ADVERTISING CIRCULATION. Straight ahead was a square room with a half dozen desks. A telephone shrilled. In one corner, the clacking Teletype spewed out paper in an endless stream. Mrs. Jacobs had brought their whole class to visit the *Gazette* last fall and she'd been most excited to show them the Teletype, the very latest news from United Press coming in over a leased wire. Only one desk was occupied. A stocky man, shiny bald except for a fringe of gray hair, typed so fast it sounded like a machine gun. Smoke wreathed upward from a pipe cradled in a ceramic ashtray shaped like the state of Oklahoma. A door in the far wall banged open. A smell of hot metal rolled toward her. An old man with long sideburns and a big white mustache stuck out his head, shouting to be heard over a clattery metallic noise. "That newsprint ain't here yet, Walt. You better check again." The door slammed, cutting off the metal ping of the Linotypes, making the newsroom seem quiet in comparison. Gretchen walked slowly toward the occupied desk. "Mr. Dennis."

He continued to hunch over the big old typewriter, eyes squinting in concentration, fingers flying.

"Mr. Dennis." His head jerked around. Deep lines grooved the editor's round face. His mouth turned down. Greenish blue eyes glittered beneath bristly brows. He glowered. "What do you want, girl?"

Gretchen wanted to run away. But he'd told Mrs. Jacobs he had to have somebody quick. Gretchen thrust out her hand with the folder holding her clips. Her hand shook. "Mrs. Jacobs said for me to bring my clips. I'm Gretchen Gilman."

He grabbed his pipe, took a deep puff. His thick eyebrows were tufted like an owl's. He snapped, "I told her I wanted a boy. She said nobody was good enough. So here you are." The emphasis on the pronoun was sour. "How old are you, girl?"

Gretchen stood as tall as her five feet three inches would stretch. "I'm almost fourteen." Well, she'd be fourteen in September. That was almost, wasn't it?

"Fourteen." He heaved a sigh. "God damn this war." He puffed on the pipe, pinned her with his glittering eyes. "Can you write, girl?"

"Yes." Her answer came out clear and definite, as definite as the crack of the exhaust when Dr. Jamison floorboarded his old car, as definite as the peal of the bells from the Catholic church on Sunday mornings, as definite as the big, black headlines yesterday about the Germans fleeing Monte Cassino.

The editor studied her a moment longer, reached out for her clips, riffled through them, stopped to read one. He took so long, Gretchen knew he was reading it twice. When he looked up, his dark impatient glance swept her up and down. "Don't believe in women in a newsroom. Except for soc." He pronounced it "sock," his voice a rasp, reflecting a newsman's disdain for the fluff of the society page. "But there's a war on." He tapped the sheet. She leaned forward and knew it was the story about Millard. "I guess you know that. Okay, girl. We'll give it a try." He handed back the clips. "You can start now. Take the plain yellow desk at the back. The metal desk belongs to Willie Hurst. Sports. He retired years ago, but he's back to help me out. Willie's off to San Antonio for his grandson's wedding. The desk that looks like a tornado hit it belongs to Ralph Cooley. He used to work for INS."

Gretchen's eyes widened. INS! She'd never known anybody who was a reporter for one of the wire services. Mrs. Jacobs had told her all about the three wire services, International News Service, Associated Press, and United Press. Nobody ever called them

17

by those long names. They were INS, AP, and UP. To be a reporter for one of them was as magical to Gretchen as owning a flying carpet.

Mr. Dennis puffed out his cheeks in exasperation. "Used to." His tone was dry and a little sad. "But I got to use him. There's nobody else left. Joe Bob Terrell got called up. He left last week." The editor jerked his head. "The desk with the rose in a vase is Jewell Taylor's. Soc. Get on the phone, call the police station, ask if there's anything new on the blotter. You can come in every afternoon after school and we'll see how you do. If you work out, you'll be full time when school's out. Five bucks a week."

As Gretchen moved past, her heart thudding, the editor glanced at her hat. "School clothes will do from now on."

And here she was, a reporter for the *Gazette*, out on her beat. Gretchen took the courthouse steps two at a time. It seemed a long time ago that she'd first walked into the *Gazette* office. Now it was a familiar place. She still tensed whenever Mr. Dennis called her name, but he didn't glower at her anymore. Yesterday, when she wrote a story on Rose Drew's plans to go to San Diego to see her husband, a navy petty officer, before his ship left port, Gretchen almost hadn't turned it in. She'd laid the story next to her typewriter and poked in another sheet of copy paper and started the kind of story she knew Mr. Dennis expected:

Mrs. Wilford Drew will take the train to California next Tuesday in hopes of bidding her husband farewell before his ship leaves for the Pacific theater. Mrs. Drew has worked at Osgood Beauty Salon for eight years. She . . .

Gretchen yanked out the sheet, threw it away. She picked up her first effort, pasted the three pages together, and placed them in the incoming copy tray on Mr. Dennis's desk. She went back to her desk and began typing up the list of civic club meetings, shoulders tensed, waiting for Mr. Dennis to clear his throat, the grumbling roar that usually preceded a spate of impatient instruction.

He cleared his throat. "Girl."

She sat still and tight. Did he sound mad? There was a funny different tone in his voice. Was he going to fire her? Why had she been so stupid? She should have written it the right way. . . .

"Girl." A bark now. "What's your full name?"

She twisted in her chair. "Gretchen Grace Gilman, sir."

"Okay." He bent back to his work.

19

When the first copies of the paper came out of the pressroom, he tossed one toward her, then clapped his panama on his head and strode out of the office, heading for Victory Café and coffee. She unfolded the paper and there on page 1, just below the fold, was her story:

ROSE DREW'S JOURNEY
By G. G. Gilman
Staff Writer

"I got to go. In my heart, I know I got to go."

Rose Drew twisted a handkerchief as she spoke. She looked at the photograph of her husband, Wilford, and . . .

G. G. Gilman . . . Gretchen clutched the newspaper. She burst out of the *Gazette* office and darted across the street, not caring that the light was red and a battered pickup honked at her. She pulled open the screen door of the café and ran to the kitchen, skidding past Mr. Dennis, who was settled at the counter with Dr. Jamison and Mayor Burkett. As she pushed through the swinging door, she shouted, "Grandmother, Grandmother, look!"

Her grandmother, yellow coronet braids

20

a little disheveled, plump face red with exertion, wiped floury hands on her big white apron. She took the newspaper, peered nearsightedly as Gretchen pointed. *"Wunderbar, mein Schatz, wunderbar."* She spread the newspaper on the wooden counter near the refrigerator. "We shall cut it out, put it up for everyone to see. *Wunderbar.*" Gretchen caught her grandmother's hands and pulled her into a circling dance around the wide linoleum-floored kitchen.

And now, here she was at the county courthouse, which looked almost like a small castle, built of big red chunks of sandstone. The courthouse crowned the slight rise in the town square, green lawn falling away in every direction. The American flag and the Oklahoma flag snapped on their poles. Dark green wooden benches were placed every so often along the sidewalks that led to the entrances on all four sides. A gazebo nestled beneath two huge cottonwoods near the corner of Cimarron and Broadway. The main steps of the courthouse, wide and shallow, faced Main Street. The county clerk, county assessor, county commissioners, and county treasurer's offices were on the first and second floors; the courtroom, court clerk, county judge, and county attorney were on the third. She'd check with the court clerk, see if any lawsuits had been filed today, then go down to the basement to the sheriff's office. Behind his office a dingy green corridor led to the barred door and three jail cells.

Gretchen reached for the big bronze door handle. She smoothed out her face. It didn't do to be proud; that's what Grandmother always said. She couldn't tell anybody what it meant, seeing her name on the story. She felt like she'd climbed onto the back of a big black stallion and was galloping up a rainbow, riding higher and higher. She glanced at herself in the smudged windowpane as she pulled the heavy door. There. She looked serious, almost stern.

The door opened into a wide corridor. The floor was a speckled marble, greenish with dots of gold. In the basement, the floor was a dark green cement. The still air in the courthouse smelled like people even when there was nobody in the hallways. There was an acrid dryness of cigarette smoke, old and new, and an undertone of varnish — the walnut walls had recently been redone — and the tickly scent of ammonia as the custodian mopped.

Gretchen's sandals slipped a little on the wet floor. She was reaching for the heavy bronze knob of the county clerk's office when a siren wailed outside. She swung around, skidded across the wet marble. She ran to the end of the hall and the landing in the stairway. She pushed up a creaky window, poked her head out. A black and white patrol car, its red light whirling, the siren rising and falling, pulled out of the parking lot next to city hall and swung onto Cimarron Street, going west. The tires squealed as it turned right onto Crawford. She lost sight of the car behind a row of elms. The city had two patrol cars: Sergeant Holliman in Car 1, Sergeant Petty in Car 2. Everybody was still shocked about Sergeant Petty. Nobody had ever heard of a woman policeman. But Chief Fraser jutted out his red chin and demanded to know what he was supposed to do with every able-bodied man in the county in the service. As far as he was concerned, if women could weld bombers, they could patrol city streets. To be sure, Sergeant Petty, a lanky raw-boned woman with a long face, had always had day duty, which made Kenny Holliman grumble, but after all, there was a war on.

Gretchen returned to the lobby, used the Cimarron Street exit. Despite the heat, she broke into a run. At the street, she waited for a horse-drawn wagon to clop past. Lots of wagons were in use now with tires and gas so hard to get. A single-story brick building housed the police station, fire station, and mayor's office. The door to the police station was closed.

Gretchen burst inside, swept the long room with a glance. There were several desks behind a wooden counter, a little like the *Gazette* newsroom, but the only sound was a muted radio and the wooden desks were neat and orderly, papers stacked, not strewn. The door to the chief's office was open. The office was dark.

Mrs. Morrison, her plump, placid face beaming, pushed back from her desk. "Hello, Gretchen. Here to check the records? I'll get the book for you."

"I heard the siren." Gretchen reached the counter and set her sheaf of copy paper on it, pencil poised. "Is there a wreck?" There was a curve as Highway 66 swung out of town and only a little stretch of shoulder before the ravine.

Mrs. Morrison carried the ledger to the counter. "No. Just a call out on Archer Street. But you won't want that. The *Gazette* doesn't carry domestic disturbance calls."

Archer Street? That was her street. A half

dozen small square frame houses straggled along the gravel road. Gretchen knew everyone in each house.

Gretchen bent to look at the list of citations. Four of them. Two speeding, one driving under the influence, a larceny. Her eyes brightened at the latter. Mr. Dennis would be interested to know somebody had stolen a scarecrow from the Hollis farm. Now that could make a good story. Why would anybody steal a scarecrow? As she printed, she frowned. "I don't see anything about Archer Street."

"That call just came in, but like I said" — Mrs. Morrison reached beneath the counter, lifted up a box of hard candy — "Walt don't carry that kind of news. Families with troubles, well, no sense in making things worse." She held the box out to Gretchen.

Gretchen smiled. "Thank you, Mrs. Morrison." She picked a sour cherry ball even though it would make her mouth feel puckery. The candy reminded her of the cherry phosphates at Thompson's Drugs. She didn't go there during the daytime anymore, not since Millard's ship was torpedoed off Tarawa. The kids all met there on Friday night, but she used to go every afternoon. She pushed back the memory of Millard, with his tight red curls and round face, correcting her in his precise voice when she'd ordered a cherry "fausfade." Funny, no one in the world knew of their joke and now only she knew. She hadn't written about cherry fausfades in her story about Millard. She'd written about how he'd tried so hard to take the place of his big brother when Mike went off to war, how Millard had learned to make black cows and hobokens, how he'd played the tuba in the band and done chemistry experiments in the shed behind the Thompson house and how he'd loved stars and music and finding arrowheads. She didn't write about how much he'd loved a senior girl and why he'd left to join the navy. That was maybe the best story of all, but that one she would keep in her heart. With the cherry fausfades.

Gretchen sucked on the candy and finished her notes on arrests. She turned her folded sheet over, looked at Mrs. Morrison. "Even so, I better get the information. Mr. Dennis says, 'Ask and you shall receive.'"

Mrs. Morrison's sweet high laughter pealed. "Don't that sound like Walt! That man has no shame. Well, it's one of those things. We got a call from Mrs. Crane that there was shouting and screaming next door at the Tatum house. Well, no telling what's wrong, but everybody knows Clyde's back for a furlough before his unit ships out and everybody sure knows Faye's not been sitting home nights since he's been gone. It may be that Clyde's heard tell of her doings. And I can't think she's set a good example for that girl of theirs." Mrs. Morrison's thin penciled eyebrows rose and her usually kindly glance was bleak as a February sunrise. "Oh, well, the war's hard on everybody, but a woman has to learn how to be alone." She turned toward her desk.

Gretchen barely heard Mrs. Morrison mutter, "Says she's just dancin' but the devil loves slow tunes." The Tatum house was three doors from Grandmother Pfizer's house. Gretchen had grown up running in and out of the Tatum house. Barb was just enough older that she treated Gretchen with casual disregard, sometimes welcoming Gretchen's wide-eyed admiration, other times brushing her off. Last year was Barb's first in high school. All the classes, from kindergarten through twelfth grade, were in the same big red brick building, but there was a divide wide as the Arkansas River between junior and senior high. Barb had gone out for cheerleader and she ran around with the older girls now. Gretchen remembered when Barb was skinny and could skip rope a hundred times without stopping. She wasn't skinny now and everyone noticed her when she came into a room. Gretchen felt a pang of envy. Barb's hair was a rich reddish brown and it curved in a perfect pageboy. Barb wasn't really beautiful, but she was interesting looking, with deep-set eyes, a regal face with high cheekbones, a way of throwing out her hands as if she were inviting the world to be her friend.

Gretchen nudged the sour ball with her tongue. She wrote down: *Tatum house. Screams. Yells.* She glanced toward the wall clock — twelve minutes to five — guessed at the time she'd heard the siren: *Car #2 dispatched 4:40 P.M.* "Who was screaming?"

Mrs. Morrison settled behind her desk. "Oh, likely Faye was tellin' Clyde off. You know, he ought never to have married her but some men got no sense about women, that's for sure. Some women are just damn fools about men and they don't get no better with age. Well, that Barb seems like a nice enough girl though she was wearing her sweaters so tight the principal sent home a note to Faye and that was another big fight. I swear, Faye's got a tongue that could strip bark off a gum tree. Well, Sergeant Petty will settle things down. And Clyde will be on his way soon enough."

28

Out in the heat, Gretchen shaded her eyes from the sun. She'd have to hurry to finish up at the courthouse before it closed. She walked fast, felt her cotton blouse sticking to her back. The main hallway was empty. At the court clerk's office, she noted that Mr. Edward Petree, 103 Cherry Street, had filed suit against his next-door neighbor, Mr. Coy Hendricks, 105 Cherry Street, for dumping out an old barrel of oil that had leaked into Mr. Petree's yard, ruining his vegetable garden. The county commissioner's office was already closed. She'd have to wait until tomorrow to check and see when they'd take the bids for that new bridge on Kershaw Road. In the basement, the door to the sheriff's office was shut and locked.

She reached the *Gazette* office a few minutes after five. Nobody was there. Mr. Dennis was probably in the press room, seeing that the papers got folded for the newsboys. She took a minute to straighten her desk, made some quick notes about tomorrow's stories — missing scarecrow, bid date for the bridge — but she needed to get over to the café. She kept her pedal pushers there. She'd change clothes and get to work. Grandmother had protested at first, saying Gretchen worked all day at the *Gazette* and that was enough, but Gretchen knew how tired Grandmother got. Gretchen started off the day at the café and ended the day there. She and Grandmother were at the café by five to get ready to open at six. Gretchen didn't go to the *Gazette* until eight so there was plenty of time to slap bacon into the huge skillets and flip eggs on the grill. Truckers coming through on Highway 66 would stop for the best breakfast on the road: bacon and eggs when they had them, hash browns, pancakes, and grits all the time. They made their own bread and rolls and corn bread. Gretchen still did most of the cleanup after she got off from the *Gazette*. Grandmother would close up and go home early if the kitchen ran out of food but in any case the door was always shut by five. There was lots to do. Mrs. Perkins might be finished up with the dishes, but Gretchen scrubbed the tables and mopped the floor and saw to the trash. There might be deliveries to unload. The meat plant in Tulsa delivered — when there was any meat — twice a week. If everything went well, maybe she'd get home by six. Grandmother would have rested for awhile and then fixed supper. Macaroni and cheese and watermelon was Gretchen's favorite.

When Gretchen finished burning the

trash in the incinerator at the edge of the lot behind the café, the sun was a hot red ball in the west. Even the scrawny bois d'arc trees cast a big shadow now. She poked the ashes to make sure there were no more sparks. Though it was still June, the county was tinder dry. Cars and trucks rumbled past on the highway. Despite gas rationing, there was more traffic than ever, most of it military trucks.

Every so often, she looked down Archer Street. The graveled street curved up and down, following the gentle contours of the hilly countryside. The windows in all the boxy frame houses were up, the front doors open, welcoming any hint of breeze. But the houses were hot, all of them, even with fans. Grandmother said people got mad easier when it was hot; mad in the summer, blue in the winter.

Gretchen gave the ashes a final poke and swung up on her bike. She rode slowly because it was hot, but she didn't care that sweat beaded her face, slipped down her back. The refrain sang in her mind: *G. G. Gilman.* She was almost past the Tatum house when she braked to a sudden stop.

The cover hung askew from the silver mailbox on its post next to the end of the rutted drive. Paint had flaked from the second T: TA UM. Dandelions poked fluffy heads from grass that needed mowing and had gone to seed. The Tatum house had a front porch. Grandmother's house had three concrete steps to the front door. Grandmother's steps were swept every day and hosed off once a week. Rambling roses bloomed on either side. The wooden steps to the Tatum porch were rickety and one plank had a broken edge. The house had a frowsy air, some asphalt shingles missing, the white paint weathered and peeling.

Gretchen swung off her bike, leaned it on the kickstand. She shaded her eyes from the crimson sun. The house looked as it always had, no different at all. Mrs. Morrison was probably right. Mr. Dennis wouldn't put anything in the paper about the call to the police this afternoon. But it wouldn't hurt to knock on the door, see if Barb was home. Gretchen walked briskly to the porch. She looked through the screen door — the front door was wide open — into the dim living room. Magazines spilled across the slip-covered sofa. An open box of graham crackers sat on the low coffee table next to an empty Coke bottle. A filled ashtray sat near a half dozen nail polish bottles and wadded tissues. There was an oval braided rug and two easy chairs, both slipcovered in shiny yellow chintz. Despite the disorder, the room glowed with color and life from the matted but unframed paintings hanging on the walls.

Gretchen knocked. The rattle disappeared into the silence quick as a frog slipping into a pond.

A quick clatter of steps sounded. Faye Tatum hurried across the living room. Faye always moved fast. She stopped midway when she saw Gretchen. Her narrow face looked hard as marble. Her blond hair fell forward, a golden strand loose across one cheek. Her green eyes smouldered like a banked fire. Crimson lips twisted downward. She carried a saucepan in one hand, a lid in the other. She wore an apron over a cotton top and shorts. The apron wasn't tied and the strings dangled on either side. There was something about the way the apron fell and the bareness of her legs that shocked Gretchen. Nobody would come outside dressed like that. It didn't look right somehow. Most women her age wouldn't wear shorts around the house, only if they were going to a picnic on a hot summer day. But Mrs. Tatum was an artist and everybody knew artists were different. Last summer Gretchen remembered coming to see Barb and finding Mrs. Tatum and Barb sitting on the living room sofa in panties and bras and how they'd laughed at her expression. It was the middle of the morning but they said it was just too hot to get dressed and after all what difference did it make because the human body was beautiful. Gretchen knew Grandmother's blue eyes would snap if she told about that visit so she'd never mentioned it. Today was hot, too.

"Hello, Gretchen." Mrs. Tatum slapped the lid on the pan. "Barb's not here." She sounded mad. And disappointed. Her lips trembled, then closed into a tight line.

Gretchen began to back away. "Please tell her I came by."

Mrs. Tatum turned without answering. She walked across the floor, pushed into the kitchen. The door swung shut behind her.

As Gretchen hurried toward her bike, she felt a rush of gladness that she was leaving. She loved the pictures in the Tatum living room, but now she remembered how often there weren't regular meals, how Barb snacked at night on peanut butter and jelly, how she liked to come to Gretchen's house to eat.

Gretchen used the rubber grips on her bike, avoided the hot handlebars. The rest of the way home, she wondered about Mrs.

Tatum. Had she shouted at her husband this afternoon? Or screamed? She was still mad when Gretchen came. But a scream was different from a shout. Gretchen glanced at the Crane house. Like Grandmother said, everything was always neat as a pin at the Crane house. The lawn freshly trimmed, though it had to be a losing battle against the blown puffs of dandelions from the ragged yard next door. Bright blue shutters framed the front windows. Begonias flourished in the flower beds. Mrs. Crane would be proud to open her front door to company any time of day or night. There would never be magazines strewn about or unemptied ashtrays or dishes in the sink.

Gretchen parked her bike behind her grandmother's house and hurried up the wooden steps into the kitchen.

Grandmother turned from the stove with a big smile. "So here you are. Just in time for supper so fine. We have salmon croquettes and fresh peas and Jell-O." Grandmother's German accent was still strong, her *w*s often sounding like *v*s. That was why she didn't like to be in the front of the café anymore and let Mrs. Perkins handle the cash register. Once last year she forgot and said, *"Danke schön,"* to a man from out of town and he threw down his money and asked how come the café had hired a Kraut instead of a good American.

Gretchen washed her hands at the sink. They sat across from each other at the white wooden table. Two more chairs were pushed against the wall on either side of the door to the living room. They pulled one to the table when her mother came on the bus from Tulsa. Jimmy's chair had been against the wall since he went overseas. His letters didn't come so often now and when they did, he didn't write much, just how he wished he could be home and when he came home the first thing he wanted to do was have one of Grandmother's big hamburgers with mustard and mayonnaise and home-made chowchow and lettuce and tomato. He said he hadn't eaten a tomato in months. And he asked after Mike Thompson. They hadn't written him that Mike was killed in the fighting in Italy, just three months before Millard's ship went down. There were two stars in the window of Thompson's Drugs. Mr. Thompson hardly ever came over to the café for lunch anymore and Mrs. Thompson's clothes sagged against her wraith-thin body.

Grandmother passed the bowl of peas. "I put your story by the cash register. Mrs. Perkins said everybody thought it was good.

She said Mrs. Jacobs had some company with her and when they paid the check, Mrs. Jacobs pointed at the story and told everyone you were one of the best students she'd ever had and you were going to be famous someday."

Gretchen's spoon stopped midway to her mouth. "Mrs. Jacobs said that?"

Grandmother nodded. "*Ja*. When Mrs. Perkins told me, I wished I'd been there to hear. But we call your mother tonight."

Calling long distance was always exciting. Of course, they might not be able to get through. Sometimes there were long waits. They didn't make long-distance calls very often. When they did or when her mother called them, they talked loud and fast against a buzzing, scratchy background. The phone company asked everyone to keep their calls to five minutes because so many people needed to make calls.

Gretchen scarcely tasted the rest of her supper though she loved salmon croquettes. She told Grandmother about her day, finishing with her last rounds. "When I got to the courthouse just before five, there was a siren so I went over to the police station. Sergeant Petty was on her way to the Tatum house. Mrs. Crane had called and said there were shouts and screams. Mrs. Morrison said that Barb's dad was home and getting ready to go overseas and maybe he and Barb's mom got mad about something." Gretchen didn't want to tell Grandmother about Mrs. Tatum being out at night since Mr. Tatum had been gone. It might not be true and that was the kind of thing that would make Grandmother say that Gretchen shouldn't go see Barb. "I stopped by on my way home. Mrs. Tatum looked like she was mad about something. So I guess she and Mr. Tatum had a big fight and Mrs. Crane called the police."

Grandmother put down her fork. "You won't put that in the paper?"

"I don't think so." Gretchen knew it wasn't up to her. "But I have to tell Mr. Dennis."

Grandmother pushed the platter with croquettes closer to Gretchen. "I know. You have your job. You must do what Mr. Dennis says. But you see, I remember Clyde when he was a little boy. He was such a friend to your mama."

Gretchen's eyes widened. "I didn't know that, Grandmother."

"Oh, they played together all through school. Clyde was a nice boy though he liked to have his own way. And he didn't like to share your mama. They'd fight about that sometimes and she'd say she wanted to be friends with everybody, not just Clyde. They were best friends until she got in the pep club. She was so busy then. Everybody was her friend." Grandmother's tone was proud.

Grandmother pushed back her chair, went to the drainboard. She cut two generous slices of watermelon, set a serving at each place.

Gretchen carefully poked out the big shiny black seeds, cut her watermelon into dripping chunks.

Grandmother settled back in her chair. "I always thought perhaps someday . . . but your mama fell in love with your daddy in high school. She didn't see so much of Clyde then."

Gretchen had only a dim memory of her father, thick dark hair and bright blue eyes and a smiling face. She couldn't quite remember her father's face, not really, but there were pictures in an album and she looked at them so often, she knew them by heart. She remembered laughter and being swung high in the air and nursery rhymes read in the glow of a flickering fire. And she remembered the gray, dark days after the accident and the fresh grave in the cemetery. They took flowers every month and put them there. Every time Mama came home from Tulsa they went to the cemetery. Her mother loved to tell stories about her dad, like the time he saw that Douglas Fairbanks movie and he made two wooden swords in shop and he and Clyde pretended they were French noblemen and everybody laughed when they staged a duel in assembly. . . . The words came back to Gretchen. She'd never thought about the Clyde in her mother's story being the man who was Barb's father.

"Anyway" — Grandmother spoke with finality — "it would never have worked out for your mama and Clyde. I'm glad it didn't because your mama loved your daddy. And once Clyde met Faye, he seemed happy as could be. She came to town when she was in high school. They got married soon after your mama and daddy. But sometimes I wonder if Clyde is jealous of Faye's painting. A man doesn't want to be second best in his home." Grandmother finished her watermelon. "Now it comes to the police being called. That's a bad way to send a man off to war. But Faye Tatum . . ." She gave a little head shake and sighed. "Well, we'd best be doing the dishes."

Gretchen popped up. She was suddenly tired to the bone, but she made her smile bright. "I'll do them, Grandmother. You go relax, listen to the radio." The six-thirty news would be on soon with Edward V. Kaltenborn. If Gretchen hurried, she'd hear most of it. And then they'd call Mother.

Grandmother bent close to Gretchen, trying to hear. She always had Gretchen do the talking. Grandmother didn't like to talk on the telephone. She always spoke too loud and very fast and her accent weighted her words.

Gretchen frowned as she tried to catch the words on the other end. ". . . not home . . . take a message?"

The voice was unfamiliar, but her mother shared rooms with other war workers and people seemed to come and go. "This is Gretchen, Lorraine Gilman's daughter. Please tell her we called." So her mother would not know for awhile about G. G. Gilman. "Tell her we are fine."

A spurt of cheery laughter. "Will do. She's fine, too. Out on a date with a navy man. Lucky gal."

Gretchen tossed restlessly on the bed. The small bedroom was hot. Not even a breath of breeze filtered through the screen of the open window. The electric fan's whir

41

was cheerful but the air didn't seem cooler at all. Disjointed words and indistinct images moved in the corridors of her sleep-drenched mind: . . . lucky gal . . . Mrs. Tatum's eyes . . . the shrill of the siren . . . G. G. Gilman . . . the smell of hot lead from the Linotypes . . . wooden swords . . . her fingers punching slowly but ever faster on the shiny keys of the tall Remington typewriter . . .

The rattle of the window screen overrode the clacking keys in Gretchen's dream.

"Gretchen, wake up!" The shrill cry rose into a nightmarish wail. "Oh, help me, Gretchen, help me!"

. . . but I don't know if he was one of your husbands. You've been married twice. Hey, Gretchen, I was always ahead of you. Four trips to the altar — and I don't know which one was the worst. Maybe you married for love. We never thought when we were girls that we'd end up — well, everybody always believed you'd succeed. Me, I was the girl in the tight sweaters — but, damn them, they all looked, didn't they? The last time I saw you was that terrible Saturday. Thirty years later I saw your picture in the newspaper. I was living in L.A. with Husband Number Three. You could have knocked me over with a feather . . .

Chapter

2

A line of bricks, some broken, edged the plot. There were — I counted and realized I'd never done that before — seven graves. The oldest was that of Grandpa Pfizer. I didn't recognize my father's grave at first glance.

The angel that had knelt on the granite stone was headless now. I'd always reached out to stroke the angel's wings. How many years had it been since anyone brought flowers for him? I was sharply glad that I could pull memories out of my past. The dead live only so long as someone remembers. When I died, no living person could — or would — picture his young face. The photos in a dark brown album in my library held only faint interest for my children, the laughing eyes of the grandfather they'd never known. The pictures were black-and-white. They'd never know — not unless I told them — that his eyes were the blue of a northern sea and his hair black and shiny as sealskin; my eyes, my hair before streaks of silver marked the passing years; my daughter's eyes, the glossy black of her hair. When I entered the cemetery, I'd looked for the family plot though I'd not come here today to visit these graves. But I had time enough to see them all. There had been no headstone on my grandmother's grave when I left town. I took a step, leaned against my cane, and bent down to touch the graven letters:

CHARLOTTE KLEIN PFIZER
Beloved wife of Karl Gerhard Pfizer
October 23, 1876–June 26, 1944

Oh, Grandmother, I loved you so. . . . `

Gretchen scrambled out of bed, reached the window. Barb Tatum, her stricken face chalk white in the milky radiance of the moon, pounded on the window screen. "Gretchen, come quick. Mama's in trouble. Oh, Gretchen, help me." Barb's pink cotton nightgown had thin white straps over her shoulders and ended above her knees.

"Barb, what's wrong?" Gretchen yanked the hook free, pushed against the screen.

Barb stumbled back. She wrapped her arms across her front. Her chest heaved as she struggled to breathe. "I ran. I ran all the way. Oh, my foot." She sank to the ground, clutched at her leg.

Gretchen darted to the wall by the bedroom door, flipped the light switch. She ran back to the window, looked out at Barb, pinioned in a square of brightness. Barb's head was bent. Her lustrous sorrel hair masked her face, tumbled over her bare shoulders. She held tight to her ankle. Blood spurted from a gash on the bottom of her right foot. "I must have run across some broken glass. I didn't even feel it." Blood puddled in the grass.

Gretchen drew her breath in sharply. "Don't move. I'll get Grandmother —"

"No!" Barb's voice was stricken. "We have to hurry. Mama needs help. Oh, Gretchen, I have to get back. I shouldn't have run away. Bring me something to bandage my foot." She pointed at the blood.

Gretchen had always wished she looked like Barb even though some of the girls didn't think Barb was really pretty. Her features were chiseled, her nose thin, her chin pointed, but her lips curved into a funny half smile whenever the boys were near, the kind of smile that promised a kiss when nobody was around to see. Her laughter, a peal of delight, made everybody crowd around her. Her blue eyes glowed as if she saw things other people didn't see. Now those eyes were glazed and staring.

"You're hurt. I'll get Grandmother." Gretchen started to turn away.

"No!" Barb's cry was desperate. "I don't want anybody to know. If you won't help me, I'll go back by myself." Barb was crying, swiping at her eyes, struggling to get up.

"Wait, I'm coming." Gretchen pulled on a tee shirt and shorts, slipped barefoot into her loafers. Her glance swept the room, then she reached for the pillow, shook the case free, rolled it into a long strip two inches wide. She carried it in one hand as she pushed the screen out, swung over the sill,

46

and dropped softly to the ground. She hurried to Barb, knelt, and peered at her foot. "You've got dirt in it. We need to wash it up. I can get some water, but we need to call Dr. Jamison."

"We can't take the time." Barb yanked the strip of cloth out of Gretchen's hand. She slung the rolled pillowcase under her foot, crossed the ends over her instep, tied them tight. "Help me up."

They stood close together. Barb's fingers gouged Gretchen's arm. "Come on. I heard Mama scream." She pulled on Gretchen's arm, leaned against her for support, and limped across the lawn.

The moon rode high in the sky. Gretchen knew it was very late. Archer Street lay quiet as a ghost town. All the houses were dark. All of them.

"Barb, what happened? Why did your mom scream?" Were Faye and Clyde Tatum fighting again?

"I heard somebody knock. Mama spoke and her voice was real loud and then the front door slammed against the wall. That's when Mama screamed." Tears streamed down Barb's face. She clung to Gretchen, tried to walk even faster. They kept to the grassy verge of the street, avoiding the gravel.

When they reached the front porch of the

Tatum house, bright moonlight showed the front door open, open to darkness within and without.

"Mama? Mama?" Barb's voice was shrill in the silence.

Gretchen pointed at the dark doorway. "Were the lights off when you left?"

Barb pressed her fingers against her cheeks. "When I got out of my window, I ran toward the front of the house. Light was coming around the shades in the living room. Then the light went out. I was scared. I turned and ran and all of a sudden I was at your house. I came to your window. Like we used to do a long time ago." One summer when they were eight or nine, they'd played a game, slipping out of their rooms late at night, going to the other house, whispering, then coming home again in the darkness and no one ever knew they'd been up and out. "Remember? Anyway, I came to your house." Barb stepped toward the screen door. "Mama? Mama?"

No answer.

Barb reached out, yanked open the screen. She stepped into the dark living room, her hand brushing to her right. When the light came on, she clamped her hand over her mouth, but the sound of her scream pulsed against the dreadful silence in the room.

After one look, Gretchen grabbed Barb's arm, pulled her outside to the porch and down the steps. The screen door banged shut. "Your dad — where's your dad?" Gretchen turned away from the house, wishing she could run and scream and cry.

Barb lifted one hand, clawed at her throat. She made a bubbling noise. She struggled to break free of Gretchen.

Gretchen held tight to Barb's arm. Gretchen's throat ached, too. No matter how hard she tried, she couldn't rid her mind of that terrible glimpse of Faye Tatum, slumped on her back near the sofa, her blond hair splayed against the braided rug, eyes wide and staring, tongue protruding from blanched lips, throat mottled with purplish bruises. Most hideous of all were the pansy purple splotches on the gray white of her throat.

Barb wavered unsteadily. "Mama."

"We have to find your dad." Even as she spoke, Gretchen realized Mr. Tatum wasn't there. If he were in the house, he'd have heard Barb's scream and their high frightened voices. And the slam of the door. It was the middle of the night. Where was he? Why hadn't he hurried to help Mrs. Tatum? "Who was in the living room with your mom?"

Barb whirled away. She ran a few steps,

dropped. "My foot." She buried her face in her hands, rocked back and forth, her shoulders shaking.

Gretchen hesitated, looking toward the house, light now spilling out onto the porch. They had to get help. But she wasn't going back inside the Tatum house. She couldn't do that. She looked across the Tatums' scraggly, moonlight-silvered yard at the well-kept house next door. Mrs. Crane was a widow and Grandmother said she was lonely. She had a long sad face and sharp blue eyes. She'd called the police yesterday afternoon about the Tatums. She talked fast, her thoughts skittering in every direction. Every year her apple pie won a blue ribbon at the county fair. She could call the police. But so could Grandmother.

Dr. Jamison knelt in front of the sofa. His graying hair was uncombed and his shaggy beard tousled. He'd only buttoned one cuff of his crumpled white shirt and his black trousers sagged without a belt. He wound a final strip of tape around Barb's right foot, then pushed himself stiffly to his feet, giving a little groan. He patted Barb's knee, gave Gretchen a swift look, his tired eyes kind and sad.

Grandmother bustled out of the kitchen.

She wore a blue cotton housedress and her everyday sturdy white shoes. Only her hair, hanging to her shoulders, indicated the oddness of the hour and the moment. "Here, Doctor, I have made coffee for you."

He took a cup. "Thank you, Lotte. Bad business. I told the chief I'd come back after I saw to Barb." He sighed. "I need this."

Grandmother held out the lacquered tray with a china sugar bowl and a silver spoon. The tray was one of her most prized possessions. Two silver dragons faced each other, their snouts bright with flame.

Dr. Jamison took a spoonful of sugar. "I've tried to give up sugar. I only use one spoonful now instead of three. My contribution to the war effort."

"You do your part." Grandmother's blue eyes were admiring, her tone firm.

He sipped, smiled. "Thank you, Lotte. So do you. Best food in the county, rationing or no. Now" — he gave a weary sigh — "will you see to Barb?"

Grandmother nodded, her hair swinging. "Oh, yes, she can stay here."

Barb pushed to the edge of the couch, the sheet that Grandmother had brought her slipping to her waist. "But Daddy will wonder where I am."

Her face heavy, her mouth drooping,

51

Grandmother looked at Dr. Jamison. Neither said a word.

"Daddy didn't come home for supper." Barb looked puzzled and frightened. "I don't know where he is."

Dr. Jamison rubbed his tired eyes and made no answer. He drank some of the coffee, put the cup on a side table. He bent over his open satchel, lifted out two small packets. He handed them to Grandmother. "One each for the girls tonight. It will help them sleep." He snapped the satchel shut, reached for his coffee.

A heavy knock thudded at the door.

Grandmother bustled across the room. "Come in, please to come in."

Chief Fraser stepped inside, ducking his head beneath the lintel. He pulled off his cowboy hat. Wiry gray hair was cut short and tight to his big head. His face bulged all over, massive forehead, distended cheeks, rounded chin. Tonight a stubble of beard emphasized the dewlaps beneath deep-set brown eyes. Gretchen had often seen him at the café, but she'd only glimpsed him at his office a few times since she started with the *Gazette*. He didn't drive a police car. Everybody in town knew his old dark green Packard, the running boards usually stained with dirt. Mrs. Morrison said he liked to be out talking to people. Since gas rationing, he mostly walked around town, sweat beading his red face, staining his shirt. "Lotte, Doc, girls." He jerked his head toward the door. "If you can get down there, Doc, take care of things? We got what we need."

Dr. Jamison drank the rest of his coffee, nodded. "All right, Buck." His mouth folded into a grim line. He placed the cup on the table, picked up his satchel. As he passed the police chief, he muttered, "Clyde anywhere around?"

"Nope." The chief's bushy eyebrows bunched in a tight frown.

The door banged behind Dr. Jamison.

Barb's head jerked up. She stared at Chief Fraser. "You have to find my daddy. He doesn't know. Oh, poor Daddy." She pulled up the sheet, buried her face in its folds.

Grandmother's voice was low. "Some coffee, Chief?"

"If it's not too much trouble, Lotte, that'd be real good." The heels of Chief Fraser's dusty black cowboy boots thudded as he walked slowly across the room. He settled into the imitation brown leather Morris chair that had been Grandpa Pfizer's fa-vorite. He dropped his cowboy hat on the floor. "Miss Barb, I reckon you know how sorry I am about your mama."

Slowly the sheet fell. Barb's pale, tear-stained face crumpled. She pressed her hands to her face.

The chief cleared his throat. "Miss Barb, if I thought it would be easier, I'd talk to you another time." The big man leaned back, kneaded his cheek with his knuckles. "But it isn't going to be easier." His deep voice was low and quiet. "Not tomorrow. Not the next day. You got to climb a hard mountain and nothing I can do will help. Except maybe I can ease some pain by finding out who did this thing."

Gretchen tried to banish her last memory of Mrs. Tatum's face. But the image throbbed in her mind. If she couldn't forget, how bad was it for Barb?

Barb's hands fell. "Who . . ." Barb shivered. She looked down as if suddenly feeling exposed and pulled the sheet up to her throat. "I don't know who came. I heard Mama's voice and the door banged and I ran away."

The chief pulled a little notebook from the pocket of his tan shirt, flipped it open. "Let's go back a little bit, Miss Barb. What did your mama do today?" The chief rubbed his nose, his eyes intent. "Start with breakfast."

Barb frowned. "I don't see what difference that makes."

He propped the notebook on the knee of his khaki trousers. "Don't do no harm to say. I want to know what your mama and daddy did today."

Barb was suddenly very still. "My daddy — he wasn't home tonight."

"We'll get to that." His tone was patient. "Now, be a good girl and tell me about this morning. Start with breakfast. You got up. . . ."

Barb wrapped her arms around the big red brocade throw pillow, propped her chin against the fringed edge. Her bandaged foot poked from beneath the wrinkled sheet. "We always get up at six-thirty. Mama's been working at the five-and-dime. Jewelry and clocks and cosmetics. She had to be there at eight. She'd come home for lunch at eleven, be back by quarter to twelve. She'd get home a little after four."

The chief pulled a pack of Lucky Strikes out of his shirt pocket, rasped a big kitchen match on the sole of his boot. He held the cigarette in nicotine-stained fingers, drew a lungful of smoke. "Is that what happened today?"

Grandmother hurried to the kitchen, returned with a big brass ashtray. She placed it on the floor next to his cowboy hat.

Barb twined her fingers in the fringe of

55

the pillow. "I guess so. I didn't get home 'til after five."

The chief settled back in the chair, looked like a big stone mountain. "So your mama wasn't taking any time off even though your daddy was home on furlough?" Cigarette ash dribbled on his shirt.

"Mama had to go to work." Barb's tone was earnest. "We needed the money. Ever since Daddy was drafted, we haven't had enough money and it made Mama nervous. That's why she got the job at Jessop's. She used to be at Millie's Gifts. She taught art classes in that little room at the back. But when Daddy was drafted, she got a job at Jessop's."

Bluish smoke hung in a haze near the chief. "Was your mama pretty sharp with your daddy about money?"

Barb stared at him, her eyes wide and frightened.

The chief reached down, tapped the cigarette against the rim of the ashtray, but he never took his eyes off of Barb. "What did they talk about at breakfast?"

Barb relaxed against the arm of the sofa. Although her narrow face was drawn and tired, she looked almost pretty, her auburn hair curling, the smooth skin of her arms pale against the red cushion. "Mama got up late and Daddy was still asleep. She had to hurry to get to work on time."

The chief slowly nodded. "What time did your daddy get up?"

Gretchen glanced at Grandmother, saw the frown furrowing her round face. It didn't sound right, a man lying in bed into the morning. Nobody did that. Of course, Mr. Tatum was home on leave. Maybe he was tired from the army.

"I don't know." Barb's fingers plucked at the golden tassels. "I left too. I've been working at Mr. Durwood's office this summer. I just barely got there in time. I didn't see Mama again until supper."

"How about your daddy?" The chief's voice was as smooth as a cottonmouth gliding through dark summer water.

Barb clasped her hands tightly together. "He didn't come home for supper." She spoke so softly it was hard to hear.

The chair creaked as the chief leaned forward. "Since he's been back, did he usually come home for supper?"

Barb stared at the floor. "Yes."

The chief ground out the cigarette. "So you didn't see your mama until you got home from work." He pulled at an earlobe. "I thought you said she came home for lunch every day?"

57

Barb brushed back a strand of auburn hair. "Yes. She did. But I didn't have lunch at home today. I went to Victory Café. I went with Mrs. Holcomb from the office."

The chief squinted at her. "But you were home for supper."

"Yes." She closed her eyes. Tears edged from beneath her dark eyelashes.

The chief leaned forward, frowning. "Miss Barb, you got to tell me what was happening at your house. Girl, I'm sorry, but I got to know what your mama did today. You say your daddy didn't come. What happened at supper?"

"When I got home, Mama was in the kitchen." Barb plucked at the sheet. Her words came haltingly. "Mama was banging the pots and pans. I asked her what was wrong and she slammed down a plate and it broke. She threw the pieces in the trash and said she didn't care. Then she took the pork chops, she'd got them special, used up all our stamps to have a good dinner for Daddy. She looked at them and then she threw them back in the icebox. She started to cry." Barb held tight to the red brocade pillow.

"How come she was so mad?" The chief squinted at Barb.

She huddled on the couch, her head bent. The chief planted his big hands on his knees. "Miss Barb, if you don't tell me, somebody will."

Barb pressed her fingers against her cheeks. "I guess it was because of the Blue Light." Her voice was low, almost a whisper. "Last night Mama and Daddy went to the Blue Light. While they were there, somebody said how Mama was the best dancer in town and everybody loved to dance with her. Daddy got mad. He didn't know she'd been going to the Blue Light while he was gone. They came home and had a fight. It woke me up. Daddy said she shouldn't have been going there by herself. It wasn't nice. Mama said there was nothing wrong with the Blue Light. People could go there and have fun and everybody ought to get to have some fun. Mama can — Mama could dance better than anybody, and she loved to dance. That's all it was. She wanted to dance. She told Daddy she didn't think much of him that he'd want her to sit around and never go anywhere and he said she had no call to be dancing with other men and she said what was she supposed to do, just stay at home night after night with no music and no one ever to talk to? She told him that's all it was, she loved to dance and there wasn't anything more to it. And she slammed off to their room. Daddy made a bed on the couch. He didn't get up this morning before we left. But Mama wasn't mad this morning." Barb's voice was eager.

"She wasn't?" The chief rubbed his red nose. "What did she say?"

"She didn't say much. But she wrote Daddy a note, left it at his breakfast place. She told me she shouldn't have gotten mad at Daddy, that he didn't understand, but it would all work out and we'd have a nice supper for him." Barb's face creased. "But when I got home for supper, she was mad again. I don't know why."

"Hmm." The chief glanced toward the cuckoo clock mounted on the wall over the mantel. There wasn't a fireplace, but a small gas heater they lit in the winter. "I guess she must have talked to your daddy." He stared at Barb, waited.

She held tight to the sheet. "I don't know," but her eyes wouldn't meet his.

The chief's eyes never left her face. "You say he wasn't there when you got home?"

"He wasn't." Barb's voice was definite. "It was just Mama and me."

"Then you and your mama had supper?" The chief hooked his thumbs behind his suspenders and gently tugged.

Barb didn't answer. She stared down at the crumpled sheet.

"Miss Barb?" The dark green suspenders wriggled over his shoulders.

Barb didn't look at the chief. "You had to know Mama to understand — whenever she got mad she talked real fast and moved real fast. She ran into her room and put on a pretty dress, her green rayon with the white flower print. She was carrying her compact when she came through the kitchen, putting on her powder, trying to make her face look like she hadn't been crying. But she was talking out loud to herself and she ran out the door." Barb took a ragged breath. "And she was mad because Daddy had the car. She'd got used to having it all to herself while he was gone. But he must have taken it."

"So your mama didn't have the car. Where do you suppose she went?" The chief loosened his suspenders.

Tears welled in Barb's eyes. "She had on her dancing shoes. I worried because it's a long way to the Blue Light. Almost a mile, but I guess she walked."

"Or maybe somebody gave her a ride. Well, we'll find out." The chief folded his arms over his chest. "And you, Miss Barb?"

"I cleaned up the kitchen, then I went over to Amelia's. Amelia Brady. She's a friend of mine. I didn't want to stay home by myself." She looked down at her hands. "I chipped the polish on my nails. Anyway, I went over to Amelia's and we did our nails and played records until real late. When I got home nobody was there. I guess it must have been almost midnight. I went to my room and went to bed."

"Did you see your mama when she got home?" The chief shook out another cigarette, lit it, but his brown eyes watched Barb.

"No." Barb slumped against the armrest.

A car door slammed outside. Steps pounded across the yard. The screen door rattled. "Chief, you in there?" The door opened and Ralph Cooley, his faded brown hat perched on the back of his head, peered inside. His skinny face was flushed, his necktie askew, his blue suit wrinkled. "There you are. H'lo, Gretchen, Mrs. Pfizer."

Gretchen had never seen Ralph Cooley when he didn't look like he'd slept in his clothes. He always reeked of whisky and cigarettes. Gretchen hadn't known what that smell, sweetish and musky, was until one day in the newsroom when Mrs. Taylor wrinkled her nose and asked him where he was getting his bourbon and Cooley laughed and said he knew the best bootlegger in town. Oklahoma was a dry state allowing 3.2 beer only and the only way to get whisky was to drive to a wet state or go to a bootlegger. Gretchen didn't know any bootleggers. No one in her family drank whisky. The Tatums drank, which Grandmother didn't like. She didn't like whisky and she didn't like people breaking the law. Sometimes there were stories in the paper about the sheriff arresting somebody for bootlegging.

The reporter stepped inside. "Mike Mackey called" — the funeral home director always let the *Gazette* know about accidents — "so I came right over. The doc says somebody strangled Faye Tatum and her daughter ran up here for help." Cooley's bleary eyes settled on Barb. "Doc said the girl cut her foot. Okay, Chief, what's —"

Chief Fraser held up one hand. "I don't have time for you, Ralph."

The reporter peered around the room. "Where's Clyde Tatum?"

Chief Fraser heaved to his feet. "Git."

Cooley backed toward the door, his gait just a little unsteady. "I'll wait outside, Chief."

"You deaf, man?" The chief's heavy face furrowed in ridges deep as sun-cracked dirt. He drew deeply on his cigarette. "I'll talk to you in the morning." Under his breath, he added, "Maybe."

Cooley moved a little faster, but his slurred words were a taunt. "I saw Faye

Tatum tonight at the Blue Light. Me and a lot of men." The door swung out. "Maybe I should talk to the county attorney."

Barb reached out a shaking hand. "You saw Mama?"

"Wait out front, Ralph." The chief spit out the words. "I'll be out in a minute."

Cooley tipped his hat, then banged outside.

The chief swung around, clumped back to the chair. It creaked as he sat. He took his time, smoked. He still looked mad, but he spoke quietly enough. "All right, Miss Barb. You been working upstairs in the county attorney's office this summer?"

Barb nodded.

"Thought I'd seen you there. Don't know how much you've learned about the law yet, but Mr. Durwood's the man who'll prosecute the case when we find out who killed your mama." He took a deep breath. "Now, Miss Barb, you're telling me you never saw your mama all day until you came home for supper and you didn't talk to her after she got back from the Blue Light. How about your daddy?" The chief took a deep puff. "What time did he get home?"

Gretchen's nose wrinkled as smoke roiled toward the couch.

Barb sat straight up, the sheet falling to

the floor. "He didn't come home. He never came home. He didn't come home for supper. And he wasn't home when I got back from Amelia's tonight."

Chief Fraser leaned forward in the imitation leather chair. "How would you know?" He tapped the cigarette on the ashtray. "You went to bed."

Barb's eyes were stricken. "I wasn't asleep. I heard Mama come in. She slammed doors and paced back and forth. I heard her go in her room and run out again. There wasn't any other sound. If Daddy was there, he would have said something." Her voice was definite. "There was a knock at the front door. I heard Mama go answer and she cried out something like, 'You've got a nerve.' Somebody came in." Barb pressed her hands against her cheeks. "There was a voice, but I couldn't hear the words. It was like somebody wanted Mama to be quiet. You know how people make a shushing noise? Then Mama yelled." Barb's face flattened in sick memory. "She was calling for help and I ran away."

"Right thing to do, Miss Barb." He cleared his throat. "You got scared and came here for help, asked Miss Gretchen to come with you. You say you didn't hear your daddy's voice?"

"Oh, I would have known if Daddy had been there." She sounded almost buoyant. "Did you ever know my daddy to whisper?"

"That's true what the child says." Grandmother clapped her plump hands together, nodded eagerly.

"No, Clyde's not much to whisper. Well . . ." The chief stubbed out the cigarette, pushed to his feet. "I guess that pretty much covers everything." He reached down a long arm to grab his hat.

Barb stood. "Chief, will you find Daddy? It's going to be awful when he finds out what's happened to Mama."

Gretchen got up, too. She realized she was more tired than she'd ever been. Her head ached, her body felt heavy. Through the screen, the night was turning gray. The sun would be up pretty soon and she and Grandmother would go to the café. They had to go whether or not they'd slept. Then she'd go to the *Gazette*. Mr. Dennis would want to know all about her and Barb finding Mrs. Tatum. But Mr. Cooley would write the story. And she'd bet he'd tell all about seeing Barb's mom at the Blue Light tonight. Gretchen thought he better not fool around with the chief. Mr. Cooley better tell him everything he knew. She wished she could hear them talk, but she'd hear all about it at the *Gazette*.

66

Chief Fraser moved slowly, lumbering like a bear across the floor, his boot heels thumping. He stopped at the front door, looked back, his big slab of a face drawn in a frown. "One more thing, Miss Barb." He spoke quietly enough, but there was an edge to his deep voice.

Gretchen blinked. Her eyes felt scratchy and bleary, but she saw Barb stiffen.

"How come" — Chief Fraser's thick gray-black brows bunched over his eyes — "the door to your room is locked?"

Barb's eyes widened and her mouth hung slack.

The silence in the room pulsed with the chief's suspicion and Grandmother's puzzled consideration and Barb's shock.

Gretchen frowned. Most people never even locked up their houses at night. Why would Barb lock the door to her bedroom? Why didn't Barb answer?

It was Grandmother who spoke. "Why, Chief Fraser," she said, her voice holding almost a tsk-tsk tone, "a girl all alone in her house late at night. That was it, wasn't it, Barb? You locked your door because your mama and papa weren't home."

"Yes." Barb bent, picked up the sheet, draped it around her shoulders though it wasn't cold and pulled it across her front. "I didn't like being by myself. I just turned the lock and went to bed."

The chief frowned. "When you got up, was it because you heard your mama come home?"

"No. I heard Mama come in and I knew she was still upset and so I lay there real still." Tears brimmed from her eyes. "She knocked on my door, but I didn't answer. I pretended I was asleep. When Mama was upset, she was hard to talk to. She rattled the knob and that's when somebody knocked on the front door. Everything happened real fast, somebody trying to shush her and Mama's cry. I knew something bad was happening and all I could think of was getting away. I got up and ran to my window and pushed open the screen and went out. I ran up the road fast as I could."

"And that's all you know, Miss Barb?" His voice was weary.

"That's all." Her voice wavered.

The chief clapped his hat on his head. "All right, girl. If you think of anything else, you call and I'll come."

Grandmother moved past him, pulled the door open.

The big man nodded. "Thank you, Lotte," he said, but his eyes still watched Barb and his heavy face was dour.

Only Gretchen could see Barb's hands clasped under the sheet, her grip so tight the knuckles blanched.

The house was hot and still. The shades were drawn but the summer sun peeked around the edges. Gretchen struggled awake. The whirr of the electric fan stirred the air, but Gretchen felt sweaty from sleep, her head aching. She looked around the room. Her clothes lay in a jumbled heap where she'd dropped them. She stared at the alarm clock and felt a shock as she realized the time. She scrambled out of bed and hurried into the living room.

"Barb?" Even as she called, Gretchen knew the house was empty. They'd put Barb in Jimmy's room, but Barb was gone and so was Grandmother. They'd left her to sleep, a dreadful hot sweaty sleep with ugly visions of Mrs. Tatum, her body sprawled on the braid rug, her face distorted, her throat marked.

The cuckoo clock chirped. Ten o'clock. She was late. Mr. Dennis despised people who weren't on time. That was part of the reason he was usually mad at Mr. Cooley, who was almost always late. Except with his stories. He still got his stories in on time — if he was in the office.

Gretchen dressed fast, in a cool summer dress with a white piqué top and red-and-white checkered gingham skirt. She slipped barefoot into her white sandals. The phone rang as she was pouring a glass of orange juice.

"Hello." She was breathless.

"Mein Schatz —"

"Grandmother" — Gretchen's voice was sharp — "you shouldn't have let me sleep. I'm late."

"That is why I have called. Do not worry, Gretchen. I spoke with Mr. Dennis and he understood that you had no sleep. I told him you would be there at eleven and he was pleased. He said" — she repeated the words uncertainly — "that there is big news on the wire and you can be of great help. Now, you must eat a good breakfast. There is a muffin and fresh strawberries. Oh, the pot is bubbling — I must go now."

Gretchen drank the juice, quickly ate the apple muffin. She gave her hair three quick swipes. It was a quarter after ten when she left the house. She could be at the *Gazette* office in less than five minutes. But first . . .

The drapes were drawn at the Tatum house. Gretchen opened the screen, knocked on the front door. The house lay quiet as death. Gretchen would have liked to whirl and run away. But Barb should be here. She wouldn't have gone to work. Maybe she'd gone to Amelia's.

Gretchen waited a moment, twisted the knob. The door was locked. Nobody ever locked their front door. Or hardly ever. The rigid knob was an unyielding reminder of the unimaginable. Gretchen clung to the handle. Yesterday she'd looked through the screen at Barb's mother, her face tight with anger, but vivid and alive. Mrs. Tatum could have had no thought that she was going to die so soon, that someone would walk through this door, this very door, and hands would clutch her throat and press until there was no more breath.

Gretchen yanked her hand away from the knob. A murderer had touched this handle, turned it. For the first time since Barb had rattled her bedroom screen, Gretchen confronted the word: *murderer.*

Who?

The chief wanted to know about the quarrel between Barb's mother and father. Barb was scared. She'd locked her door. Was she afraid of her father?

Gretchen stepped back. The screen door sighed shut. She hurried down the steps, then hesitated. What if Barb was inside, all alone in the house where her mother had died? Gretchen glanced at the front windows. The shades were down. She started toward the sidewalk, stopped, shook her head, hurried around the side of the house. A recently painted white picket fence marked the boundary of the Crane yard. She glanced past a clothesline. Sheets flapped in the midmorning breeze. A Venetian blind jiggled in the first window, providing a slit just big enough to look through. Gretchen wondered what Mrs. Crane had told Chief Fraser. Gretchen passed a tipped-over hay wagon, a pile of weathered lumber, a rusted butter churn, a washtub sprouting ivy. She reached the backyard, skirted an overgrown garden.

The door to the screened-in porch wasn't latched. Gretchen listened hard then slipped inside. "Barb?" Her loud voice startled a cardinal in a wisteria bush. The sweet scent of the wisteria mingled with the sharper smells of paint and turpentine. Slowly, Gretchen walked toward an easel and looked at the half-done painting. A woman in a white dress rested languidly on a white wicker sofa. The only color was the red rose in one trailing hand and the red cushion bunched behind her head. The woman's face was only partially glimpsed behind an open book held in the other hand. There was a sense of white and peace, red and vigor.

The kitchen door squeaked open. Barb stood in the doorway. "Mama was a good painter." Barb brushed back her tousled reddish brown hair, stared at the unfinished painting with red-rimmed eyes. "She was happy when she painted."

Gretchen took two quick steps to stand just in front of Barb. "Why did you go off without telling me? Why didn't you answer the door?" She knew she sounded angry. She was. She hated the thought of Barb alone in the house.

Barb slumped against the wall. "I came home. I had to." Her voice was dull. "I want to be here for Daddy." She took a deep breath. "But he hasn't come. I don't know what to do." She wore a blue shirtwaist dress and white sandals, the bandage bulky on her right foot. Yesterday she would have been beautiful. Today her face was puffy and pale, her hair haphazardly brushed. She didn't even have on any lipstick.

Gretchen picked her way carefully because this might be the wrong thing to do, all wrong, but it might be the best thing to do. "Maybe you ought to go on to the courthouse. When there's any word, they'll know in the county attorney's office."

Any word . . . Gretchen knew the police were looking for Mr. Tatum to tell him about Mrs. Tatum's murder. And, she thought coldly, feeling an icy heaviness in her chest, to ask him where he was last night and how mad he had been at his wife and whether he'd come in the front door and quarreled with her. Gretchen frowned. "You said somebody knocked on the door. Your dad wouldn't have knocked."

"No, it wasn't Daddy." Her voice was dull, but determined. "Daddy wouldn't knock. He'd just come in."

"You're sure you heard a knock?" They stood so close together, Gretchen heard the soft, quick breath Barb drew.

Barb's eyes brightened, widened. "Somebody knocked. That proves it wasn't Daddy." Barb gave a sigh of relief. "I told the chief, but I'm going to tell Mr. Durwood. He can make the chief understand. Of course he will. I'll go now." She turned away, limping on her bandaged foot.

Gretchen was almost all the way to the *Gazette* office before she wondered: What if no one believed Barb?

. . . when I saw your picture on the page with the editorials. I remember you won a prize for an editorial in the Wolf Cry. You were always winning prizes. Anyway, there you were in the Times. *The headline said: Around the World . . . by G. G. Gilman. You were in Rome and it was something about happy Italian memories. That's nice, to have happy Italian memories. I wish I did. I had some good times — when I didn't remember home. That was always the trouble . . .*

Chapter

3

"Gretchen, *mein Schatz*." I heard Grandmother's voice in my memory. It was as if she were here and speaking to me. No one had ever said my name in quite the same way. Was it her German accent or was it the love that made the intonation so utterly unmistakable? In my heart, I felt like a girl again. Gretchen. That's how Grandmother knew me. I'd been

G. G. Gilman in newsrooms around the world for most of my life. The nickname, derived from my initials, sounded like Gigi, appropriate for a fluffy white Angora cat or a fan dancer. I like to believe I carried it off with flair. No one patronized me. Or, to be honest, no one ever tried it twice. I hadn't been so tough in the beginning. The toughening started that sultry summer when Barb Tatum ran through the night to bang on my window screen. . . .

"Pretty ugly, huh kid?" Mr. Dennis's rounded face sagged into creases like an old bloodhound. He leaned back in his swivel chair, arms folded, pipe clenched in one side of his jaw. "You feel like telling me?" His tone was quiet.

Gretchen stood by his desk. She didn't answer. She couldn't answer.

Jewell Taylor, her bluish white hair in a French twist, stopped typing. She made a soft, sad noise. The feather on her wispy hat trembled. "Walt, don't make the child talk about it. Let Ralph handle it."

"Gretchen was there." The editor's tone was sharp.

Gretchen stood still and stiff, reliving the night, how Barb's fingers on the screen sounded like June bugs, the smell of newly mown grass at the Crane yard, the light spilling down from the pink ceiling fixture onto Mrs. Tatum's sprawled body. . . .

"But maybe not." The editor puffed on his pipe and the sweet woodsy scent was comforting, like the crackle of a fire in winter. "Okay, Gretchen, I've got a couple of stories for you. Billy Forrester's family brought him home from the army hospital in Kansas City. He lost both legs. They say he wants to go to college. And the First Baptist Church has a new pastor. And there'll be a Red Cross bus to take volunteers to Tulsa Saturday to donate blood for the wounded overseas. We'll do a box on page 1 for that. But first, clear the wire." He jerked his head toward the clacking Teletype, paper oozing from the top, sloping down, and mounding on the floor.

Mrs. Taylor brushed back a loose tendril of her snowy hair. "Have I got room today for that mug of the garden club president?"

Dennis glanced toward the page layouts spread across his desk. "Nope. Too much jump from the Tatum story."

"All right." Mrs. Taylor was always good-humored. In her world, if a story didn't run one day, it would the next. As far as she was concerned, big stories came and went but weddings and funerals and club meetings were the heart and soul of the *Gazette*. As she'd earnestly said when she handed Gretchen the list of this year's graduating class, "What matters are people's names. That's what they look for in the paper."

But Gretchen knew that everyone would read about Faye Tatum in this afternoon's *Gazette*. And, as Mr. Dennis observed, Gretchen had been there.

Gretchen took a step toward the editor. "Mr. Dennis, maybe if I wrote it all down. About last night."

He said quietly, "I'm not asking you to do that."

She rubbed tired eyes. "I know. I want to." If she put the fear and horror into words, the words would be separate and distinct from her, leeching the harsh images out of her mind and onto paper.

"Sure. Then see about the wire." He swung his chair around, faced his typewriter.

Gretchen slowly walked to her desk, sat down. For awhile, there was no sound except for the rattle of typewriter keys. Occasionally, Mr. Dennis grabbed the phone, barked out a number to the operator, asked quick, short, crisp questions. Gretchen heard his gruff voice in the background and felt safe. Mrs. Taylor talked to herself as she worked. Her cheerful chirp had become a familiar background noise to Gretchen.

Gretchen stared at the yellow copy paper. She started, stopped, started again. It took almost an hour. Finally she had three double-spaced pages. At four lines to an inch, it ran sixteen and a half column inches. She pasted the sheets together, laid them in the incoming copy tray. Mr. Dennis nodded his head in acknowledgment. Mrs. Taylor reached out to pat Gretchen on the arm as she walked back to her desk. Gretchen felt drained, but there was a sense of relief and release. She reached for the slender phone book with a picture of the First National Bank on the cover. She looked up the number of the Forrester house, and picked up the phone. When the operator answered, she said, "Three-two-nine, please."

A woman answered. "Hello."

"Mrs. Forrester? This is Gretchen Gilman for the *Gazette*." She always emphasized the name of the newspaper. She was still amazed at the effect of her words, how nice most people were, how eager they were to be helpful and answer her questions. "Would it be okay for me to come over and talk to Billy? I'd like to do a story about him." No legs. Never to be able to walk or run or climb. But he was home. What if Jimmy got hurt like that?

"A story about Billy?" Mrs. Forrester's voice quivered. "There used to be a lot of stories when he was the quarterback. They won state. It was three years ago. Only three years . . . Oh, God." The phone was fumbled, dropped.

Gretchen felt the hot prick of tears in her eyes.

"Hello?" The voice was thin, but loud. Manly. "Billy here. Mr. Dennis?"

"No, this is Gretchen Gilman. I'm working for the *Gazette* this summer and —"

"Jimmy's little sister, right?" A laugh. A nice laugh that sounded like Jimmy when he read about Archie in the comic strip, Archie and Jughead and Veronica. "I remember Jimmy. Best punter I ever saw. Where's he now?"

"In the South Pacific. We had a letter from him last week." Such a short letter, mostly about how much he missed Grandmother's hamburgers. "Billy, can I come over and talk to you?"

There was silence on the line.

Gretchen thought she understood, hoped she understood. "About your plans for going to college?"

"College." The little sound over the telephone wire could have been a cough or a sigh or a sob. "Yeah. Sure. Come anytime. I'm here."

Gretchen heard his pain and frustration in those two small words. *"I'm here."* Where else would he be unless someone took him, the fast quarterback who'd fallen back behind the line once, so deep, then outrun them all past the goal line.

"I'll be there in a little while. Thank you." As Gretchen was putting the phone down, she heard his thin voice, "Oh, Ma, don't cry. Please, Ma . . ."

The *Gazette* front door banged. Ralph Cooley strolled in, hat tilted to the back of his head, cigarette in his mouth, hand clutching a fistful of copy paper. He flapped the sheets. "Read all about it. Cops Hunt Killer. Dogs Called In."

Mr. Dennis's chair squeaked as he faced the door, leaned back. His face had a look Gretchen recognized. Whenever Mr. Cooley ambled across the newsroom cocky as a rooster, Mr. Dennis's face turned sour, like he'd eaten bad barbecue or maybe smelled a skunk. "Christ, Ralph, what's kept you? You went over there at nine." Mr. Dennis glared at the clock. It was just past noon.

Mrs. Taylor fluttered across the room.

81

"Here's the story on the Colman triplets. Did you know they named them Franklin, Winston, and Charles? Oh, I've got to hurry. It's the Ladies of the Leaf luncheon. Gladys Rogers is going to review Pearl Buck's new book." Her high heels tapped as she hurried out.

Gretchen checked the clock. Not quite noon. She grabbed her pica pole, the thin metal ruler with type sizes marked on the left and inches on the right, and hurried to the Teletype. Using her pica pole, she ripped the stories free, sorted them by origin. Each story had to be spiked. There were four spikes, one each for local, state, national, and international. The spikes were long, sharp nails that had been pounded through metal jar lids, then hot lead was poured in. When the lead cooled, the nails stood upright to serve as spikes for copy.

Cooley grinned as he strolled past Mr. Dennis's desk. He slouched into his chair, tossed some crumpled notes by the typewriter. "Patience, Walt. Nobody wanted to talk to me and finally I told the chief's secretary I was going to run a story that law enforcement in the county had no news about Faye Tatum's murder. That got me into his office. There are currents, Walt. Tricky currents. Lots of door banging. The stalwart chief and the ambitious prosecuting attorney are toe-to-toe, ready to fight. Lurking on the sidelines, ready to jump in the ring, is the sheriff. This is going to be one hell of a battle and I'm just the man to ferret out the real story. Did I ever tell you how goddam lucky you are to have me? Nobody ever got better stories for INS than I did. I ought to be the bureau chief in Dallas. I ought to have got the job in Washington. If I had, I'd be in London now or the Far East. Somewhere."

"Yeah." That was all Mr. Dennis said, his face still sour.

Cooley's pleased look slid into a frown. He puffed his cigarette, shot the editor a brooding glance. "I can handle my whisky."

Mr. Dennis picked up a pencil, grabbed a sheet of paper. "What's the chief got, Ralph?"

Cooley shrugged out of his suit coat, draped it over the back of his chair. He spread out his notes, rolled a sheet into the Remington. "The chief is going to feel a lot of heat if he doesn't find the husband pronto. The county attorney's been on the phone already and he's pushing the chief hard. No love lost between Durwood and Fraser. No trace yet of the husband. The sheriff's got some men out with dogs. Anyway, I've got a hell of a lead."

Cooley typed and talked at the same time: " 'Well-known artist Faye Tatum was strangled in her home Tuesday night after dancing the evening away at a local nightclub, according to Police Chief Harold "Buck" Fraser. Chief Fraser said police are seeking the victim's soldier husband, Sgt. Clyde Tatum, for questioning.'

"How's that? I'd say it looks bad for the husband. . . ." Cooley talked, typed, talked, typed, his words coming almost as fast as the staccato bursts of his typewriter keys. His cigarette smouldered in a butt-filled ashtray.. "The cops can't find the poor bastard anywhere. Tatum's car is parked in the lot at the Blue Light. Has the keys in it. That doesn't make a hell of a lot of sense, but nothing ever makes much sense with murder." Cooley yanked out a sheet of copy paper, rolled another into the typewriter. "And, hold on to your hat, Walt, I had a ringside seat last night. See, you got to be part of the community to know what's going on." There was a sardonic edge to his voice and he slid a taunting glance toward the editor.

Gretchen recognized the refrain. That was what Mr. Dennis always told them. But

84

he wasn't talking about spending time at the Blue Light. The editor ignored the gibe, held his pencil poised to write.

"Anyway" — Cooley's voice still had an edge — "when I got to the Blue Light, Tatum was drinking at the far end of the bar. I didn't know who he was then, but I knew he was trouble. He was surly as hell and everybody gave him a wide berth. He's a big man. Six feet, two hundred pounds. Seemed like he was waiting for somebody. Faye showed up about six-thirty, looking like a million dollars with her hair in a pompadour and a fancy dress and . . ."

Gretchen frowned. She remembered the green print. The shirtfrock dress was perfect for work or going shopping. It wasn't fancy. It was nice.

". . . she and Tatum had a shouting match. The chief says somebody at the barbershop told Tatum yesterday afternoon that his wife was having gentlemen friends over at the house since he'd been gone. . . ."

Gentlemen friends . . . That was awful. If Clyde Tatum had been angry that Faye was dancing at the Blue Light, how had he felt when he heard this? Gretchen worked out the time in her mind. If he was at the barbershop late in the afternoon and somebody told him about his wife, he could have gone to the house and been waiting for her when she got home from work. If he asked her about men coming to the house, well, that was sure a reason why they might have yelled at each other loud enough for Mrs. Crane to call the police.

"Well . . ." Cooley leaned back in his chair. "Faye screamed that it was a lie. She told Tatum he had a nasty mind and as far as she was concerned he couldn't get out of town soon enough and she was going to have a good time, no matter what. That's when Lou Hopper came around the bar and took Tatum by the arm. Before you could snap your fingers, Lou had him out the door. You know her. She runs the Blue Light like a drill sergeant."

Gretchen knew all about the Blue Light. It was the biggest beer joint in the county with a live band every night. Of course, she'd never been inside, but Millard had played in the band, sneaking out of his room at night and not telling his folks. That's how he got crossways with them and ran off to join the navy. Millard had liked Mrs. Hopper. Gretchen had spoken to her after Millard left, asked her to let Millard know he could come home, his parents weren't mad anymore. Mrs. Hopper hadn't made any promises but it wasn't too long after

Gretchen had gone to the Blue Light that Millard wrote, sending a picture of himself in his white navy uniform. The Thompsons had that picture of Millard and a picture of Mike in his army uniform at the drugstore, up on the wall behind the cash register. Millard had told Gretchen that Mrs. Hopper was strict with the band but fair. Gretchen wasn't surprised Mr. Tatum had done what Mrs. Hopper told him to.

"Lou doesn't want any trouble out there." Mr. Dennis made some notes. "Okay, Lou shoos him out. What time was that?"

"Maybe seven. Anyway, everything settled down. Everybody was jitterbugging, having a hell of a time." Cooley scooted his chair closer to the desk. The Remington keys rattled. "Including Faye Tatum. She danced every dance. But with everybody. You know what I mean, no particular guy." He took a drag from his cigarette, frowned at the words on the sheet. "She danced with a bunch of guys." He gave a wolfish smile, whistled. "I couldn't miss her. Nobody could. Then or later. She put on quite a show. Jitterbug. Tango. Foxtrot. Good gams."

Gretchen had a snapshot-quick memory of the body sprawled in the untidy living room, legs agape. If Mr. Cooley had seen that, he wouldn't sound like he was talking in a movie about somebody who wasn't real.

"She lived up the street from me." Gretchen was surprised she'd spoken. Mr. Cooley blinked, like it was the first time he'd noticed she was there. He gave her a funny look, almost a sneer. Gretchen ripped off more wire copy. "She was exciting to be around. All the kids liked her. She used to fix homemade strawberry ice cream for Barb. That's Barb's favorite." She stopped at a story about the fighting in Italy. Any news about the Forty-fifth Division was important. The Forty-fifth came from Oklahoma.

Cooley gave a husky rasp of laughter. "Just a dandy American mom — when she wasn't being a barfly."

Gretchen spiked the story. She whirled toward the reporter, her face burning. "Mrs. Tatum wasn't like that. Barb said her mom just loved to dance. That's all. Barb said her mom told her dad all she wanted to do was dance."

"Oh, sure. And there are leprechauns in my desk drawer." Cooley's mouth curved in a mocking grin. "Anyway, I can tell you that Faye was higher than a kite last night. Then she got loud and weepy and pretty soon she was at the bar, going up and down, asking people what they'd do if somebody said they were running around on their wife or husband. Then she got belligerent, asking if anybody knew who'd said those things about her. That's when Lou talked to her. Faye quieted down. The last time I saw her, she was in that hallway back by the bathrooms and she was leaning against the wall, holding on to the receiver at the pay phone. The chief wants to know who she talked to. He says that could be the key to the whole thing. The county attorney isn't impressed. Durwood says it looks pretty clear that the Tatums were having trouble. Seems there was a disturbing the peace call from the next-door neighbor late in the afternoon. Durwood said the chief needs to check that out. The chief said he goddam well knows how to run his own investigation and when he needs help from the county attorney, he'll call on him. The sheriff's already been out to see Lou Hopper. I called the Crane house, but I didn't get any answer."

"Faye didn't get killed yesterday afternoon." Mr. Dennis's voice was mild. "Hey, Gretchen, check the morgue for mug shots of Chief Fraser, Sheriff Moore, and Donny Durwood, the county attorney. I'll run a sidebar: Lawmen Seeking Killer."

Gretchen walked to the big wooden filing

89

cabinets in the corner near the Teletype. She pulled out the drawer marked D-E-F.

Cooley yanked the last sheet from his typewriter. "She sure as hell croaked last night — and that happened after she and Tatum had their dustup at the Blue Light." Cooley scribbled a slug on the sheets, pushed back from his desk, and rolled his chair the two feet to the editor's desk.

Gretchen picked two photographs out of the files in D-E-F, found the sheriff's file in M-N-O. Chief Fraser looked like an old bulldog, but not as tired as he had last night. Sheriff Paul Moore's long face reminded her of a sheriff in the westerns, maybe because his eyes had a flat, cold stare and he wore a string tie, real old-fashioned. Donald Durwood, the county attorney, gazed straight at the camera, stalwart as an Eagle Scout, short blond hair, regular features, firm chin.

Mr. Dennis reached out for Cooley's copy. "Did Faye leave the Blue Light by herself?"

Gretchen placed the photos on his desk.

"She went out the door alone. Who knows?" Cooley rubbed his nose, gave a big yawn. "Anyway, she went home and got herself strangled. If you ask me, she was asking for it."

"Nobody asked you." Gretchen's voice was wobbly, but she glared at him, her gaze furious, and his eyes dropped first. "She was nice."

Cooley laughed. "She was an easy —"

The editor rattled the sheets. "That's enough, Ralph. Gretchen knew the woman. Let it go."

Cooley rolled his chair back to his desk, his glance at Gretchen sardonic. "The facts speak for themselves, kid."

"She loved to dance. But the way you say it . . ." Gretchen felt sick inside for Barb. Barb would read the paper. Of course she would. She would read in the *Gazette* that her mother was strangled after dancing the evening away in a local nightclub. . . . It sounded bad. Gretchen took a step toward Cooley. "Did you put anything in the story about Mrs. Tatum? About what kind of person she was?"

Cooley raised an eyebrow. His hands were poised above the keys. "What did her kid say? That she loved to dance?"

She loved to dance. That's what Barb had said. But that wasn't everything. If that was all he wrote . . . "She was an artist." There was a painting right now on the screened-in porch that Gretchen couldn't describe, not really, not the way it made her feel to look at

91

it. As much as she loved words, sometimes there were things words couldn't capture. But the painting made her feel like she was looking at a heartbeat or a song, things you couldn't see but you felt inside.

Cooley picked up his suit coat, slipped into it. He yawned. "I'm going to get some lunch, then I'll nose around the courthouse, see what else they've found out. Maybe they've got a line on her boyfriend." He shook out a cigarette. "Though I don't suppose that matters now."

The Teletype began to rattle. Gretchen ignored the paper coming out. She spoke loud and fast so she could get it all out. "Mr. Cooley, you could talk to some people who knew her. Some of the people who took art from her. Or somebody at the five-and-dime. They'd tell you what she was really like." About the way her laughter sounded light and free as a silver spoon striking a crystal glass. Or the way she would rush out into the yard on a summer night and catch hands with Barb and the other girls playing in the yard and swing in a happy dance, singing that silly song, "Mairzy Doats."

Cooley poked his hat to the back of his head. He gave her a hard stare. "Who, me? I'm no sob sister, kid. That kind of story belongs to Jewell. Or maybe you'd like to do it. Make everybody get their hankies out."

When the front door slammed behind him, Gretchen slowly turned toward Mr. Dennis. "He's going to make her sound cheap. Like she should have died." The pictures were back in her mind: Mrs. Tatum sprawled on the floor, Barb with her face puffy, her eyes stricken.

Mr. Dennis leaned back in his chair. He folded his hands behind his head, frowned at her. "There's nothing in his story but the facts."

"The facts . . ." Gretchen stopped. She didn't know how to make him understand. Then she looked into bleak green eyes and knew that he understood everything.

Dennis nodded slowly. "That's right, kid. You're getting there faster than most. Depends upon which facts, doesn't it?" He poked at Cooley's copy. "Every fact in here is true. Ralph may have a smart mouth, but he gets it right. But you don't think the Blue Light and alcohol and people mad at each other tell the whole story about Faye Tatum. I'll tell you what, you go get a story about Faye. Only one thing you have to promise me."

"Yes, sir?" She stared into his mournful, skeptical, somber eyes.

"You got to promise that your facts will be true, too." The chair squeaked as he turned back to his desk.

"Won't you have another glass of lemonade, Gretchen?" Mrs. Forrester's brown hair puffed in thick rolls, framing a gentle face. She had milk white skin and light blue eyes. Her pink shirtwaist dress was crisp with starch. It might have been any summer day on a screened-in porch, bright with white wicker and navy cushions, except for the misery in her eyes and the young man in a wheelchair, a pale green spread draped to hide his missing legs.

Gretchen's stomach ached. She didn't know whether the ache came from the tart lemonade or from the pain and heartbreak and courage at the Forrester house. Or from the nagging worry that she'd promised to find out the truth about Faye Tatum and she didn't know where to start. "No, ma'am. Thank you. Do you know when you will be able to go to school, Billy?"

His hair, cut short, was a golden brown too and his freckled face thin. Too thin. His short-sleeve cotton shirt was too big for him. "They haven't told me when they're going to operate again." He frowned. "There's this place that doesn't heal. Once I

94

get past that, I know exactly what I want to do. I've got it all planned." His voice lifted with eagerness. "They say it's a sure thing that the president's going to sign that bill for veterans to go to college. I'm going to go to A&M and be a vet."

Gretchen's uncle Sylvester was a veterinarian and he was always being called out in the middle of the night when a cow was having trouble delivering a heifer or a quarter horse came down with colic. Gretchen thought about the rough uneven ground out on farms and ranches, the ruts that crisscrossed a barnyard.

Mrs. Forrester pressed a crumpled handkerchief to her eyes. Her shoulders shook.

Billy gripped the arms of his wheelchair. "I'm going to get artificial legs. I'm going to walk." He didn't look at his mother.

Gretchen glanced down at her notes. She mustn't cry. She wrote quickly: *artificial legs.* "Why do you want to be a vet?"

Billy's hands relaxed. "Animals don't . . ." His voice trailed off.

Gretchen waited.

He took a deep breath. "I want to help things live."

"Animals don't . . ." she repeated.

His mouth twisted. He stared at the throw which lay in a revealing drape, no bulges for legs, nothing to mar the smooth cotton. "Animals don't toss grenades. Animals fight." He nodded, his face wrinkling. "Sometimes they kill. But they don't set out to destroy everything in their path. I like animals. All kinds. So, that's what I'm going to do . . ."

Gretchen wrote fast. She scarcely heard his final words, he spoke so softly: ". . . or die." She looked up quickly. She didn't write those words down. He hadn't spoken them to her. Or to his mother. He'd spoken to himself.

He clapped his hands together, grinned at her. "How do you like working for the *Gazette*, Gretchen?"

"I want to be a reporter" — she met his gaze directly — "as much as you want to be a vet."

He reached out and they shook hands.

Mrs. Forrester exclaimed, "A reporter? Oh, Gretchen, I hope not. I thought you were just working there for the summer and writing some nice stories about people like Rose Drew. You don't want to be a real reporter, do you? There are so many terrible things in the papers. Why, we heard on the radio this morning about Faye Tatum." Her face tightened in disapproval, sharp lines cutting from her nose to her mouth. "You shouldn't have to know about things like that. Or women like her."

"Oh, Ma." Billy's voice was sharp. "Mrs. Tatum was nice. Whenever I used to go see Barb, she was as nice as could be."

"Nice women don't go to taverns by themselves." Mrs. Forrester's mouth folded into a thin, tight line.

Gretchen gripped her pencil so hard her hand hurt. "She loved to dance. That's all. Barb said she just loved to dance." She stood, folded her sheets of yellow copy paper.

Mrs. Forrester stood, too, her face as cold as a frozen pond in January. "She was a married woman. She shouldn't have run around like she was single."

Billy slammed his hand on the arm of his chair. "Ma, there's nothing wrong with dancing."

"Dancing's just an excuse, Billy." Her pale eyes glittered.

He fingered the hem of the throw. "I used to dance. I went to the USO all the time." He ignored his mother's muffled cry. They didn't dance or drink in the Forrester family. "Maybe Mrs. Tatum was scared. Or lonely. Or feeling blue. When they play the music loud and fast, everything else goes away, at least for a while. If all she did was dance, there's nothing wrong with that."

"She wouldn't be dead if that's all she did." Mrs. Forrester tossed her head like a horse scenting a snake.

Gretchen paused at the door. "Nobody knows for sure what happened. The police don't know. They're trying to find out. I'm going to write a story about Mrs. Tatum. I'm going to talk to the people who knew her best."

"Least said, soonest mended, I should think." Mrs. Forrester's tone was snippy.

Billy rolled his chair forward. "Gretchen's got a job to do. I think it's swell. Barb can help. She'll know who her mom's friends were. Gretchen, please say hi to Barb for me. Tell her I'm sorry about her mom. Real sorry." His eyes held memories of death.

"I'll tell her." Gretchen hoped she could make Barb know that Billy understood. But Gretchen wouldn't say a word about Mrs. Forrester, who stood like a stone in her pretty pink dress as Gretchen pushed through the screen door. Mrs. Forrester had made up her mind. She believed that Faye Tatum was a bad woman and that was why she came to a bad end. Gretchen could imagine Mrs. Forrester talking to her friends, their voices low and secretive, and the knowing looks they would exchange.

Gretchen walked fast despite the heat.

She was in a hurry. Maybe nothing would change Mrs. Forrester's attitude. Everybody in town would be talking about Faye Tatum and the Blue Light and Faye's quarrel with Clyde. But Gretchen was determined that there would be something more to remember about Barb's mother. Thanks to Billy Forrester, Gretchen knew where to begin. Barb knew her mother's friends. That was the place to start. With Barb.

When she passed Victory Café, she frowned at the streaks of dust on the plate glass. Tonight she'd scrub the front window. The café was crowded, all the seats at the counter taken, most of the booths full. It had been that way ever since the war started, even though many days they didn't have any meat. But Grandmother's spaghetti and homemade tomato sauce and her macaroni and cheese were big favorites. Funny, she didn't even know what the special was today. This must be the first morning in forever that she'd not opened up with Grandmother. Right now her achy stomach felt hollow, but she kept right on walking. She'd eat later.

At the courthouse, Gretchen went straight to the third floor, which housed the offices for the court clerk and the county attorney and the judge. Past the courtroom at the far end of the broad marble hallway, a clump of young men clustered near the closed door to the draft board. Three big ceiling fans stirred the hot air. The windows at either end of the hall were pushed high.

On the wall opposite the frosted glass door of the county attorney's office, there were big photographs of the county judge and the county attorney. Judge Alonzo Miller was old with a wrinkled face, thick glasses, and a weedy mustache. Donald Durwood looked young and handsome and kind of noble, like Alan Ladd in that movie where he'd been a soldier for money and then he knew he had to do the right thing. There'd been a lot of pictures in the county attorney's file at the *Gazette* from the days when he played high school football and later at A&M. He looked more stern in this picture, steely gaze, jaw set. She opened the door, stepped into a small anteroom. The door to the county attorney's office was to the left. It was closed. Wooden filing cabinets ranged against the opposite wall. The anteroom held three desks, the largest a brown walnut. On the big desk were a typewriter, a telephone, in and out boxes, a brown leather desk pad, and neat stacks of correspondence. A Coke bottle sat next to a blue pottery plate with a sandwich, potato chips, and a dill pickle. A long golden oak table stacked with brown manila folders was pushed next to the wall beneath the three big windows, open to catch any breeze. Mrs. Holcomb, a buxom woman with shiny brown hair bunched in sausage-thick curls, held a fly swatter high above her head, poised to strike.

As the door clicked shut, she whispered, "Wait, Gretchen. Hush. Oh" — a sigh of frustration — "it's moved. If you hadn't come in just now . . . I hate wasps. What a morning." Abruptly, she lurched forward, swung. The wasp tumbled to the shiny wooden floor. She bustled to the walnut desk, plucked a tissue from a drawer, gingerly picked up the insect, flung it into a green metal wastebasket. "There." She paused, pushed back a tendril of loose hair. "Come in, my dear. I'd close the windows, but then it's worse than a sweatshop in here. There must be a nest of them right under the eaves. I was just having my lunch. Do you suppose wasps smell food? What can I do for you? Mr. Durwood isn't here. If you're here about Mrs. Tatum's murder — oh" — her voice dropped — "it's so awful. Poor little Barb. But Mr. Durwood did the right thing, hard as it was." She dropped

101

into her chair, but made no move to pick up her sandwich. "The look on her face when she came out of his office just broke my heart. I wanted to grab her up in my arms, but she just walked past me like I wasn't even here. She went over to her desk and grabbed her purse from the drawer. I understand she's staying at your house. Will you tell her I wish I could help?" She picked up the Coke bottle, took a deep swallow. "I don't know if anything can help with the police looking for her father. It seems pretty clear he was the one that did it. I'll tell you, Gretchen, drinking leads a man straight to hell."

"Why was Barb in Mr. Durwood's office?" Gretchen glanced at the closed door. "What happened?"

The secretary scooted her chair closer to her desk, took a bite of her sandwich. "He had to let her go." Mrs. Holcomb's tone was mournful. "I mean, he has to do the right thing. That's what he told me when he came out. If ever a man looked unhappy, it was him. But like he said, there can't be any appearance of favoritism before the law and if Barb worked at his office, why, people might think he wasn't going to do his job and make sure the police arrest Mr. Tatum if he turns out to be the guilty party."

Gretchen heard the buzz of a wasp. She waved it away with her handful of copy paper.

"Another one!" Mrs. Holcomb came to her feet. She squealed as the wasp came near her, tried to make herself small as she darted toward the swatter atop a filing cabinet.

"What if Mr. Tatum is innocent?" Gretchen raised her voice. "Barb heard someone knock on the front door. Her dad wouldn't knock."

The swatter slapped against the table, killing the wasp. Mrs. Holcomb edged the head of the swatter beneath the wasp, scooped it up, dropped it in the wastebasket.

"Her dad wouldn't knock," Gretchen repeated, remembering the certainty in Barb's voice.

Mrs. Holcomb dropped the swatter on a cabinet. She shrugged. "Oh, my dear, there's all kinds of reasons he might knock. Maybe Faye locked the door. You know, they had a big fight at the Blue Light. Everybody heard her yelling at him. And there she is, dead not much later. Of course the police think Clyde's the one. Mr. Durwood says Barb didn't understand how her daddy's the main suspect. He hated having to tell her. She was real upset."

★ ★ ★

Out on the sidewalk, Gretchen heard the jukebox, Judy Garland singing "The Last Time I Saw Paris." Mrs. Jacobs had told the class that she'd never been to Paris but she cried every time she heard the song. Gretchen opened the screen door, stepped into a tumult of noise, people talking as they ate, the clatter of dishes, a rumble of laughter from a booth at the back. Gretchen squeezed behind the counter, heading for the phone beside the cash register. Mrs. Perkins gave her a harried look. "Gretchen, listen, can you take some orders? We're swamped."

Gretchen hesitated. She hadn't had lunch yet, and it was past one o'clock. Mr. Dennis wouldn't mind if she took a few minutes to help out. She reached under the counter, found an apron, slipped it on. But she kept her eye on the clock. She wouldn't take more than half an hour. She tried the Tatum house twice. Each time the operator said there was no answer. Was Barb there and refusing to pick up the phone? No, she wouldn't do that. She'd answer in case it might be her dad.

In one of her trips to the kitchen, Gretchen fixed herself a bowl of the special — stewed okra and tomatoes with corn bread — and called hello to her grandmother. Grandmother smiled but she was too busy to talk, moving swiftly from stove to counter, ladling up the special, cutting more corn bread just out of the oven, pausing to flip grilled cheese sandwiches. There were no hamburgers today, but big red franks split wide sizzled on the griddle. Gretchen ate a few bites from her bowl each time she darted in to pick up orders.

She checked the clock. Half past one. She reached back to untie her apron, then let her hand fall. The screen door banged and the county attorney and the sheriff came in. Gretchen bent her head to look past them. Chief Fraser wasn't with them. Maybe that was to be expected considering how Ralph Cooley said the prosecutor and the chief weren't getting along. Durwood was talking fast and gesturing energetically to Sheriff Moore. She looked up and up to see the crown of the sheriff's hat. Durwood was looking up too. As the men crossed the floor, they stopped at almost every table. Durwood's curly blond hair was damp with sweat. His white dress shirt clung to him. As he reached out to shake hands or clap friends on the back, heavy gold cuff links glistened. The county attorney looked tense and worried, the sheriff grim. Gretchen had often seen them here at the café. Durwood always had a friendly word for everybody. Some-times his wife, Sheila, met him here for lunch and that was exciting because she was a Winslow. Every town has its aristocracy. The Winslows lived on Hickory Hill. Everyone stood a little straighter when Sheila Dur-wood came by, gracious and always elegant. Grandmother said Mr. Durwood and his wife were one of the town's finest young cou-ples. Durwood almost always had a smile on his face. There was talk of him running for the state senate. Everybody said he was a nat-ural. Gretchen wasn't sure exactly what that meant, but the men admired his athletic phy-sique and women smiled over his curly blond hair and blue eyes and ready grin. He wasn't smiling today.

Sheriff Moore swept off his Stetson. His face was all points and angles, the bones jut-ting from his cheeks, his chin sharp as a V. His gaze swept the café. He hulked behind the younger man, dark brown eyes peering out from beneath bushy gray eyebrows. The curving mustache that ended near the jawline was gray, too. His bony face was tanned the color of mahogany except for a thin white band near the hairline marking the fit of his cowboy hat.

"Hidey, Donny, Sheriff." A voice rose above the greetings. "What's the latest on the murder?" Mayor Burkett came to his feet. He tossed his napkin onto the table, reached out to shake Durwood's hand, then the sheriff's. "This has been a shock to all of us. Are you making progress?" His plump face creased in concern. Mayor Burkett always wore a white suit and a straw boater in the summertime.

Gretchen edged nearer. She held the order pad.

Durwood's cheeks puffed in exasperation. "Some of us are." His tone was sour. "I can't get a straight answer out of the chief. Looks to me like he's wasting a lot of time out at the Blue Light. Wants to know the name of every man Faye Tatum talked to or danced with. But Paul and I" — the county attorney jerked his head toward the sheriff — "are doing everything we can. We've driven a lot of back roads. The sheriff's got two search teams with dogs out. Nobody's seen Tatum since he left the Blue Light last night. His car's still in the parking lot so we think he's on foot."

The mayor rocked back on his heels. His frown deepened. "Don't like the sound of it, a dangerous fugitive at large. What if he comes up to a farmhouse with only women-folk there?"

The sheriff shifted the lump of chewing

tobacco in one cheek. "Radio's telling everybody to keep their doors locked, not answer to a stranger. I don't think people need to be scared. He isn't armed, so far as we know. Nobody saw a gun at the Blue Light and he was in his uniform. No place to carry a gun. Now that would be a horse of a different color —"

J. B. Miles, the cattle auctioneer, boomed, "The posse would be shooting at the twitch of a bush if Clyde had a gun."

Sheriff Moore smiled but his eyes were as hard as agates. "We'll pick him up pretty soon. We're checking the bus and train stations in Tulsa. We'll find him if he's still around here." The sheriff flung a knobby hand toward the door of the café. "But he may have thumbed a ride on 66."

Mayor Burkett reached into his hip pocket for his wallet. "One thing seems mighty clear. An innocent man would have come home, no doubt about it. I sure don't like the idea of Tatum running around loose. I told Chief Fraser how I felt about it and I'm telling you. I've called a special meeting of the city council for Friday night if we don't have this thing cleared up by then." The mayor's bulbous eyes challenged the county attorney and sheriff. "The council expects to hear from both of you."

"You can count on us." Durwood met the mayor's gaze. "We'll be at the meeting. And we'll have plenty to report." It was the mayor who looked away, began to count out his change.

The sheriff cleared his throat. "I expect it will all be over by Friday night. See you, gentlemen." He jerked his head toward the booths. "Come on, Donny."

Gretchen followed them.

Durwood slid into the booth. He pulled a handkerchief from his pocket, swiped at his face.

The seat squeaked as the sheriff sat down. He gave a little bark of laughter. "Getting to you, Donny? You gotta get a thicker skin if you're going to stay in politics."

Durwood jammed the handkerchief into his pocket. "The mayor doesn't worry me. It's damn hot today, Paul." He looked up at Gretchen, smiled. "What's good today?"

The sheriff picked up the menu. "Get yourself some summer shirts. Those long sleeves would make anybody sweat."

The county attorney reached for the ice water, took a big gulp. "Hey, I got to wear these shirts." He held out his arm. "Look at that." He moved his wrist and the gold cuff link was bright as a piece of sunshine. "Birthday present from Sheila. Lion heads."

109

The sheriff glanced at the links. "I'd save 'em for winter." His short-sleeve khaki shirt was open at the throat. "Let's see, young lady. Got any fried baloney today?"

Gretchen took their orders. When she brought their lunches, fried baloney and turnips for Sheriff Moore and the special for Durwood and two iced teas, she put the glasses, each with lemon wedges and fresh mint, and plates on the table. She looked at the county attorney. His face was somber. He picked up his tea and drank it halfway down.

"Mr. Durwood." Gretchen's fingers curled around the edges of the serving tray. "Do you know where Barb is?"

"Barb?" He looked at Gretchen sharply.

The sheriff turned cold, inquiring eyes on Gretchen.

"Barb Tatum. I went to your office looking for her this morning. Barb said she was going to tell you about hearing a knock on the front door last night." Gretchen balanced the tray on one hip.

"Barb Tatum?" The sheriff raised a bushy eyebrow. "I hadn't heard about this."

Durwood fingered one of his cuff links, his face drawn in a tired frown. "The knock on the door? That's what she told me." His voice was skeptical. "But what else could she say? Poor kid. Of course she claims somebody knocked on the door. She's trying to protect her dad. But the minute she told me, I knew I had to let her go." Though he sounded hard and determined, his face was sad. "She didn't take it very well. I tried to explain, but I don't think she ever got it. She's been working in the office this summer and so far as I know, she did a good job but" — he spread out his hands palms up — "here she was, trying to give evidence in a case I'll be handling. Obviously, we couldn't have her in the office. There's plenty of confidential material when I prepare a case and right now it looks like Clyde Tatum's going to be arrested for the murder of his wife and I'll prosecute. Still, I hated to tell her that." He massaged the side of his face. "She was crying when she left. I asked my secretary to call around, see if she can line something up for the girl. Of course, a job's probably the last thing she's worried about right now. I don't know if there's any family here. Maybe she'll be leaving town." He dipped his spoon into the bowl.

The sheriff cut his bologna into quarters, speared a piece. "My son-in-law's been looking for help. Colonial Insurance. They got a lot of papers to handle at his office."

"I'll tell Barb." Gretchen hesitated, then

111

said quickly, "Last night Barb came to my house for help. She told me then that she'd heard a knock on the door. And later Barb told the chief her mother answered the door and said, 'You've got a nerve,' and then there was a struggle and Barb ran away."

" 'You've got a nerve,' " the sheriff repeated. "Hmm. Could be somebody Faye didn't know well. Or didn't expect to see. On the other hand, after the fight she and Clyde had, maybe that's exactly what she'd say to him."

Durwood spread the orangey oleo on his corn bread, stared up at Gretchen. He took a bite, spoke indistinctly. "So you were with Barb? Did you see anybody near the house?"

Mrs. Perkins clattered from behind the counter. "Gretchen, can you come help? We need you."

Gretchen turned and saw her grandmother with her back to the dining area, holding the telephone and talking and Mrs. Perkins fluttering her hands toward the kitchen.

Gretchen glanced at the clock. Almost two. She needed to check in with Mr. Dennis, tell him she'd talked to Billy Forrester and she was getting started on the story about Faye Tatum. She would stay late this evening to make up for the time here at the café. So, if Grandmother needed help for a few more minutes, that was okay.

Behind her, she heard the sheriff's gruff voice saying, "I suspect she died pretty quick. Tatum's a big, strong man. I'd guess he was long gone when the girls got to the house. He probably blundered out of the house and into the woods. That's where we'll find him, huddled in a thicket somewhere. Won't surprise me if he's dead."

Gretchen stopped at the kitchen door, turned her head to listen.

The county attorney had lifted his iced tea, but stopped without drinking. "Dead?" He sounded startled.

The sheriff speared another piece of bologna. "Remorse. Clyde's no killer. I've known him since he was a boy. A woman can drive a man a long way down a dark path. I reckon right now there's no one sadder than Clyde." He chewed, swallowed. "Except his little girl."

. . . remembering. You were nice to me, Gretchen. You tried to make me feel better about Mama. But you didn't know how awful it was, how bad I felt. That first day after she died, the whole world caved in on me. Daddy was missing. I didn't know then that everybody thought he'd killed Mama. I went to the county attorney's office to tell him about the knock on the door. He didn't believe me. He told me it looked like he was going to have to try and send my daddy to jail. He told me the police were looking for Daddy. But he didn't tell me why. I didn't find out until the chief came to your house that evening. Donny Durwood only said he was sorry and I couldn't work for him anymore. I walked out of his office and I couldn't feel a thing. It was like nothing was real, not him or the streets or the cars or the people. . . .

Chapter

4

A cardinal flashed through the air, red as a

dancing flame. He and I and a chittering squirrel were the only living creatures in the cemetery, but familiar figures moved in my memory, as real as the bright bird and the darting squirrel. Grandmother smiled at me, blue eyes shining, as she swiped floury hands on a blue apron with white scalloped edges. Mr. Dennis bent over yellow copy paper, marking, changing, correcting, then looked up with his sardonic, disbelieving, hopeful face. Donald Durwood sighed and I heard his sad murmur, "Poor kid." Chief Fraser stood on the platform of the gazebo on the town square, big head thrust forward, eyes blazing, chin jutting, defying them all. I stood amid the graves, surrounded by ghosts. . . .

Mr. Dennis wrinkled his nose, plopped down the coffee mug. "Cold." He scratched at his bristly chin. By the time the press run ended, he always looked wilted, his fringe of gray hair tousled, his sagging cheeks drooping, his shirt wrinkled. "Just like the trail for Clyde Tatum. Colder than a white-bellied wide-mouth bass tossed on the dock." He pointed at the front page of the *Gazette*. The first issue lay on his desk with its distinctive smell of paper and fresh ink. Faye Tatum's murder was the lead story. A three-column spread at the bottom of the page detailed the search under way for Clyde Tatum. Both stories had Ralph Cooley's byline. My story about Barb coming to my window and our grisly discovery was just below the fold. It read: *By G. G. Gilman.* The sidebar about the chief and the sheriff and the county attorney had no byline because Mr. Dennis wrote it. The photos were stacked: grim-faced Chief Fraser, slate-eyed Sheriff Moore, sternly confident County Attorney Durwood. The Allied attack on Cherbourg rated a 36-point, two-column head at the upper left. The murder had pushed inside the latest news of the heavy Japanese losses at the Battle of the Philippine Sea.

Gretchen felt wilted, too, from her rush through the boiler-hot afternoon. Her dark hair hung in damp ringlets and her dress stuck to her back. She stood by Mr. Dennis's desk and wished for a big glass of iced tea. "They haven't found Mr. Tatum?" She didn't know whether to feel glad or sad. It was terrible to know the police and the sheriff and his deputies were hunting Barb's daddy to arrest him for her mother's murder, but it was almost worse not to know where he was. Every minute Mr. Tatum stayed gone made him look that much guiltier.

Gretchen took a deep breath. She had to

push out the words. "Sheriff Moore thinks he may be dead."

Mr. Dennis's green eyes raked her face. He leaned forward, round furrowed face intent. "What have you got, girl?" He listened until she was done. "Hmm. Sheriff may be right." The editor gave a dry bark that might have been a laugh or might have been a cough. "Or he may be wrong. Let's say Clyde didn't kill Faye. Since he hasn't shown up, he most likely heard about her murder." He tilted his head to one side, stared up at the ceiling fan. "He may be hiding out because he's scared. Or it could be that he doesn't know yet. He may have gotten the hell out of town last night because he's mad at her. He may show up down at Sill, ready to ship out. I'm with the chief. There's a lot of stuff we don't know. A lot of could bes and may bes." Dennis's gaze dropped to his desk. He stared at the front page. "Goddam. Broken font in the Cherbourg story." He picked up a red pencil, circled the head. The H in HARBOR was chipped. "Looks good otherwise." He tossed down the red pencil.

"Mr. Dennis, I haven't found Barb anywhere. Mr. Durwood didn't know where she'd gone. I went to her house and I called some of her friends." Gretchen felt the crumpled sheets of copy paper in the pocket of her skirt, the sheets that were still blank. "She can tell me about her mom's friends."

The editor frowned.

Gretchen spoke fast. "That's how I can find out about Mrs. Tatum. For my story." She looked at him anxiously. Didn't he remember how Ralph Cooley had sneered and how people would read Cooley's story in this afternoon's paper, all about Mrs. Tatum dancing away her last hours at the Blue Light? "Is it too late now for me to do the story?"

Mr. Dennis picked up his story log. "Try for Friday, Gretchen. That gives you tomorrow to find people. You can hold the Forrester story until next week. And Gretchen, that was good work to talk to the sheriff and the county attorney." Dennis raised a bristly eyebrow. "So the mayor's going to demand answers at a specially called city council meeting." His voice was thoughtful. "Durwood's been aching to tangle with the chief. If they don't find Tatum before then, the chief's going to have trouble. I'll tell you what, Gretchen. You can come to the council meeting with me Friday night and . . ."

Every Friday night in the summer, Gretchen and a bunch of friends — Wilma and Judy and Louise and Betsy and Rhonda and Arlene — went to Thompson's Drugs to sit at the counter and have a sundae or soda. Then they would walk together and as they passed the Bijou, Gretchen always looked into the dim cool interior for a glimpse of Tommy Krueger. If he was taking tickets, their eyes would meet and there was a promise in his. She'd see him Saturday night when everybody went to the show for the double feature. This coming Saturday the double bill was *What a Woman!*, starring Rosalind Russell and Brian Aherne, and *Guadalcanal Diary*, with Preston Foster and Lloyd Nolan. Friday nights the girls usually ended up at a slumber party at one girl's home. Sometimes they stayed up all night playing bridge.

". . . and you can do a color story." He glanced at her, then continued smoothly, "I'll cover the meeting while you take a look around, pick up the attitudes, describe the way people look and act. Write it so that the reader sees the council chamber, smells the cigar smoke, hears the tone in people's voices." He barked again and this time she knew it was a harsh laugh. "I double guarantee, there'll be plenty for you to write about."

Gretchen tossed away her plans for Friday

night without a qualm. She forgot that she was hot and tired, pushed away the thought that she'd hoped to see Tommy. After all, she'd see him Saturday night. Tommy was two years older. He ran track and he was tall and thin and bony with a shock of curly brown hair and quizzical blue eyes and a spattering of freckles. He had a habit of shoving his fingers through his wiry hair. They'd met at the library last summer. They both loved *The Moon Is Down* and *The Human Comedy*. Sometimes when the movie was under way and Tommy didn't have to take tickets, he and Gretchen talked in soft whispers behind the thick velvet curtains. Last week they'd stood very close, wrapped in a fold of the curtains, and she'd smelled the spicy scent of his hair oil as he bent down and his lips brushed hers. For that sweet instant, she didn't hear the tinny sound of music from the movie or the crackle of candy wrappers or the murmur of voices, on the screen and off.

A color story . . .

Gretchen brushed back a limp curl. "Why is Mr. Durwood against Chief Fraser?"

The editor's green eyes glinted. "Smart girl. That's the right question. The chief thinks Durwood's reckless and too quick to interfere with the police. Durwood's a gunslinger, always ready to prosecute, and he thinks the chief is too cautious, wants too much evidence before he'll make an arrest. The mayor likes to keep them head to head, says a good healthy competition is best for the town. Of course," Dennis observed as he leaned back in his chair, his lips curled in a sardonic grin, "depends on whose ox is being gored, doesn't it? There's a rumor the chief's encouraging Beau Bradley to run for county attorney. That might be okay with Durwood if he makes up his mind to try for the state senate. And it might be damn annoying to Durwood if he wants to stay on as county attorney. Bradley's done a fine job on the school board. So" — Dennis pushed up from his chair, picked up the fresh paper — "you might get to see a little drama Friday night." Mr. Dennis reached up to the hat tree for his panama. "But for now, you get on home."

The sun was a brilliant red in the west. Gretchen's skin felt like wax paper shriveling in a campfire. She wished she'd taken the time to drink more water at the café, but she'd hurried to get the floors mopped and the tables and booths set for tomorrow. Now Archer Street shimmered and the three blocks home seemed endless. Tired, she was so tired. She needed to think about the story on Billy Forrester and she had to talk to Barb — where could Barb be? — so she could find people who knew Faye Tatum. Faye Tatum . . . Already it was hard to remember her face when she was alive.

A horn honked twice and the chief's big green Packard nosed toward the shoulder.

Gretchen stepped up to the open window.

The chief's smooth-crowned cowboy hat almost touched the interior roof. His heavy face was perspiring. He looked tired, worried, and somber, but he almost managed a smile and his deep voice was gentle. "I'm on my way to your house, Miss Gretchen. Can I give you a ride?"

"Yes, sir." She pulled the door open, yanking back her fingers from the hot metal. She slid gingerly onto the leather seat. The big seat was hot, but she sank back against the softness. She pulled at the door, but it didn't quite close. He reached across, slammed it shut.

As the big car rumbled down the street, Gretchen frowned. "Why are you coming to my house?" She sat bolt upright. "Is Grandmother all right?"

"Your grandma's fine. I'm coming to see Miss Barb." He slowed, eased the shift into second as the Mallorys' red springer spaniel ambled across the street. The Packard picked up speed and he shifted into third.

Gretchen smoothed her damp hair back from her face. "I've been looking for Barb all day."

"So've I." He turned into the graveled drive at Gretchen's house. "Seems like she's been in the woods over near her house . . ."

Gretchen looked back at the patch of scrub oak and piney woods that spread up a slope from the Tatums' backyard. She'd never thought to look in the woods when she stopped at the house earlier.

". . . and she came straggling out a little while ago. Sergeant Petty's been keeping an eye on the house. I guess Barb was waiting for her papa to come home."

He reached over, gave a pull on the handle. "That door sticks. There you go, Miss Gretchen."

His boots crunched on the gravel. Gretchen hurried ahead to open the front door. "Grandmother? I'm home. Chief Fraser's with me."

Her grandmother hurried out of the kitchen, face red, apron askew, a pot holder in one hand. "Chief Fraser, I was just getting our supper ready. Will you stay and eat? We have tuna fish sandwiches and tomato soup tonight."

He stood in the doorway, holding his big hat. His eyes scanned the living room. The radio was on and a smooth deep voice announced the news: ". . . V-1 rockets struck in the heart of London today and Londoners once again raced for cover just as they had during the Blitz. . . ." "No, ma'am, but thank you. Is Miss Barb handy?"

"That poor child." The older woman's dumpling face creased in concern. "So pale and tired and nobody to help her. The only family is Faye's sister, Darla Murray. She's down in San Antonio, Texas, with her husband at the air field. She can't come until Friday. She told me to call Reverend Byars." She gave a little headshake. "That's the church they grew up in, though Faye hadn't been in a long time. But I didn't feel it was my place to say anything. Anyway, I talked to Reverend Byars and he'll see to the funeral. They're thinking it will be Friday afternoon. He said Barb can come and live with them. They've got a houseful of kids and that big old rambling house. He's coming over tonight to see her. I told Barb to rest for awhile in Jimmy's room —"

The hall door opened. Barb still wore the blue shirtwaist dress. Sharp wrinkles marked the starched cotton. She held a fabric-covered satchel with leather handles. "Have you found my daddy?" Her voice was tense and anxious.

"Not yet." The chief dropped his cowboy hat on an end table. "I need to speak with you, Miss Barb." His voice had a determined edge.

She stared at him, her eyes forlorn, then slowly walked, still favoring her sore foot, to the channel-backed chair next to the sofa. She passed through a shaft of sunlight streaming through a west window. Barb wasn't wearing a slip. The chief's gaze dropped to the floor. She sat on the edge of the slick damask cushion, stiff and straight, still clutching the handles of the satchel.

". . . President Roosevelt is expected to sign into law this Thursday the G.I. Bill of Rights, which will . . ."

Grandmother bustled to the radio and turned it off. "Gretchen, if you will come with me to the kitchen —"

The chief lifted a big hand. "That's all right, Lotte. I'd be pleased for you and Miss Gretchen to stay. You're the closest Miss Barb has to family right now. I'm thinking she needs folks to stand by her."

He waited until Gretchen and her grandmother sat on the brown angora mohair sofa. Gnarled hands clasped behind his back, he walked heavily across the room to look down at Barb, his protuberant cheeks red, his thick lips folded tight. Abruptly, he cleared his throat and swung one hand toward her, pointing. "Who was the man coming in the night to see your mama?"

Barb sat frozen, her face stricken, her shoulders hunched. The handles of the satchel fell from her hands and the cloth bag thudded to the floor. "Man?" It was a tiny gasp of sound, barely audible.

The chief rocked back on his heels. "You didn't tell me that's why your mama and papa had a fight."

Barb came to her feet, grimacing as she put too much weight on her right foot. "That's not why! Daddy was mad because she was going to the Blue Light. That's all that it was. I swear it. It's because she was dancing. I promise. And Mama left him a nice note before she went to work." Barb clasped her hands tightly together.

The chief's face furrowed with disbelief. "Miss Barb, I got to tell you I got plenty of witnesses at the barbershop yesterday afternoon who heard your daddy explode. Seems he was lathered up getting a shave and Ed Newton came in for a shoe shine. He made a crack to somebody about Faye Tatum's mystery boyfriend and Clyde came out of his chair like a stung bronco.

He pinned Ed up against the wall and had him by the throat. Took two men to get him off. Ed got mad too and told Clyde it was all over town that some man was visiting his house late at night and Clyde sure wasn't in town and maybe Clyde should ask Faye what's what. Clyde wanted to know who was saying this. Ed wouldn't ante, said it didn't matter and surely Clyde was man enough to find out the truth himself. Clyde stormed out of the barbershop, half his face still lathered. Now this is gospel truth, Miss Barb. I got to know, who was coming to see your mama?"

Barb turned away. She sank blindly into the chair, hid her face in her hands.

Grandmother drew her breath in sharply. She leaned forward. "Chief Fraser, please, she is just a child. Why do you have to ask her things like this?" Her voice quavered. "This is so awful, her mama dead, her daddy gone, and now for you to treat her so." Grandmother clutched the folds of her apron, her blue eyes anxious.

"Lotte, I got to ask." His voice was harsh. "I've hunted to hell and gone out at the Blue Light. I thought maybe somebody followed Faye home. She'd had a lot of beer. Things can happen. I've checked out every man who was out there. If anybody came out after Faye, nobody saw it. Somebody would have, just like somebody saw a man sneaking into Clyde's house while Clyde was gone. I'll tell you, Miss Barb" — he swung back toward Barb, who looked up at him in sick horror — "I got to know who that man is. He may be in danger." His face looked older than time and full of sorrow. "I didn't want to believe your daddy killed your mama. Maybe a police officer shouldn't look at crime like that, but I've known your daddy since he was a boy. He was in my Scout troop. But I got to deal with what's happened. Clyde knew about the man and Clyde's run away. If he's innocent, he's got to come home and tell us where he was last night. If he's guilty — well, the man your mama was seeing has to be warned. So you've got to tell me, Miss Barb, who he is."

Tears spilled down Barb's face. "Daddy thought Mama . . . Oh, I didn't know. Oh, God." She huddled, her body folding in on itself. "Somebody told him . . . and he thought . . ." She spoke in wrenching spurts, then moaned, a writhing cry of heartbreak.

Worst of all was the moment that Barb recognized what the chief's words meant. Her dazed look changed to fear, hopeless, aching, unbearable fear.

Gretchen knew that Barb was stricken by horror, clearly aware that her father might be guilty.

The chief's big shoulders slumped. "God almighty, Miss Barb, I'm sorry. But you see, I got to know. Who was the man?"

"It isn't true." Barb swallowed jerkily. A sob shook her shoulders. "I tell you it isn't true. Nobody came to see Mama. Mama wouldn't do that. It's a lie." She dissolved into hiccoughing cries.

Grandmother rose. She was heavy, but she flew across the room, knelt by the chair to pull Barb onto her shoulder. She twisted to look up at the chief. "Of course this child doesn't know. No woman would let her daughter see that kind of thing."

Barb pulled away. Her face was blotchy and red. "I tell you, it isn't true." But her voice was faint. Fear flattened her features, made her body shake.

The chief heaved an irritated sigh. "I guess that's right. I guess a woman letting a man steal into her husband's bed would sure keep it quiet. But I'm going to keep looking." He swung around. In two steps he was at the door and scooping up his big hat. He pulled open the screen. He gave Barb one last look, shook his head, and slammed out.

★ ★ ★

"Try to eat a little soup, my dear." Grandmother spoke as if to someone who had been very ill for a long time.

Barb touched the spoon, left it lying on the table. "I can't. I keep thinking about Daddy."

Gretchen picked up half a tuna fish sandwich. The crusty bread was sweet and fresh, the filling zesty with pickle juice and chopped green onions. "Look, Barb, you told the chief it wasn't true. So it will be all right. They'll find out what happened." Gretchen was suddenly voraciously hungry.

Barb pressed trembling fingers against one cheek. She spoke almost in a whisper. "It wasn't true. But if Daddy thought it was . . ."

Grandmother pushed the platter of sandwiches closer to Barb. "We can't change what's happened. None of us made this happen. So you must not worry. You must trust in God. Please try the soup. It will be strengthening for you."

Barb picked up the spoon, slowly began to eat. She finished half the bowl, ate part of a sandwich, then pushed back the plate.

"That is such a good girl. Now I will see to the dishes and you and Gretchen listen to the radio." Grandmother started to rise from the table, then hesitated, one hand pressed against her chest. She wavered on her feet.

"Grandmother!" Gretchen stood so quickly, her chair tumbled to the floor. She reached the older woman, now breathing quickly. "Are you sick? I'll call Dr. Jamison."

Grandmother sank back into her chair, reached for her glass of iced tea, drank deeply. "No, no. I am fine. Just a little catch in my chest. It will go away." She put down the glass, took another deep breath.

"You're tired, Grandmother. I'll help you to your room." Gretchen took a tight grip on her grandmother's soft arm. "You've had too hard a day. You can lie down. Barb and I will do the dishes."

Grandmother slowly stood. "Yes, I will rest for awhile. Thank you, Gretchen."

Gretchen helped her grandmother walk slowly down the hall to the bedroom at the back. She settled her in the big green rocker next to her table covered with pictures in heavy brass frames and the leather-bound family Bible. "I'll bring you some tea, Grandmother."

The old woman sagged against the cushions of the rocker, closed her eyes. One hand still pressed against her chest. "No, *mein Schatz*. I will just be quiet for a few minutes."

By the time Gretchen reached the kitchen, Barb had cleared the table and stacked the dishes. Gretchen got the dishpan out from beneath the sink, put on a kettle of water to boil. Gretchen washed, then scalded the dishes with the boiling water. Barb dried, stacking the dishes and cutlery near the breadbox.

When she was done, Barb flung the dish towel on the counter. "Gretchen, can I use your phone?"

The phone was on the wall near the door to the living room. Gretchen pointed to it. "Sure. I'm going to see about Grandmother." The kettle still held hot water. Gretchen poured the water into a cup with a Lipton tea bag. When it was steeped dark as pine tar, she discarded the tea bag. She added two heaping teaspoons of sugar. They were almost out and the grocery hadn't had a sugar shipment for almost a month. At the phone, Barb gave a number to the operator. As Gretchen stepped into the hall, she heard Barb ask quickly, "Is Amelia there?"

In Grandmother's room, Gretchen placed the cup and saucer on the table. "Grandmother?"

Her eyes fluttered open. Her face was pasty white. "Oh, Gretchen." She tried to smile.

Gretchen felt her stomach twist. Grandmother looked so sick. "Grandmother, I'm going to call Dr. Jamison —"

Alarm flaring in her face, Grandmother lifted both hands. "No, no, you must not. I need only to rest. The tea will help." She took a deep breath, placed her hands on the chair arms.

The front doorbell rang.

Grandmother struggled to get up. Her breath came in short, quick gasps.

"I'll see." Gretchen stepped closer, put her hand firmly on the older woman's shoulder. "Stay here, Grandmother. Drink your tea. I'll take care of it."

"Yes, please." Grandmother closed her eyes. Her arms rested on the chair, limp and heavy.

Gretchen hurried into the living room. Barb waited in the kitchen doorway. She stared toward the front door, her eyes empty, her face rigid. Gretchen thought of the newsreel pictures of bombed-out children, lost, alone, hopeless.

The doorbell jangled again. The Reverend Byars peered through the screen. "Miss Gretchen, I've come to see Miss Barb. I know you and your grandmother have opened your hearts to her. I've come to offer her our house as her new home."

Gretchen ran to the door. "Grand-mother's resting. Please come in." She stood aside for him to enter. The fiery evening sun bathed the dusty yard in a brilliant orange light. Birds cawed as they wheeled around the elm trees, ready to roost for the night. The hot air shimmered though it was almost eight. Cicadas rasped, their summer song so loud it masked the squeak of the screen door hinges.

"Thank you, Miss Gretchen. We won't disturb your grandmother. True to my word, I've come to offer sanctuary to Miss Barb." He looked at the stone still figure. "Miss Barb." The preacher's voice was as thick and slow and sweet as molasses. Each word hung in the air like a dancer in a spot-light, eager for applause. Blond hair swooped in a high pompadour above an unctuous face. He lifted plump hands, palms up. "Let us pray." His head sank and his voice soared. "Dear Lord, we gather here in thy name always reverencing thee and knowing that thou does hear thy children's call. Lo, we can be sure that in times of trouble and sorrow thou art near. Be with us now as we grieve for a lost soul and pray that your child Faye shall be gathered up by an-gels and lifted out of sorrow and sin. We know that the sins of the world do mock your goodness and we must be ever vigilant against the vices that the devil casts among us, leading us away from the path of righteousness. Evil surrounds us . . ."

Gretchen felt buffeted by the sonorous flow of words. Was he saying that Barb's mother was bad?

Barb pressed her hands against her cheeks.

The deep, rich voice rolled on: ". . . dance and drink and lust have ever paved the way to hell. I tried to counsel our sister Faye and alas she didn't heed my voice or that of her Savior. She went her own way and we see the fruits of that decision. As it says in First Samuel, fifteenth chapter, twenty-third verse: For rebellion is as the sin of witchcraft, and stubbornness is as iniquity and idolatry. Because thou hast rejected the word of the Lord, he hath also rejected thee from being king." He paused, clasped his hands together. "But with your help, Good Lord, we shall surround her dear child, Barbara, with your loving care and safeguard her from the temptations of the world and the devil. Amen." He lifted his head, his face wreathed in a forgiving smile. He walked toward Barb, his hands outstretched. "Miss Barb, I've come to take you home."

Barb took a step back. "My daddy will come. I know he will. I'm going to stay at a friend's house tonight. I've talked to Amelia Brady and I'm going there right now." She turned away from him, walked determinedly to the sofa, and picked up the cloth bag.

"Miss Barb." His deep voice swooped low. His face held a look of forbearance, though his eyes were cold. "We cannot refuse to accept what life brings to us. We cannot shut our eyes to facts. There's no question that last night's brutal act sprang from disorder between a man and wife, disorder that . . ."

Barb clutched the valise against her, wrapped her arms around it as if it could shield her from Reverend Byars's words, his relentless, smooth-toned, crushing words. "It wasn't Daddy." Her voice shook. "I tell you, it wasn't Daddy. I would have known." But her eyes were full of fear. "It was someone else."

". . . can be predicted when a woman forgets her marriage vows. As we are told in the sixth chapter of Romans, verse twenty-three: The wages of sin is death."

"Mama wasn't . . . she didn't . . ." Barb pulled up the valise, hid her face.

"We won't say more." His resonant voice filled the little living room. "It isn't for girls to know about these things. And now" — he cleared his throat, frowned as the old grandfather clock chimed the hour — "I must get back to the church. I've left the assistant pastor with the young people, but I must be there for our closing prayers. Perhaps, Miss Barb" — and he spoke as if bestowing a great gift — "you will be happier to stay with your friend tonight, but we stand ready to welcome you. At any time." He bowed his head, clasped his hands. "Dear Lord, give us strength to go forward and face down the forces of evil which beset us. Remind us ever that only thy goodness and mercy will save wretched sinners from lives of torment and everlasting perdition. Gird us for battle. In Jesus' name we pray, amen." He nodded in satisfaction and moved briskly toward the door, pompous and confident, impervious to Barb's pain. He stopped for an instant in the doorway. The last red rays of the evening sun flooded around him, glistened on his hair, turned his skin pink as a pig's. "Give my best wishes to your grandmother, Miss Gretchen. Good night, young ladies."

Gretchen didn't watch him go. Instead, she took a tentative step, then another, toward Barb.

Barb still stood with the valise hiding her face, her fingers arched like claws against the flowered fabric. She didn't move until the sound of his car backfired its way into the street. Abruptly, she flung the bag onto the floor. Her eyes glittered with tears of rage. Her face twisted. "Mama laughed at him. She said he was a silly little man who spent his life trying to scare everybody into heaven, saying nobody should drink or smoke or dance, and that women in shorts were asking for trouble and deserved what they got. He told Mama she shouldn't paint the kind of pictures she painted because they made people think about things they shouldn't do. Mama said his problem was he wanted every woman he saw. She told me that Lucille, one of her friends at work, sings in the choir and one day Lucille was in the choir room early and he came in and pressed himself up against her and she could feel him, hard as a rock. Mama told me never to get in a room with him by myself, that she'd heard about others he'd touched and nobody could say anything because who would believe it about the preacher? Now he's acting like Mama got killed because she went to the Blue Light to dance." She took a deep, shaky breath. "And worse. He's saying Mama . . . he's saying Mama was a bad woman. And there isn't anything I can do." She doubled her hands into fists.

Gretchen reached out, gripped a thin arm rigid as a metal pole. "Yes, there is, Barb. Yes, there is."

"Barb didn't go with Reverend Byars?" Grandmother held the cup of tea with both hands, looked worriedly at Gretchen.

"She won't ever go there." Gretchen knew the words were true as she spoke them. Barb would never, never, never go to that house. "She's gone to spend the night with Amelia Brady. Reverend Byars said . . ." Gretchen frowned. "He prayed for Mrs. Tatum, but he made her sound bad."

"Oh. I see." Grandmother's face looked old and worn and infinitely sad. "Poor Barb. To have to listen to such as that. And truth to tell, he didn't like Faye. He scolded her for her painting and she defied him. She didn't go back to church again. And in his anger he doesn't think how Barb must feel. Of course she will not want to go there. We will tell her she can stay with us as long as she wants."

"Barb says her daddy would never hurt her mother. Barb says he will come home." Gretchen heard her words curl up into a question.

Grandmother finished the tea, set the cup on the saucer. She didn't look at Gretchen.

139

"Poor Clyde. Poor Faye." The words were heavy with sorrow. She rested her head back against the chair, her eyes mournful.

"Let me help you get ready for bed, Grandmother." Gretchen went to the closet, found Grandmother's pink cotton night-gown. It smelled sweet and fresh, from the wind that fluttered the wash as it dried on the clothesline. "I'll brush your hair. And bring you a glass of warm milk."

Grandmother lay heavy and still against the plumped cushions of the rocking chair, her muscles inert, her breathing slow. She looked small. She'd never looked small to Gretchen before. A smile curved her lips. "You're a good girl, Gretchen." Her voice was just above a whisper, light as the far-away whoo of an owl. "Please put my gown on the bed. I will rest a while longer. You have had such a long day, a hard day. And to have seen what you have seen." Her voice was filled with pain.

Gretchen's hands clenched for an instant, then she willed away the image of Faye Tatum sprawled in death. Gretchen stepped to the bed, spread the gown out, tried to smooth the wrinkles where she'd clutched the thin fabric.

"Oh, dear child, I would have spared you if I could. Gretchen . . ." Grandmother pushed back a wisp of hair from her face. "Don't remember the way Faye died. Remember the way she lived. She is in heaven now, splashing paints on canvas, brighter paints on a bigger canvas than she ever had here on earth, and there is no more sorrow or fear or unhappiness." Grandmother nodded solemnly. "The Bible tells us: God shall wipe away all tears from their eyes; and there shall be no more death, neither sorrow, nor crying; neither shall there be any more pain. . . ."

"Grandmother" — Gretchen's voice trembled — "I wish Barb was here. Reverend Byars talked about God, but it didn't help. And you help." Gretchen rushed to the rocking chair. She knelt, buried her face against warmth. She cried.

"Mein Schatz, mein Schatz . . ."

With tears came release. Or was it Grandmother's faith? Her sweet voice opened a vision of eternity, a glimpse beyond sorrow and evil and horror. The words glowed in Gretchen's mind: *neither shall there be any more pain.* Gretchen felt her Grandmother's hand gently stroking her hair. And heard the faint peal of the telephone in the kitchen.

Gretchen lifted her head.

Grandmother gasped. She stared toward the hall, gripped the arms of the rocking chair.

Gretchen wiped her face, jumped to her feet. "Grandmother, it's all right. Don't be scared. I'll go." She hesitated in the hallway, knew she was right: Grandmother was frightened. Why should the telephone upset her?

The ring was louder in the hall.

Gretchen skidded into the kitchen, lifted the receiver. "Hello."

The operator's voice was thin against the scratchy background noises. "A collect call from Lorraine Gilman. Will you accept charges?"

Gretchen felt a surge of happiness. "Yes, oh, yes."

"Gretchen, honey, oh, my God, I just saw the paper. I was late getting home from my shift. I can't believe —"

Gretchen clung to the telephone. Her mother's quick, light voice raced, as it always did, words tumbling over the wire fast as the click of castanets. "Mother, oh, Mother. Can you come home? It's been so long. You haven't been home since May." Gretchen pictured her mother that last visit, her shiny blond hair in a new French twist, her blue eyes sparkling as she watched Gretchen's delight in the sack of new books she'd brought all the way from Oliver's Bookstore in Tulsa. Her mother had worn a new blue dress to church that Sunday with three-quarter-length sleeves and a batiste collar. Her white and blue spectator pumps and fabric handbag were new, too. She'd laughed and said she'd used up all her ration points for the year but it was worth it to have a new outfit, her first since the war began. Gretchen had gone over and over that weekend in her mind until it glowed like a special rock polished by time. They'd laughed and eaten a big Sunday dinner with fried chicken and mashed potatoes and green beans. The pineapple upside down cake was light and airy and the brown sugar topping perfect. It had been almost like old times.

"Baby, I am coming home. On Saturday. I've got the day off. I've been planning —" She broke off. "But first, tell me what happened. About Faye. It's awful to read. The paper says she was strangled and they're looking for Clyde. But there was a story written by you. G. G. Gilman." She spoke the name almost in awe. "I couldn't believe it. When I read it, I knew it was you. All about Barb running to get you and the two of you finding Faye. It made me feel like I'd been there and the police chief coming to talk to Barb. How did your story . . ."

Grandmother walked slowly into the kitchen, her face anxious.

Gretchen pointed at the phone and smiled. "Mother," she whispered.

". . . get in our paper?"

Gretchen held tight to the receiver. "You saw my story? Mr. Dennis must have sent it out over the wire. Oh, Mother! I didn't know he would. He's supposed to give the wire service any story he thinks they might use."

"I've been half crazy ever since I read it." Her mother's voice wobbled. "You shouldn't have gone with Barb. Not when she said her mother screamed. Oh, Gretchen, I'm frightened for you and Mother. I wish I could come home right now. Is Mother all right?"

"Grandmother's fine." Even as Gretchen spoke, she knew that wasn't true. Grandmother looked old and ill. But it wouldn't do any good to worry Mother. "We're all right."

"You and Barb didn't see anybody?" Mother's voice was sharp.

"Nobody. Barb had cut her foot and I had to wrap it . . ."

"Thank God." Her mother was grim.

". . . so by the time we got to their house, no one was there."

"So the police really think Clyde killed Faye. Oh, my God, I can't believe it." She half covered the receiver and her voice was

144

muffled, but Gretchen heard her tell someone, "Gretchen's all right. She didn't see anybody." Another huge sigh of relief. Her voice came back loud and strong over the crackling on the line. "I don't believe Clyde hurt Faye. And Faye — well, she might thumb her nose at bluestockings, but she wasn't a tramp. She wouldn't . . ." Her voice trailed off. Suddenly, the vigor fled and her tone was uncertain. "But who can say now, with the world the way it is. Who can say?"

"Mother, the story in the *Gazette* tells how she danced away her last hours at the Blue Light. It makes her sound cheap. But Mr. Dennis said I could write a story" — Gretchen felt like she was standing on a little boat in a big lake during a storm and she wasn't sure she could make it to shore — "about what she really was like, how she loved art and what a great mom she was to Barb and how she laughed a lot." Could she do it, could she, could she?

The silence on the line grew until it swirled around Gretchen, dark as the night that pressed against the windows of the kitchen. "Mother . . ."

A quick indrawn breath, a muffled sob. "Oh, baby, I'm sorry. You made me think about Faye and the night she and Clyde got married. Your daddy and I went to the wedding and Faye and Clyde danced the Anniversary Waltz. Every time I hear that song, I think of them. I remember when Faye threw her bouquet. She threw it straight to Nita McKay and when the flowers came up against Nita she looked so startled and joyous and her smile was like a sweet, sweet baby's, so open and trusting and loving. Nobody ever thought Nita would be able to get married. She's been blind since she was a little girl. She cried out, 'For me? For me?' and Peter Thompson was standing by the door and he looked at Nita. They got married six months later. And you know, I don't think it would ever have happened if Faye had thrown those flowers to someone else. Your daddy always said I was silly —" She broke off, gave a little laugh, murmured to someone, ". . . like to be silly . . ." and came back to the line. "Anyway, I believe life is like that." Her voice was suddenly serious. "You walk down a certain street one day or you go out to a dance and nothing will ever be the same again. Gretchen, life changes. I —" A quick breath. "Listen, honey, I've got to get off the phone. People are waiting. You know how it is. But I'll be home Saturday morning. Gretchen" — a pause and then a rush of words — "I'm bringing a friend. I

146

know you'll like him a lot. See you, sweetie."
The line went dead.

Slowly Gretchen hung up the receiver.

"Gretchen, what is wrong?" Grandmother reached her, gripped her arm. Her voice rose. "Is something wrong with your mother?"

"No. She's coming home Saturday." *I know you'll like him a lot. . . .*

Grandmother's eyes lighted. "But that is good. She is coming home."

"She's bringing someone with her." Gretchen tried hard to keep her voice even. "Mother said we will like him a lot."

. . . worst of all was knowing Daddy thought Mama made love with somebody else. Daddy was jealous about her dancing at the Blue Light but if he thought there was a man . . . When the chief said somebody told Daddy about a man going into our house late at night, I felt sick, like my insides were being torn to pieces. You thought I stayed at Amelia's house that night. I didn't. I went for awhile, but her mother made me mad. I told them I was going to your house, but I hid in the woods. . . .

Chapter
5

Could have, would have, should have. Does everyone look back over life with aching regret? Oh, yes. If you live long enough, there will be sadness and hopeless longing for the mistakes, large and small, some well meant, some malicious. If you are lucky there will not be so much pain that your spirit creaks and breaks beneath the burden. If only I had . . . But what could I have done? Grandmother did her best. I did my best. We didn't know a life hung in the balance. What would have happened if I had talked to Grandmother? I understand now that Grandmother had great courage. I see her as she was then, a woman of late middle age, her heart already weakening, daring to reach out with love from that great, good, and generous heart. Oh, yes, she displayed enormous courage because she was a woman with many fears, intimidated by authority, anxious to fill out paperwork correctly, trying always to please. In the timeless silence of the cemetery, I remembered her . . .

Gretchen lay rigid as a board. Night pressed against the window, dark as a highwayman's cloak. Why did Mother have to bring someone home with her? It wouldn't be the same. Why did she say that things change? Hadn't everything changed enough with her mother gone to Tulsa to work in the war plant and Millard dead and Grandmother painting *Victory Café* on the plate glass because people didn't like German names?

Gretchen felt the hot prick of tears. Millard, so sweet and funny and nice to her, her best friend in all the whole world. What good did it do to talk about him being a hero? He didn't want to be a hero. He'd wanted to go to college and learn about the stars. When they were little kids, he'd point up at the Big Dipper and explain in his patient, kind way, "That's in the constellation Ursa Major, Gretchen. That means the Greater Bear. Over there . . ."

It was too hot for covers, so hot the bed felt damp beneath her. She'd tossed the top sheet to one side. She grabbed the edge of the sheet, pressed it against her eyes. She barely heard the click of the door. The drone of the cicadas rose and fell, rose and fell. As the rasp diminished, she heard the floor creak. She lay still, the sheet gripped in her fingers, and peeked through half-closed eyes at the open door and the shaft of light spilling in from the hallway. Grandmother stood just outside Gretchen's room, head bent as if listening.

Gretchen frowned. Grandmother wore a dark housedress and her sturdy, low-heeled work shoes. She held a wicker basket in one hand. Slowly, she stepped back into the hall and softly shut the door. The room was dark again.

Gretchen rolled over on her elbow, peered at the closed door. Why was Grandmother dressed? Gretchen slipped out of bed, hurried to the door. As she eased it open, she heard the unmistakable click of the front door lock. That was almost as startling as Grandmother slipping quietly out into the night. They never locked the doors to the house. Why would they? And where was Grandmother going?

Gretchen ran down the hall and looked out a living room window. Grandmother walked slowly down the front walk. Occasionally, like the flicker of fireflies, a light shone for an instant, then was gone. She was using a flashlight to find her way.

Gretchen raced back to her room, flung off her gown, pulled on a blouse and pedal pushers. She stepped barefoot into her loafers, not taking the time for anklets. She moved swiftly to her window, unlatched the screen, dropped to the ground. Last night a milky radiance had poured over Barb. Tonight the moon was hidden behind thick clouds and shadows bunched dark as crow feathers.

When she reached the front yard, she saw Grandmother at the end of the street, walking away from town. Grandmother walked slowly, so she was easy to follow. Gretchen slipped from shadow to shadow. Grandmother turned to the right at Maguire Road. There were occasional farmhouses set back from the road, which ended in a couple of miles at Hunter Lake. Gretchen followed cautiously, ducking behind trees when Grandmother paused to look around her. They passed the Turner farmhouse. No lights shone. A pickup truck was parked in the side yard. Two chained dogs howled. Grandmother scuttled faster but around the bend she stopped and leaned against the trunk of a big sycamore, her breath coming in short, quick gasps. Finally, wearily, she trudged forward.

They walked for another ten minutes and came over a rise. Grandmother stopped once again to look around, then she turned off the road, taking a path that plunged into a thicket of shrubbery.

Gretchen lost sight of Grandmother. She ran lightly to the path. She hesitated, looking into darkness, but she heard a rustle ahead of her. She wished she had a light, but she took slow, careful steps and gradually her eyes adjusted to the velvet thick gloom. Suddenly there was a flicker of light. Gretchen edged behind a tree trunk. Only a few feet ahead, Grandmother played the light of the flash across the weathered wood of a ramshackle cabin. Once there might have been a clearing. Now grass had grown waist high like a meadow. Shrubbery and a tangle of vines pressed against the cabin walls. A huge tree loomed over the rotting roof.

The door creaked open. A big man in a crumpled khaki uniform was outlined in a dim glow of light. "Mrs. Pfizer." His voice was eager, uncertain. "I wasn't sure you'd come after what they've been saying on the radio. They said the police are looking for me. I thought you might believe what they're saying."

Grandmother placed a hand against her chest. "I know what they have said." She spoke quietly, her voice low and sad. "And I have remembered how you came to my house and the little boy who was so good a friend to my Lorraine. And I receive the call from the young woman who would not say who she was but she said you needed for me to come, that you were innocent. And I listen to my heart and it tells me you did not do this awful thing. So I have come and I have brought you food." She held up the basket.

He came down the steps, took the basket. Grandmother's breathing was quick and fast. "Are you all right, Mrs. Pfizer?" He gripped her arm, helped her up the steps.

She clicked off the flashlight. "I will be fine." The words were labored. "I have walked fast and I am not used to coming so long a way."

They stepped inside. When the door was closed, once again the cabin was featureless, dark, an abandoned, decrepit structure. Gretchen thought the old place belonged to the Purdys. She was almost sure this was part of their land and once a tenant farmer had lived here. There was a stream that wound through bottomland on the other side of the cabin.

Gretchen crept up the steps. She eased along the porch, her fingers touching the wooden boards. Suddenly, she felt emptiness, then wool. Kneeling, she brushed her fingers across the material. A blanket! There was a blanket spread across a window. Cautiously, slowly, Gretchen pulled the covering away from the frame, peered inside.

Most of the tiny room was jammed with discarded furniture, a tabletop leaning against the wall, old straight chairs stacked one atop the other, an easy chair with its stuffing oozing from cracked imitation leather, a harp with most of the strings missing. Smudges on the floor marked where boxes and castoffs had been moved to make room for two chairs on either side of a scarred maple table. A kerosene lantern sat atop a dingy iron range. The wick blazed, casting a fitful orange glow. Barb's father hunched over the basket and flipped open its lid, pulling out a drumstick and a wedge of corn bread, and eating and talking, his mouth full. "God, I'm so hungry. . . . I haven't eaten since yesterday . . . lunch, I guess. . . . Got water from the creek and boiled it . . . a wood-burning stove. I found the lantern half full of oil. It stinks" — he gestured with one bare arm, the gnawed drumstick pointing at the coil of smoke — "but it still works." He looked dirty, tired, disreputable, like the hoboes who huddled in winter at one end of the freight yard, waiting to sneak aboard a train to take them somewhere, anywhere, nowhere. Clyde's black hair was cut so short it looked like sheared bristles on a hairbrush.

Gretchen searched for the handsome, dapper man she and Barb used to watch tinkering with the engine of his Ford and dancing cheek to cheek with Barb's mom to music playing on the Victrola. It was almost the face Gretchen remembered, curved high forehead and straight nose and square chin. Mother once said he looked like Tyrone Power. Not tonight. His puffy face, blurred by a spiky growth of beard, looked beaten and drained, his hollow eyes wild and glazed. Creases marred the stiff cotton of his short-sleeve uniform shirt.

Grandmother folded her hands. "I packed bread and dried fruit and cheese and pecans. There is food for several days. But, Clyde, you must come home." She looked around the dusty room. "You cannot stay here. This will not help you. And Barb needs her father."

He put down the drumstick, half eaten. "They're hunting for me. For *me*." His face puckered in disbelief. "They think I hurt Faye." His lips began to tremble. He buried his face in his hands.

Gretchen gripped the windowsill.

Grandmother struggled to her feet. She came around the table, touched his shoulder. "Do not think about it, Clyde. It does no good —"

He slammed his hands on the table, his stricken face twisting in sorrow. And in fury. "I got to think about it. Don't you see? They're all wrong. They think I hurt Faye. I wouldn't do that. I didn't. I was mad at her but that's because it broke my heart to think about her and another man. But if I'd gone home last night . . . oh, God, she would be all right. And now she's dead. If I'd gone home . . ." He stared at Grandmother with tear-filled eyes. "I shouted at Faye and she shouted back, said it was all a lie. Maybe it was. But then who hurt her? Did some guy hear us quarrel, follow her home? Or was there somebody else and she told him she was through because it was me she really loved?" He touched a silver identification bracelet on his left wrist. "Faye gave me this before I left for basic training. I took it off last night. I was going to throw it away. But I couldn't." He held tight to the silver links. "Faye loved me." His voice shook. "I know she did. The way she came to me . . ." He lifted his hands to his face, massive hands with broad wrists and thick forearms.

Gretchen shuddered. His hands were so big, the skin on his arms smooth and taut over muscles strong enough to crush a woman's throat. She pushed away the thought of Faye Tatum's dead face. Gretchen didn't want to think about the hands that had choked her life away.

Grandmother walked heavily around the table, sank into the chair. "The young woman who called me . . ." Grandmother's eyes fell away from Clyde. "If she can tell the police that you were with her . . ."

Clyde dropped his hands, shaking his head. "I can't tell the police about her. See, her husband's overseas and his folks would be wild if they even knew she'd been at the

Blue Light. If they ever knew I'd come home with her, God, they'd probably try to take the kids away and he's a jealous . . ." His voice trailed away. He gave a crooked smile. "Kind of like me. But there wasn't anything to this. We were friends a long time ago, like me and Lorraine. Just friends. She felt sorry for me when I got tossed out of the Blue Light. She came out after me. I was pretty drunk." He touched his head, winced. "We took a drive. She had a little extra gas. We didn't go far. Just out to Hunter Lake. And she said Faye danced with everybody, that there wasn't a special guy, same as with her. She said she'd never seen Faye leave with anybody or anybody go out after her. Anyway, I fell asleep in the car and she drove home. She brought out a blanket to me and that's all I knew until this morning. She came running out and shook me awake and said I had to leave. She'd heard on the radio that somebody had killed Faye and the police were looking for me. She said I had to get away from her place. She begged me not to tell anybody I'd been there. I promised her I wouldn't. But I made her promise me she'd call you. I was thinking pretty fast by then. I knew I couldn't go home. The police would arrest me first thing. If they arrested me, nobody would be looking for the man who killed Faye. I thought of this place and I told her how to tell you to find me. I said if she'd keep quiet about me, I'd never tell anybody I'd been with her, no matter what. Because I'd figured it out by then. My being in her car didn't prove anything. The police would just say I went home and killed Faye and came back to Su — to her car." He clenched his hands. "This morning I could see in her eyes that she was scared of me, that she thought maybe that's what I'd done. She kept backing away from me. She said she knew the county attorney and she'd call him for me, that he was a nice guy and she could set it up for me to meet him, tell him I was innocent. But she kept backing away. You'd think she could have looked at me and known I hadn't gone any-where. How could a man go and kill his wife and come back and lie down in a car and go to sleep? I can't sleep now thinking of what's happened to Faye. If I'd gone home . . ."

"But Clyde," Grandmother said patiently, "don't you see? It is that you have not come home. That is why the police hunt for you. If you were to tell the police what you have told me, then they would know to look for someone else."

"Tell them I got drunk and fell asleep in somebody's car? Do you think they'd believe me?" His tone was bitter.

Grandmother said eagerly, "But the young woman who called me —"

"I promised her I wouldn't ever tell anybody. It could ruin her life. And all she did was be nice to me." He shook his head. "No, I got to find out what happened. It's up to me." He pushed back his chair, stood, and his big dark shadow fell across Grandmother. "No matter what happens, no one will ever know you came here tonight. I promise."

Slowly Grandmother rose. "Clyde, I pray you will be careful. I am afraid you are in great danger."

"Danger? Oh. You think they'd shoot at me?" He spoke the words as if they were strange. He jammed his hands in the pockets of his trousers. "I'll be careful. I just need to talk to some people." He gave a little snort of laughter. "Maybe they'll be scared too, like Su — like this morning. Anyway, I don't have any time to waste. I've only got three days until my leave is up. But I've got some ideas. And if I find out who hurt Faye . . ." He broke off, his face crumpling.

Grandmother came around the table, put her arms around him.

His face bent forward. He rested his fore-head against the top of Grandmother's head. His racking sobs hurt Gretchen deep inside.

"Clyde, please, let us pray." Grand-mother's voice trembled. "Our Father who art in Heaven . . ."

He pulled away. "I can't pray." He shook his head, his eyes glittering. "No."

Gretchen felt frozen. What did he mean?

Grandmother reached out, clung to one big hand. "We are called upon to forgive so that we may be forgiven."

"Forgive?" Clyde's face hardened. "How can I forgive?"

Grandmother squeezed his hand, let it go. "To step into heaven, Faye has forgiven all that she suffered. We must do the same."

Clyde's big head sank forward. He jammed his hands into his trouser pockets. "But it's my fault. If I'd gone home . . ."

Grandmother sighed. "And you must for-give yourself."

He didn't answer.

Grandmother turned toward the door.

He called after her, his voice soft. "I'll al-ways be grateful that you came. And I promise I'll come home when I find out who hurt Faye."

Gretchen whirled and hurried to the steps. She slipped into the darkness.

★ ★ ★

The sound of the shot exploded in Gretchen's mind. She knew it was the crack of a gun. One shot. Not like when she and Millard used to go into the woods with Jimmy and Mike and watch while their big brothers used old cans perched on a fence for target practice. One shot . . . and then shouts.

Gretchen rolled out of bed, ran to her window. She pushed out the screen. Up the street, a flashlight swept across the Tatum yard. "Kenny? Rosa?" Chief Fraser's deep voice boomed. The light swung up and down as he ran heavily toward the house.

Once again Gretchen dressed quickly. She was almost to the window when her door opened and the light came on.

Grandmother's hair was tousled, her face puffy from sleep, her eyes wide with fear. "Gretchen, what is happening? Where are you going?"

Gretchen poked her head out the window. She held up a hand for quiet as she listened to barking dogs and a woman's cry, "Kenny, Kenny, answer me." Lights flared on in the houses on either side of the Tatum place. Mr. Kaufman stood on his front porch in white boxer underwear and no top, his pink belly poking out, yelling, "What's going on out there?"

162

The woman yelled, "Chief, I can't find him."

Gretchen pushed out the screen.

"Gretchen, I heard a shot. You must not go out." Grandmother hurried across the room and her soft hand clutched at Gretchen.

"Just one shot. And no more." Gretchen was impatient. "I heard Chief Fraser. I think he's with Sergeant Petty and they're looking for Sergeant Holliman." She pointed up Archer Street. "Look, there's the chief, running toward the backyard." He was clearly outlined by the wash of light from the Kaufman front porch, a flashlight wavering in one hand, a gun held steady in the other. "I've got to find out what's going on. Grandmother, please call Mr. Dennis. Tell him something's happened at the Tatum house."

"And wake him up?" Her tone was scandalized. "At this hour?" Gretchen's Big Ben alarm clock showed the time: 3:40.

Gretchen swung her leg over the sill. "He won't mind." She was sure of it. She dropped to the ground. She wished she had a pencil and paper. She would have to pay close attention to remember everything right. She heard Grandmother's protest, but Gretchen kept on going. The Crane house had lights at the back, but the front door was closed. The Tatum house was still dark. The

Kaufman house was lit from front to back and Mrs. Kaufman, in a pink nightdress, her hair rolled in curlers, peered out the front door. "Larry, you come back here."

A flashlight bobbed toward the back of the Tatum house. Another shout, this one excited and shrill. "Chief, I've found Kenny. He's hurt. We've got to get help."

Gretchen ran faster. She caught up with Chief Fraser as he strode along the side of the Tatum house. "Chief, has someone been shot?"

The chief flapped a long arm at her and the flashlight beam speared into the night sky. "Get back, girl. I don't know what's happened."

Mr. Kaufman slammed the gate of his backyard. "What the hell's going on?"

"Call an ambulance, Larry." The chief's voice was brusque. "I've got a man hurt. Sergeant Holliman."

Kaufman craned to see. "Jesus!" He swung heavily about and ran toward his house.

The chief called after him, "Stay inside until we've looked around. Rosa, where are you?"

"Back here. By the porch steps. I think it's okay." Her tone was careful. "I don't see or hear anybody."

The chief disappeared behind the house. Gretchen hurried to the end of the wall, peeked around. A flashlight lay on the first tread of the wooden back steps. The light flooded over Sergeant Petty, who was kneeling by a still figure. Sergeant Holliman lay on one side, an arm outstretched, legs bent at the knees. A revolver was within inches of his lax fingers.

Sergeant Petty held a gun in her right hand. Her eyes rapidly scanned the night, checking the yard, the woods, the houses next door. She used her left hand to explore the face and head of the downed man. Her fingers moved along the shoulders, across the chest, around the back. "I don't find any blood. There's some swelling on the side of his head. He's unconscious, but he's breathing steady." She pulled a handkerchief from a back pocket, gripped the barrel of Holliman's gun, lifted it to her nose. "Kenny didn't shoot this gun. That shot . . ." She put the gun down and turned toward the dark woods. "Chief, I don't know what happened. I was over there." She gestured toward the weeping willows that marked the property line between the Tatum and Kaufman yards. "I didn't see a thing, but I thought I heard something funny. I called out real low for Kenny and there wasn't any answer. I didn't like that so I started over this way. All of a sudden there was a bunch of noise all at once, a kind of banging and scrambling and a thunk like somebody got hit and the shot. It all came at once. I got out my gun and started running this way. I didn't see anybody." She gestured at the trees and their thick tangle of undergrowth. "If anybody got in there, we won't find them now."

"Nope. Not now." The chief's voice was dour and angry.

"Gretchen!" Grandmother came around the side of the house. "Where are — oh, there you are. Please, I called Mr. Dennis and then I got dressed." She stopped, pressed her hand against her chest, tried to catch her breath.

"It's all right, Grandmother. I'll come home in a little while. Mr. Dennis might need me. Please."

Grandmother looked about. "Is it safe to be here?"

A car screeched around the corner onto Archer Street, jolted to a stop. Mr. Dennis slammed out of a black Ford. He left the headlights on and ran across the lawn. "What's going on, Chief?"

"Sergeant Holliman's hurt." He jerked his head toward the Kaufman house. "They've

called an ambulance. We had the house surrounded, Holliman in the shrubs by the
back door, Petty over in the willows, me in
the oak tree in the front yard."

A siren rose and fell.

Chief Fraser hurried to the side yard. He
swung his flashlight in an arc.

The ambulance bumped over the curb,
came along the side of the house, stopped
within a foot of the chief. The driver poked
his head out the open window. "Gunshot?"

Sergeant Petty pushed up from the
ground. "Don't think so, Timmy. Think
he's just knocked out. He's over here."

The driver and his assistant, both middle
aged, moved stiffly but quickly. They carefully eased Sergeant Holliman onto a
stretcher, lodged him in the ambulance, and
roared off down Archer Street on their way
to the hospital.

Mr. Kaufman came up beside Gretchen
and her grandmother. He was still shirtless,
but he had pulled on a pair of dark pants.
"You all hear the shot, too?" He didn't wait
for an answer. "What happened to Kenny?
Did he get shot? What was he doing?"

"They were watching the Tatum house."
Gretchen spoke softly. She didn't want to
attract the chief's attention.

"Oh, waiting for Clyde to come, I guess.

Did he?" Mr. Kaufman craned to look past the chief and Sergeant Petty.

Gretchen didn't answer. Why would Clyde Tatum come to his house? He'd told Grandmother he had some ideas. But what would he hope to find out here? Or to do here?

"Clyde?" Grandmother's face was stricken. "Was it Clyde? And a gunshot?"

"Nobody saw him." Gretchen wanted to take that scared look away from Grandmother's face. "That's just a guess."

"I'd say it has to be a pretty good guess," Kaufman snapped. "Who else would want in there? After a murder and all?"

Gretchen patted her grandmother's shoulder, whispered, "It's all right. Go on home. I'll be there in a little while."

Mr. Dennis was right behind the chief and Sergeant Petty as they moved the beams of their flashlights across the ground. The springy grass was crumpled where Holliman had fallen. His revolver glistened in the light.

"No blood," Kaufman whispered. "That's good."

"Get the gun, Rosa." The chief swung his flashlight toward the back porch. Faye Tatum's painting glistened, the oil fresh and bright. The beam moved, revealing the open door into the kitchen. "Looks like somebody got into the house. Holliman heard something, came up this way, and somebody knocked him down."

"The gunshot?" Sergeant Petty tucked her gun into its holster, held Holliman's by the barrel.

The chief lifted his big shoulders, let them fall. "When Kenny comes to, maybe we'll find out. Come on, Rosa, let's take a look inside." He stopped on the bottom step, turned his flashlight on Mr. Dennis. "Police investigation. Nobody else can come in." The beam moved, lighted Gretchen, danced around her, touched on Grandmother and Mr. Kaufman. "Lotte, you're here." His face creased in a frown. "And Miss Gretchen."

Grandmother took a step back.

The chief looked around the yard. "Where's Miss Barb? She can help us check out the house, see if anything's missing."

Gretchen stepped forward. "She didn't stay with us tonight. She's at Amelia Brady's. Do you want me to call and ask her to come?"

He thought about it, yawned, shook his head. "No reason to wake her up, haul her out at night. I'll talk to her in the morning." He rubbed at his eyes. "If anything's gone, we can't do anything about it now. Come on, Rosa." He paused on the steps. "You folks can go home now. Appreciate your help." He glanced at Mr. Dennis, held up his hand. "I'll talk to you in the morning, Walt. Ten o'clock."

"Aren't you going to call the sheriff? Get some deputies out here to look through the woods?" Mr. Dennis waved his hand at the dark mass of trees.

The chief scowled. "Don't need any help." He turned, stumped up the steps. Sergeant Petty followed. They moved across the porch. In a moment, lights flowed from every window of the little house.

Mr. Kaufman scratched his chest. "Too little, too late if you ask me. Guess we won't know what happened until Kenny comes to. If he does. Well, I think I'll get back to bed. 'Night." He turned away.

Grandmother took Gretchen's arm. "Let's go home now. It is very late."

Mr. Dennis trotted to them. "Thank you for calling me, Mrs. Pfizer."

Grandmother pushed back a tendril of loose hair. "I would not have done so but Gretchen insisted."

The editor nodded at Gretchen. "Good job. And Gretchen, here's what I want you to do in the morning. . . ."

Gretchen kept her eye on the clock. She worked fast, turning the bacon as it sizzled, grating potatoes for the hash browns, beating eggs to scramble. Even though she and Grandmother had only had a little over an hour's sleep when they got up at five, Gretchen wasn't tired. She looked across the café kitchen. Grandmother's shoulders sagged and she moved as if she had weights tied to her legs. Gretchen made up her mind. She had to get some help for Grandmother.

"Be right back," she called softly.

Grandmother scarcely noticed as Gretchen pushed through the swinging door into the front of the café. The lights were off but sunlight slanted through the plate glass, pooling on the wooden floor in a lake of gold. Gretchen hurried behind the counter. She picked up the phone, gave the operator a familiar number.

"Hello." Alarm lifted the high, strong voice.

"Cousin Hilda, this is Gretchen. I'm sorry to call so early, but I wondered if you could help Grandmother at the café today." Gretchen picked up a cloth, wiped a smear from the counter. "She's hardly had any sleep the last two nights. There was more trouble at the Tatum house last night."

171

A quick indrawn breath. "More trouble? Lord have mercy. What's happened now?"

"Somebody broke into the house and there was a shot and Sergeant Holliman's in the hospital. But he wasn't shot so nobody knows exactly what happened. But it woke us up and —"

"Ach, and I suppose you and Lotte had to go see what happened? It would have been better to stay in your house and be safe. I saw the story in the newspaper with your name." There was no approval in the heavily accented words. "A young girl should not know about such things. That woman — going to a tavern and dancing with men. No wonder her husband was angry. It said in the newspaper someone told him there had been men at their house while he was gone. That will drive a man to drink and when men drink and lose their tempers, these kinds of things happen."

"But he —" Gretchen snapped her lips shut. She'd come so near letting out the truth. She must never tell anyone of Grandmother's visit to the Purdy cabin, no matter what anyone said about Clyde Tatum. Abruptly, she understood Grandmother's insistence that he come home. He must return and tell people he was innocent. If he didn't, everyone would be sure of his guilt.

Gretchen said quickly, "They don't know what happened to Mrs. Tatum. They think a man may have followed her home —"

"If she had not been at a tavern without her husband, she would not have been in danger, would she? Now what is this you are calling about?" Suddenly the hardness fled. Cousin Hilda's voice was full of concern. "Is Lotte sick?"

"She's tired and her chest hurts." Gretchen looked toward the kitchen door. "She doesn't know I've called, but I have to go to work —"

"To that newspaper office? I tell you, Gretchen, I do not think that is a good place for you." Cousin Hilda gave a decided cluck, just the way she always preceded any pronouncement with which she expected everyone in the family to agree. "Family comes first. That is what you must tell them. It is not a place for a nice girl. Or for any woman. I've heard about newspapermen and how they act. I've seen that Ralph Cooley walking around town with a swagger as though he is so big a man. And he smells always of whisky. So, it is your duty to stay with your grandmother. Perhaps this is a blessing in disguise —"

Faye Tatum's murder? Clyde Tatum's running away? Grandmother's hurting chest?

Sergeant Holliman's injury? Gretchen gripped the receiver, felt a wash of panic. Give up her job? She had a quick painful memory of Grandmother's tired face and the slow way she walked. But Grandmother had been so proud of her story with the byline. Grandmother wouldn't ask her to quit. She wouldn't ask . . . Gretchen drew her breath in sharply. "Cousin Hilda, I've got to go. But Grandmother needs to go home and go to bed. I hope you can help us." She hung up. Her hands were hot and sweaty. Give up her job . . .

She walked into the kitchen and checked the clock. Almost six. Almost time to open and Mrs. Perkins wasn't here. Gretchen couldn't leave her grandmother alone to manage the cooking and the serving. But Mr. Dennis was counting on Gretchen finding Barb this morning before the chief saw her. And Gretchen wanted to get started on the story about Faye Tatum so everybody wouldn't be like Cousin Hilda and think Faye was a bad woman because she went to a tavern without her husband. Almost six . . . they would be up for breakfast now at the Brady house. Gretchen was determined to call and talk to Barb.

The back door opened and Mrs. Perkins, her long face drooping, scuttled inside.

"Sorry I'm late. Morning, Lotte, Gretchen. I'll get out front and get the lights on and the door open." She ducked away, not looking toward either.

Gretchen would have spoken up, reminded Mrs. Perkins that she had been late three days running, but Grandmother shook her head. As the door swung shut behind Mrs. Perkins, Grandmother said quickly, "Everyone does their best, *mein Schatz.*"

At least Mrs. Perkins had come. Quickly, Gretchen untied her apron, pulled it off. "Grandmother, I need to go now." She crumpled the apron in her hands. "Will you be all right?" Should she stay?

Grandmother turned from the stove. Her face was still gray though tinged with pink from the heat of cooking and her exertion. "I will be fine. You go now. You have much to do." Her tone was proud. "And we will have such a happy time when your mama comes home."

Gretchen darted across the kitchen and hugged Grandmother. She hung her apron on its hook and hurried out the door.

Gretchen rode her bike to the *Gazette* office, but didn't stop when she saw the windows were still dark. She'd thought perhaps Mr. Dennis might have come in really early, but he was probably tired this morning. He would likely be there by seven. She turned onto Archer Street. She would use the phone at home to call the Brady house. She sure didn't want to miss Barb.

She eased her bike to a stop in front of the Tatum house. She didn't see any trace of police. Did the chief still have someone watching the house? Maybe, maybe not. Everyone last night believed the unseen intruder was Clyde Tatum, coming home for something he needed. If that was true, there wouldn't be any point in a police watch now.

Gretchen stared at the dark windows. The house already had the abandoned air of a boarded-up shanty on a country road. If she were Barb, she would never spend a night there. How could Barb bear to go inside that house, knowing what had happened there?

Gretchen pushed up on the bike seat, began to pedal, careful to keep her skirt away from the chain. She glanced at the Crane house. Mrs. Crane must have heard the uproar last night, but she hadn't come outside.

Gretchen turned into her driveway. A slim figure rose from the swing on the front porch. Barb wore a striped cotton blouse and blue shorts. Her russet hair looked mussed and wilted.

Gretchen put on a burst of speed. What luck that Barb had come. It wouldn't be necessary to call the Brady house after all. "Barb . . ." Gretchen dropped the bike beside the steps, hurried onto the porch. "I'm so glad you're here. I was going to call you at Amelia's. Listen, somebody broke into your house last night and Chief Fraser wants you to go through the house with him and see if anything's missing."

Barb frowned, looked down the street. "Broke into our house? Why? Who did it?"

"Nobody knows. Come on, let's call the chief." Gretchen opened the front door. "You didn't need to wait on the porch."

Barb stepped inside. "I didn't want to go in when nobody was home. I was thinking about coming to the café, but I decided to rest for awhile." Her voice was dull. She lifted the canvas bag. "I brought my stuff. I thought maybe I could stay here during the day. Amelia's mother —" She broke off, pressing her lips together.

Gretchen grabbed the bag. "Why don't you spend the night, too? You can stay with us as long as you want to."

"Oh, that's okay. I'll go back to Amelia's tonight. But last night Mrs. Brady talked and talked and talked and her voice was just so soft and sweet" — Barb's tone was mincing and saccharine then hard with bitterness — "and she's just like Reverend Byars. She's saying Mama —" Barb broke off, pressed her hand against her mouth.

"Oh, Barb, I'm sorry." Gretchen almost told Barb not to pay any attention to Mrs. Brady. But how could Barb ignore ugly words about her mother? If Barb knew what Cousin Hilda had said . . .

"I don't care." Barb's eyes blazed. "I know better. Mama was — oh, Gretchen, you know how Mama was. You're going to write that story about her, aren't you?"

"Yes." Gretchen wished she could go to the *Gazette* office right this minute and start calling. Would Faye's friends be willing to talk about her? Could she get the story done in time for tomorrow evening's paper? But first . . . "Barb, we have to call the chief and see —"

Barb lifted a trembling hand to her face. "Would it be okay if I had something to eat?" Her voice was small.

"Didn't you have breakfast?" Gretchen's voice was sharp. Why hadn't the Bradys offered Barb anything to eat? And last night Barb had scarcely touched her dinner.

Barb shook her head. "I left real early. I didn't want to be there. I told them I'd promised to come back here for breakfast."

"Come on." Gretchen hurried toward the kitchen, dropping Barb's bag next to the sofa.

The white curtains at the kitchen window were freshly washed and ironed. They fluttered in the gentle breeze. The drainboard was clean, the sink empty, the dish cloth draped over the faucet. The kitchen table was bare except for a plate of cinnamon rolls, covered with wax paper.

Gretchen pointed at the plate of rolls. "I'll get some milk and butter." She brought a plate and silverware and the pitcher filled to the brim with fresh milk from Cousin Ernst and Cousin Hilda's farm.

Barb slipped into the chair, ate quickly. She didn't speak. She looked sad and drained.

Gretchen looked away. She knew she could make Barb feel better. She could tell Barb her father was safe, that he was hiding in the Purdy cabin. She could tell Barb that he had said he was innocent. Gretchen moved to the sink. She picked up the dish cloth, scrubbed at the clean sink. But if the police ever found out that Grandmother had gone to the cabin, that she knew where a wanted man was hiding, she would be in terrible trouble. They would question her and she would be frightened. Gretchen couldn't

do that to Grandmother, no matter how unhappy Barb was. It wasn't — Gretchen
struggled to understand a nebulous thought
— Grandmother's fault that Mr. Tatum had
run away.

". . . Gretchen? Won't you help me?"
Barb's voice was uncertain. "Of course if
you don't want to . . ."

Gretchen jerked around. "What did you
say? I was scrubbing" — she held up the
dish cloth — "and I didn't hear you."

Barb got up. She picked up her plate and
glass, came to the sink. She avoided looking
at Gretchen. "You said the chief wants me to
look through my house, see if anything's
missing. Will you come in the house with
me?"

"Sure." Gretchen took the plate and silverware, turned on the water. She busied
herself with the small wash. This was what
Mr. Dennis had wanted. Gretchen wished
she didn't feel as if she were cheating Barb.
After all, Barb needed someone with her.
But didn't she have a right to know that
Gretchen would be there for the *Gazette*
too?

Gretchen squeezed the dish cloth. Fair
was fair. And somehow, she thought Mr.
Dennis would understand if Barb said no.
Gretchen slowly turned. "Barb, listen, I

don't mind going with you. But whatever the chief finds, I'll have to write a story about it for the *Gazette*." There. She'd probably lost her chance to get a good story. But now she didn't have a sick feeling in her stomach.

Barb's shoulders lifted, fell. "Everything else is in the paper." Her mouth twisted. "Why not that? I don't care. And besides, I don't think it will amount to anything." Her gaze burned into Gretchen's. "It wasn't Daddy. I know it wasn't Daddy."

The old green Packard rumbled into the Tatum drive. Gretchen and Barb stood near the front steps. It was already hot. Today would be a scorcher, likely reaching a hundred by afternoon. Cicadas whirred.

Chief Fraser walked slowly, his boots striking up little puffs of dust from the dry ground. Barb waited, her face bleak. Crows cawed, lifting in a black swarm from the elm tree nearest the house. The Kaufmans' German shepherd barked, lunging against his chain.

"Morning, Miss Barb, Miss Gretchen. Appreciate your help." He held a tagged key in his right hand. "You know about last night, Miss Barb?" He tilted his big head to one side, looked at her with somber eyes.

"Gretchen said somebody broke in." Barb glanced toward the closed front door. "Do you know who it was?"

"No. But maybe we'll figure something out when we look around inside." The chief moved past them. He banged back the screen, unlocked the front door, held it open.

Barb gripped Gretchen's arm, her fingernails sharp as little knives. They stepped into the living room. Chief Fraser clicked on the light. Barb leaned against Gretchen and turned her face away from the center of the room where they'd found her mother's body. Gretchen couldn't pull her eyes away from the rumpled rug. They'd taken Mrs. Tatum away, but no one had straightened the rug. The house was hot and still with all the windows shut. There was a faint smell of paint and turpentine and a lingering scent of old tobacco smoke.

"Miss Barb," Chief Fraser said briskly, "please look around the room. Do you see anything missing, anything out of place?"

Barb stepped away from Gretchen. She folded her arms tight across her front. Her gaze moved from the easy chairs to the fireplace. Silver candlesticks flanked a pink Dresden china clock on the white mantel. A small green hat with an orange feather dangled from one candlestick. Two balls of yarn were tucked next to the clock.

The coffee table was just as it had been when Gretchen stopped by the house on Tuesday afternoon, magazines in a disorderly stack, the open box of graham crackers, the overflowing ashtray, the bottles of nail polish and used cotton balls.

"Nothing's changed." Barb took a deep breath.

The chief led the way to the narrow hall. "This first room . . ." He looked at Barb inquiringly.

"Mama and Daddy's room." Barb walked slowly inside. Chief Fraser was close behind.

Gretchen stood in the doorway. The bed was unmade. A cotton nightgown was tossed over a rocking chair. Faye's clothing lay on chairs, hung from the bedpost, poked from open drawers.

"Were her things usually strewn around?" Chief Fraser frowned at the disarray.

Barb fingered the lace edge to the collar of a blouse. "Mama was always in a hurry. There was never enough time to do everything she wanted to do. She wanted to be with people, me or Daddy or friends, and talk and laugh. Or she wanted to paint. Clothes" — Barb waved her hand — "she'd straighten everything up every so often and she'd be real proud of how tidy it was — and then the next minute she'd toss something down and not give it a thought."

"So I guess there's no way to tell if anybody looked for something." He rubbed his face. "Though what in time anybody'd look for, I don't know."

Barb pointed across the room. "Look! There's Daddy's duffel bag." The brown bag lay in a heap on the floor next to the closet. "And there on the dresser" — she ran across the room — "there's his hairbrush and comb. So it wasn't Daddy who came. He'd take his things, wouldn't he?"

The chief frowned. "You'd think so, if it was him. But tell me this, Miss Barb, where's your daddy's gun? Where does he keep it?"

Barb turned to the closet. The door stood open. She stepped inside and reached up on the shelf. "He keeps it up here. . . ." She paused, stood on tiptoe, swept her hand back and forth. "Why, it's gone. Daddy's gun is gone!"

. . . I got a cot out of the shed and set it up back in the woods. I thought Daddy might come home, but I couldn't make myself stay in the house. I didn't think I'd fall asleep but I did. A shot woke me up. I climbed a big cottonwood. Flashlights swung everywhere. One swept toward the trees. I saw a man in dark clothes running on the path to Creek Road. I couldn't tell who it was. I didn't come out. I didn't want to tell what I'd seen. I mean, it could have been Daddy. I didn't know. I snuck up and heard everything the police said. That's why I came to your house in the morning. Anyway, I'd told Amelia I was staying with you. When the chief came and we went to my house, I couldn't believe it when I looked in the closet and Daddy's gun was gone. . . .

Chapter
6

. . . and felt for a shining incalculable instant that Grandmother was beside me, her faith and goodness a bastion and a beacon. The feeling passed and I was alone in the chill world of the dead, surrounded by souls, jostled by memories. The last time Mother came home, we didn't bring flowers for Daddy. I'd resented it then. How hardhearted I'd been. I'd not realized, never for a moment recognized, that Mother was still young that summer day in 1944. So very young. In her late thirties, impulsive, open to emotion, ready for laughter and love and happy days. Shiny blond hair frizzed around her eager bony face. She moved fast. She was too thin, as if her energy and enthusiasm had refined her body to a minimum of flesh. She loved bright colors. Pink and purple were her favorites. To me, she always appeared elegant and stylish. I would never forget the yearning look . . .

The teletype clattered. Gretchen worked fast, sorting the stories, the continuing siege at Cherbourg, updated casualty figures from Saipan, Red troops at Viborg, V-1 rocket attacks in London, U.S. bombers hitting robot roosts in Pas de Calais, the signing of the G.I. Bill. It was already hot in the newsroom. The ceiling fans creaked, stirring the steamy air. Ralph Cooley, his hat tipped to the back of his head, a cigarette dangling from the side of his mouth, sat hunched at his typewriter. His wrinkled suit coat hung from the back of his chair. He had a pack of cigarettes tucked in the pocket of his short-sleeve white shirt. Mr. Dennis stood behind him, round face puckered in a frown beneath a green eyeshade, pipe clenched in his teeth, arms folded.

". . . the chief won't say Tatum's armed and dangerous, but hell" — Cooley's bony shoulders rose and fell — "anybody can figure it out. Holliman admits he didn't see much. He heard a noise from inside the house and went up to the back porch to take a look. Somebody came busting out the kitchen door and whammed him on the head. Holliman said he thought he was a dead man because his head hurt like hell and he heard a shot and smelled the gunpowder. The chief thinks whoever it was" — Cooley drawled the indefinite phrase — "Bugs Bunny maybe" — the reporter gave a snort of laughter — "cracked Holliman on the head with a gun and the gun went off. So . . ." Cooley's tone was mildly regretful. "It doesn't look like Tatum tried to shoot Holliman. Anyway, with what she got this morning" — Cooley jerked his head toward Gretchen — "it seems pretty clear the gun belongs to Tatum. I mean, we got a gun going off and Tatum's gun is missing from his house. One plus one . . ."

Mr. Dennis took his pipe, held a match to the tobacco, drew hard. "The chief says an unidentified prowler broke into the house and a gun appears to be missing."

Cooley swiveled his chair, looked up at the editor. "So —" It was a challenge. "What's the chief thinking? Some stranger broke in and went straight to the place Clyde kept his gun?"

Mr. Dennis puffed on his pipe. "You got a gun, Ralph?"

Cooley looked startled. "Me? Hell, no. Damn things go off."

The editor's eyes glinted with disdain. "A lot of people do. Including me. You know where I keep my gun? On the shelf in the closet of the bedroom. Unless you live on Hickory Hill . . ."

The town's big houses sat on the crest of a wooded hill.

". . . and have a gun room with racks or a case, you keep your gun on a high shelf in the closet, away from the kids."

Cooley's eyebrows shot up. "So Bugs Bunny decides he needs a gun and why not try the Tatum house?"

"Shit." Mr. Dennis turned away, walked to his desk.

"Face it, Walt." Cooley's raspy voice was a taunt. "Your Boy Scout is looking for trouble. If I were the guy who was screw—" Cooley glanced toward Gretchen and continued, "fooling with Faye, I'd get the hell out of town for now. Anyway, I've got a quote from the sheriff." Cooley cleared his throat. " 'Sheriff Paul Moore Thursday advised county residents that fugitive from justice Sgt. Clyde Tatum, wanted for questioning in the murder of his wife, is believed to be armed and dangerous.' " Cooley took a deep puff on his cigarette. "And that's my lead."

Jessop's Five and Dime at the corner of Main and Crawford was four doors down from Victory Café. Gilt gingerbread topped the brick wall above the plate glass windows. The fire engine red entrance framed double doors. Gretchen pushed inside. The coffee shop counter with six leatherette swivel seats was on the left. The menu included hamburgers (the ground beef mixed with oatmeal to stretch the meat), grilled cheese sandwiches, and soups. Everybody knew the food couldn't compare to Victory Café's. Shelving filled the middle of the store. Glass-topped counters ran along the wall to Gretchen's right and the rear wall. Jessop's sold cosmetics, utensils, dishes, toys, jewelry, fine candies, everything that wasn't carried at Thompson's Drugs or Miller's Hardware.

Gretchen said good morning to Mrs. Jessop, who taught the junior high Sunday school class, and hurried down the central aisle. The jewelry counter was at the back. Lucille Winters wiped a cloth reeking of ammonia on the glass above the watch display. She looked up at Gretchen's quick steps on the wooden floor. Lucille's dark hair swept up in a high pompadour above a broad, open face, the cheeks bright with rouge. Big dark eyes, the lashes loaded with mascara, widened. "Oh, Gretchen," she cried. "You were with Barb when she found her mama. Was it awful?" She peeked past Gretchen's shoulder, gestured for Gretchen to come close, and whispered, "Mrs. Jessop doesn't want us to talk about it. I've felt so bad ever since I heard. How is Barb?"

Gretchen came close to the case, which was filled with Benrus and Orvin watches. She carefully didn't lean on the sparkling glass top though she bent near and spoke softly. "Sad. Scared. Worried about her dad. Furious over what they're saying about her mom. That's why I came to see you. I want to write a story about what Mrs. Tatum was really like."

Lucille put down the cloth. She reached down, opened the back of the case, picked up a tray of lapel watches. "Pretend you're looking. Mrs. Jessop's coming this way." She unloosed a bow knot-style pin with the small watch dangling. "This is ten-carat rolled gold plate. It would be lovely for your mother. Is this what you're looking for?"

The floor creaked. Mrs. Jessop's heavy steps came near, turned away. Her broad back in a stiff gray dress made Gretchen think of a battleship in the newsreels, overpowering, unstoppable, unyielding.

Lucille's fingers closed around the watch. "Mrs. Jessop said we wouldn't mention Faye again. She said, 'That kind of woman deserves what she gets,' " the clerk whispered. "None of it's true. About Faye and another man. I know it's not. Faye and I had a lot of time to talk." She studied Gretchen. "You wouldn't know . . . not yet . . . when you're older you'll understand. Women talk about men. Especially when a man is gone. Faye was crazy about Clyde. It was the way she said his name, the way she talked about him coming home and how they'd —" Her eyes fell. She opened her hand, carefully replaced the watch in the tray. She glanced around, checking for Mrs. Jessop. "Listen, it may get me in trouble. If you put it in the paper, she'll know we were talking about Faye and she'll say I was on company time. But I don't care. I've been thinking about going to Tulsa. They're always looking for somebody at the Douglas plant. Anyway, I'll speak up for Faye and look everybody in the eye. I tell you, she loved Clyde and nobody else. Here's what she told me and everybody who wants to think she was a bad woman can just put this in their pipe and smoke it. . . ."

Shielding the fan of copy paper with her body, just in case Mrs. Jessop looked toward them, Gretchen wrote as fast as she could.

Jim Dan Pulliam rolled the tire toward the jacked-up car. He moved with muscular grace. Smears of oil streaked his hands and lower arms. The sleeves of his tee shirt were rolled to the shoulder. The thick mat of golden hairs on his arms glistened in the noon sun. His jeans hung low on his hips. He squatted and bounced the tire on the axle. As he slapped on the lug nuts with easy familiarity, he used the back of his hand to wipe sweat from his face, leaving an arrow-head-shaped splotch of black on one cheek. "Barb said her mother thought I was the best?" His voice was soft and he darted a shy look at Gretchen.

Grasshoppers buzzed in the waist-high

weeds behind the rutted, oil-stained patch of ground. Gretchen was intensely aware of Jim Dan, of his nearness, the smoky blue of his eyes, the thick tangle of chestnut hair that fell across his forehead, the way his jeans clung to his body. She dropped her eyes to the fan of copy paper. "Yes." Her answer seemed to come from a far distance. "Barb said her mother was sure you'd be an artist. A wonderful artist." She pushed away the sensations that had taken her by such surprise. She would think about them another time. Jim Dan, Tommy . . . Right now she needed to find out about Faye Tatum. She held fast to that thought, listened to Jim Dan's tentative, gentle voice.

". . . she never laughed at anybody." He picked up a wrench, tightened the nuts, one by one. "I mean, it was funny, she laughed a lot but when she looked at your work, she was serious as she could be. Funny thing is, I was in a lot of trouble at school but she didn't care about that. She . . ."

Gretchen nodded, her pencil flying.

Cousin Hilda slapped tuna fish salad on thick white bread. Tall, angular, her steel gray hair drawn back in a skintight bun, she moved in quick jerks, her stiffly starched apron crackling. "I sent Lotte home and I put a sign out front: SANDWICHES TODAY. Chips and pickles." Her thin voice was as remote as a dove's cry. "I brought in four quarts of my own bread-and-butter pickles." She used the wooden spoon to point at the long line of bread. "Tuna fish. Chicken salad. Egg salad. Bacon, lettuce, tomato. And plenty good enough, I say. I'll thank you to see about the coffee and tea and take orders. That Mrs. Perkins is slower than a sinner coming to the altar. Too busy listening to everybody talk, if you ask me. Tried to tell me about Faye Tatum's fingernails and I shut her up pretty quick, I can tell you. Do I want to know about things like that?" Her pale green eyes bulged, her lips pursed. "Now let me see . . . Lordy, that bacon's crisp as peanut brittle. . . ."

Gretchen checked the first order clipped to the line, swiftly fixed three plates. She loaded the tray. When she pushed through the door, Mrs. Perkins bustled toward her. "Gretchen, is Lotte all right? That woman" — she jerked her head toward the kitchen — "came in here like a Sherman tank and first thing I know, Lotte's gone home and I'm supposed to race around like a greyhound and every time I open my mouth she shuts me up."

"Cousin Hilda means well." Gretchen heard the echo of her grandmother's voice in her own. "Please don't pay any attention to what she says. And she is good to come so Grandmother can get some rest. She hasn't had much sleep since Mrs. Tatum was killed, what with everything that's happened on our street."

Mrs. Perkins's brown eyes gleamed. "That's right. You live almost next door, don't you?" She shivered, bent close to Gretchen. "Do you know what I heard the sheriff —"

"Mrs. Perkins, I'll take a piece of Lotte's apple pie," Mayor Burkett called out from table one.

Mrs. Perkins swung around, hurried behind the counter.

At the third stool, his regular place, Dr. Jamison finished his bowl of vegetable soup. "Hmm, that looks good. Cut one for me."

Every table was taken, every booth filled. A group of officers from Camp Crowder had pushed two tables together. Gretchen darted in and out of the kitchen, taking orders, filling cups and glasses, clearing tables. She took bites from a BLT as she came and went.

Mrs. Perkins pushed through the door, carrying a full tray of dirty dishes. She emptied the scraps and stacked the plates by Cousin Hilda, who bent over the sink, water rushing. Cousin Hilda, her face flushed from the heat, gestured at the garbage pail with a spatula. "That's full. Dump it."

Mrs. Perkins's face closed up like a box turtle.

Gretchen hurried to the pail. "I'll get it." She grabbed the metal rung and pulled.

Mrs. Perkins stood still for a moment, then, with a sniff, joined Gretchen. The two of them slid the pail across the floor. When the screen door banged shut behind them and they thumped the pail down the steps into the alley, Mrs. Perkins muttered, "If I didn't like Lotte, I'd go home and let *her*" — the pronoun bristled with resentment — "see how she'd like doing this by herself. Maybe she could learn how to say please."

Gretchen watched the back door. She whispered, "Mrs. Perkins, what did the sheriff say?"

The alley pulsed with heat. Mrs. Perkins lifted her hand to brush a strand of lank brown hair away from her flushed face. "Oh, it was awful, but I couldn't help hearing. He was telling Mr. Durwood about the autopsy report they did on poor Faye." She shivered. "The sheriff said they found skin and blood underneath her fingernails."

"Skin and blood . . ." Gretchen repeated slowly. "I don't understand."

"Oh, don't you see?" Mrs. Perkins slipped behind Gretchen, clamped her fingers on Gretchen's throat.

Startled, Gretchen lifted her hands, reached back, fastened on Mrs. Perkins's bony arms.

Mrs. Perkins loosed her grip. Her arms fell. She stood so close, her breath was warm on Gretchen's face. "Faye tried to get the hands off her neck. The sheriff said she fought real hard. She had long nails. He said Faye must have marked him up pretty good."

"Well, I'll be damned." Ralph Cooley thumped his desk with his fist. "Now it makes sense. I thought the chief had lost his mind. Last night he showed up at the Blue Light, made every man jack hold out his arms for a look-see. Nobody could figure out what the hell. But he was looking for scratches. He didn't find any. That pretty much shoots a hole in his theory that somebody followed Faye home Tuesday night. 'Course, it could have been somebody who isn't a regular. But I'd think the chief would know pretty much who was there Tuesday night and probably checked on all of them."

197

Cooley's eyes narrowed. "Maybe he'll trade off. Give me some good stuff if I don't use this. Thanks, Gretchen." He lit a cigarette, looked pleased.

Gretchen turned away. She didn't like Ralph Cooley. She didn't like the way he talked, the way he looked, the way he thought. Faye Tatum's murder was a game to him. His words hung in her mind; all he cared about was the story he could write. She walked slowly to her desk, sat down. She needed to make some calls. But the cold, quiet question slid into her mind. What did she care about? The story she would write . . .

Betty Steele bustled onto the screened-in porch, placed the tray on the wooden table next to the swing. "It's sweetened tea, Gretchen. With fresh mint." Soft curls framed a sweet, eager face with mild blue eyes and pink cheeks.

"Thank you, Mrs. Steele." Gretchen accepted the big glass. She liked tea better without sugar but she took a sip, then another, and the sweet cold drink poured energy into her body. "Barb said you took a lot of her mom's classes at the gift shop." She put down the glass, picked up her pencil and the fan of yellow copy paper.

Sudden tears glistened in Mrs. Steele's eyes. "Faye was the most alive person I ever knew. She loved painting and teaching people how to do it. I never knew anybody who loved painting as much as she did. . . ."

Gretchen rested her bike against the trunk of the big cottonwood that shaded the back steps of the Blue Light. The back door was open. A radio played Glenn Miller's "Mood Indigo." A half dozen cars were parked in front on the beaten-up ground that served as a parking lot. Gretchen didn't have a clear picture of what went on in a tavern. People drank beer and listened to music and danced, and lots of people in town, like Reverend Byars, wrinkled their faces like prunes when anybody talked about the Blue Light. Gretchen wasn't sure why she'd come. She'd talked to Mrs. Hopper last fall when she'd tried to get word to Millard that his folks weren't mad at him anymore. Gretchen remembered a big woman in a purple dress with a dead white face and bushy red hair and tired eyes. She'd brushed Gretchen off, but a few weeks later Millard had written his folks. Maybe . . .

Gretchen knocked on the screen door. It rattled on its hinges. A sour smell overlain by sizzling onions and hot grease rolled over her. She peered through the screen into a long kitchen. Her nose wrinkled. The dingy room looked dirty; the garbage was overflowing; food-crusted dishes were stacked on an uneven wooden counter. She knocked again.

"So what's the damn hurry?" A skinny little woman in a tattered shirt and stained skirt stamped to the door. "Go away, kid. We don't need whatever —"

"Mrs. Hopper." Gretchen lifted her voice. "I need to see Mrs. Hopper."

The woman snapped a dish towel at flies buzzing over the dishes. "You selling something?"

"No. Please. Tell Mrs. Hopper" — Gretchen knew this wasn't the time to say she was from the *Gazette* — "that I'm here for Faye Tatum." A slight breeze rattled the leaves of the cottonwood, but not even the thick blanket of shade lessened the moist heat of the late afternoon. Gretchen's tongue felt thick she was so thirsty. Even in the shade, the air felt hot as exhaust from a tailpipe.

"The one that got herself killed?" The bony woman wiped her face with the cloth. Her gnarled hand was soapy. "Lou don't know nothing about that. I can tell you she don't want to talk about it."

Gretchen almost turned away. Even if Mrs. Hopper would come to the door, she'd likely send Gretchen away. But maybe . . . "Please, go ask her if she liked Faye. If she did, she'll want to talk to me."

The sharp-featured woman shrugged. As her shoes clumped on the wooden floor, Gretchen jumped off the steps onto hard-packed dirt. She hurried to the water faucet that poked from the side of the foundation. She crouched, turned the handle, let warm water slip through her fingers until it cooled, then pooled water into her hands and drank thirstily.

"Josie" — the voice was deep and explosive — "what kind of game — oh, there she is." The screen door banged. Lou Hopper stood on the top step, her hands splayed on her hips. Mercurochrome red hair flared in thick curls to the sides of her head. Thin black eyebrows, shiny as tar, arched in half moons above dark eyes cold as a winter pond.

Gretchen scrambled to her feet. She wiped her hands on her skirt as she moved toward the steps. "Mrs. Hopper, I'm Gretchen Gilman and —"

"I remember you." The rough voice was brusque. "Millard's friend." Mrs. Hopper pressed her lips together in a tight line.

Gretchen looked up and their eyes met. Gretchen waited, not moving, knowing that the hard-faced woman's silence was a tribute to Millard. For an instant he was there with them, his round face bright with happiness.

"Goddam war." Mrs. Hopper jammed her hands in the pockets of her emerald green skirt. She cleared her throat. "Josie said you asked if I liked Faye Tatum. Why?"

"People are saying a lot of bad things about Mrs. Tatum." Gretchen looked into cold, empty, remote eyes. "Mostly because she came here to dance. I want to write a story for the *Gazette* telling people what she was really like. You can help me."

Bright red lips twisted. "Gilman . . ." Her eyes glittered like coins tossed on a table. "G. G. Gilman." She gave a hoot of laughter. "So people'll think you're a man." She lifted her big shoulders in a shrug. "Why not? Why the hell not? It's always a man's goddam world, isn't it? Give 'em hell, kid. I'm all for you. But I don't talk to cops and I don't talk to reporters."

As the screen door squeaked open, Gretchen called out, "If you liked Faye, why won't you say so?"

Mrs. Hopper looked over her shoulder. "I run a beer joint, kid. Who cares what I say? I

202

don't want to get mixed up in anything. People come here to have a good time. They want to laugh and dance and forget the war. I don't talk about 'em."

"All I want to know is what you thought about Faye Tatum. Everybody says she was a tramp because she came to the Blue Light. If you say that isn't so —"

"Like that will make a difference?" Her voice was sharp. "Do you think anybody in town will believe what I say? Or care what I say? Poor Faye. She wasn't looking for trouble." Mrs. Hopper let go of the screen, turned to face Gretchen. "All right." She came down the steps, her face bleak. "I'll talk to you. About Faye. Nobody else. But funny enough, that won't be hard. And I don't give a damn what the bluenoses think. Because you know something, they're wrong. . . ."

Closed windows. Closed doors. The Tatum house baked in the unrelenting blast of the sun, a hot red ball in the western sky. The crackling dry heat in the shut-up rooms would be suffocating, sickening, stifling. Were the doors locked? Probably. But who would go inside? Maybe Barb's aunt would stay there when she came up from Texas. But Barb had packed up more clothes this morning, enough clothes for several days. That visit seemed a long time ago.

Gretchen glanced at the folded copy of the *Gazette* in the basket of her bike. Every night she proudly carried the paper home, eager for Grandmother to see her stories. She didn't want to show tonight's *Gazette* to Grandmother. Grandmother would read the lead story by Ralph Cooley, saying that Sgt. Clyde Tatum was now believed to be armed and dangerous.

Gretchen rode slowly, her legs aching with weariness. She was almost past the Crane house when she realized the front door was open. Gretchen slowed, stopped. She looked up the neat walk. Water glistened on the rose bushes in the flower bed by the front porch. Gretchen swung off her bike, leaned it on the kickstand. She'd talked to Lucille who had worked with Faye Tatum and Jim Dan who would be an artist because of her and Mrs. Steele who had learned about art from her and Mrs. Hopper who ran the bar where Faye Tatum had loved to dance. Mrs. Crane had been the nearest neighbor to the Tatums. Mrs. Crane had called the police Tuesday afternoon and started the trouble. No, that wasn't right. It wasn't Mrs. Crane's fault that the Tatums had quarreled. But Mrs.

Crane clearly kept an eye on the house next door.

A ruffled white curtain moved at a front window.

Faye Tatum's neighbor . . . Gretchen started up the walk. She wished she wasn't so tired. She felt burdened not only by fatigue but by too many words and emotions and faces. She had enough now for a good story, but it wouldn't be complete if she didn't talk to Mrs. Crane.

She lifted her hand to knock, but quick footsteps sounded. Mrs. Crane looked through the mesh of the screen door. Permed gray hair in tight curls bristled from her narrow head. Skin sagged from sharp bones. Her mouth drooped as if she'd just said something sad. The brightness of pansy blue eyes was almost startling in the seamed face. She held up the evening paper and pointed at the headline: ARMED AND DANGEROUS. "Gretchen, do you know about this?" She yanked open the door, her movement sharp and jerky. "I was going to come and see you tonight. Since you're working on the paper, I hoped you could tell me." She took a deep breath, her words spewing like shelled peas tipped into a pot. "I'm so upset. I wish I'd gone to spend the summer with my daughter in Perry, but I thought I should be here to help with George's children. Come in and let me get you some iced tea. You sit down and I'll be right back."

As Gretchen stepped inside, she smelled talcum powder, starched cotton, furniture polish, and fresh-cut watermelon. The living room was almost a twin in size to that in the Tatum house, but here everything was fresh and clean, washed and polished, the chintz-upholstered furniture adorned with doilies, the windowpanes sparkling, the curtains crisp as altar linen. The dark walnut dining room table glistened. China and silver shone through the glass of a breakfront. A portion of the kitchen table was visible through an open door. Slices of watermelon on a green pottery platter looked fresh and succulent.

Gretchen sat on the blue chintz sofa in a pool of summer heat. The electric fan whirred, stirring the air, making it seem cooler for an instant. Mrs. Crane kept on talking as she bustled about the kitchen, her high, tremulous voice slightly breathless. ". . . I've felt so bad about Faye but I never thought anything like that would happen. When I called the police, I was frightened for Clyde" — her shoes clattered on the wood floor — "because Faye was out of control. I never heard anything like it in all my life. I've never heard anyone scream like that." She pattered into the living room, placed the tray on the coffee table. She stared at Gretchen. "You look so hot and tired, honey. Here." She held out the glass, ice clinking, fresh mint poking from the tea. "I brought you some watermelon, too."

"Thank you." Gretchen lifted the glass, welcomed the thickly sweet, bitingly cold tea. The watermelon was sweet, too, and crunchy, Gretchen's favorite taste of summer.

"Anyway, my husband, William, I don't know if you remember him, Gretchen, but he always said to me: Least said, soonest mended. And, oh" — tears welled in her eyes — "I'm so ashamed. If I hadn't told Penelope — you know her, my sister-in-law Penelope Newton — about seeing that man late at night, maybe none of this would have happened. I should have known that Penelope always tells Ed everything and Ed was at the barbershop . . ."

The words buzzed like flies swirling over a picnic. Gretchen sipped the tea and pieces of Faye Tatum's last day clicked into place like clothespins snapping garments to a line.

". . . and he's such a loudmouth, showing off, telling everybody there about a man

207

coming to see Faye with Clyde off in the army. Of course, Ed didn't know Clyde was right there in Moss Wilson's chair. I shouldn't have told Penelope, I know I shouldn't, but I kept thinking about George and how it would break his heart if Jennie ever fooled with a man. Not that Jennie would do a thing like that. She's been the best wife and mother a man could ever have and I've loved her like she was my own and not just my son's wife. But thinking about George off in the Pacific, fighting those awful Japs, why it just made me mad at Faye even though before I would have said she was a good woman even if she was an artist. I was thinking about George and Jennie when Penelope came over that afternoon and I told her what I'd seen and how bad I thought it was. Penelope promised not to tell anyone, but she never could keep a thing from Ed. But I swear" — those bright eyes bulged — "I was scared to death Tuesday afternoon when I heard those screams and shouts. I was in the kitchen with the window open" — she gestured toward the back of the house — "and I heard the back door slam and Clyde yell and pretty soon Faye's voice was shrill and loud, louder than you'd think anybody could be, and she said he was" — Mrs. Crane paused and a pink flush deepened the rose of her cheeks — "anyway, she was saying he was awful, so bad and mean and that it was all a lie and what kind of man was he, to believe that kind of garbage about his wife and she'd been so glad he was home and now he'd ruined everything. Clyde yelled that she was a" — another pause — "a bad woman, though that's not the word he used, and a minute later she shouted she was going to kill him, that she'd get the gun and shoot him dead and show him what happened to liars. That's when I ran to the phone and called the police. Before Sergeant Petty came — and I don't think it's right to have a woman in pants like that, I don't care if that's what war workers wear —" She lifted her hand, pressed it to her lips, then cried, "Oh, I'm sorry, Gretchen, I know your mother works at the plant in Tulsa and it's real important to have people working to make the airplanes and I know she has to dress that way, but Sergeant Petty looks almost like a man and she walks like one, too. But the back door banged and Clyde came out and his face looked like he was trying not to cry, you know how men can look, their faces all bunched up tight like a wild horse pulling on a bit. Anyway, he was gone before the police car got here. I was watching out the window" — she pointed across the room where the curtain had twitched — "and Sergeant Petty went right up to the front door and knocked. There wasn't any answer. She went around to the back of the house. I was so glad Clyde had already left. I'll never forget how Faye sounded, screaming that she was going to shoot him dead. When I called the police that's what I told them . . ."

Gretchen remembered the wail of the siren as the cruiser pulled out of the dusty lot.

". . . and the police car got here real fast but Clyde was gone. In a little while, Sergeant Petty drove off. Now, you being on the paper and all, I thought you would know. How come she didn't get that gun away from Faye? I told them about the gun." The tears made her eyes shiny like purple flowers wet with rain.

Gretchen finished the watermelon. She took another gulp of tea, carefully placed the glass on the tray. It wouldn't do to set it on the table and make a ring on the wood. "I don't know, Mrs. Crane. I'll ask Mr. Dennis." Ralph Cooley had missed this. Gretchen felt confused. Faye Tatum threatened Clyde? "Are you sure it was Mrs. Tatum who —"

The gray curls bounced as she nodded vigorously. "I know what I heard. Just like I know what I saw late at night at that house." She sat up very straight and her cheeks flamed. "No one can call me a liar. That's what I told Faye when she called —" She gave a tiny gasp and her eyes widened.

Gretchen frowned. "Mrs. Tatum called you?"

Mrs. Crane's face congealed like day-old Jell-O.

"From the Blue Light?" Gretchen's voice was eager. "The chief wants to know who she called that night."

"Oh, Gretchen." Mrs. Crane's voice trembled. "It was awful and she made me so mad. She'd been drinking and she was all upset. She'd talked to Ed Newton and he told her what I'd said to Penelope." Tears trickled down the worn cheeks. "Oh, how I wish I hadn't done that. I made up my mind I wouldn't ever tell anybody about what I'd seen, not ever again. I didn't tell Chief Fraser. I told him how Faye said she was going to shoot Clyde. That's the only reason I phoned the police Tuesday afternoon. I didn't tell him Faye called me from the Blue Light. I don't want to be mixed up in anything. But when she asked me why I lied about her, I told her it wouldn't do any good to pretend with me because I saw what I saw and I told her chapter and verse. She got real quiet. I guess she knew it wasn't any use calling me a liar. She held on to the phone without saying a word. I heard music and voices and somebody singing. Finally she hung up. But none of that matters now. She made mistakes. I don't know anybody in this lifetime who hasn't." Mrs. Crane looked toward the starched curtains at the window, her face drooping in sadness.

Gretchen frowned. "Chief Fraser said it could be real important to know who she talked to." But if it was just Mrs. Crane, it didn't make any difference at all.

Mrs. Crane folded her plump arms across the starched front of her blue housedress. "Least said, soonest mended." Her lips folded into a tight line, resistance in every line in her face, in the stiffness of her body. "Don't you go and tell anybody what I said. You hear now? I'm not going to say anything bad about Faye. She's dead and gone. Let her rest in peace. She was a good mother and a good neighbor."

"Chief Fraser's scared something might happen to the man." Something? Gretchen knew better than that but she didn't want to say it aloud in this calm, clean, homey room, didn't want to picture Clyde Tatum, un-shaven, weary, heartbroken, knowing in her heart what the chief feared: Clyde Tatum killing the man who had made love to his wife. She willed away the image of Clyde, hunkered by the scarred wooden table in the hot, dirty cabin. "You need to tell the chief. He's trying everything to find out who was coming to see Mrs. Tatum and —"

"Oh, no." Mrs. Crane's eyes were huge. She held up her hands in protest. "No. I won't talk to him. No, I won't." She took a deep breath and the words tumbled faster than starlings skittering in the night sky. "It won't do Chief Fraser a bit of good to come see me. I know there was a man. I saw him plenty of times, but" — she took a deep breath, clasped her hands tightly together, her eyes big with fear — "who it was is God's business, not mine. I don't recall now who it was. And I've said all I ever intend to say." She folded her lips tight as a closed coin purse.

The silence between them was heavy with fierce decision and puzzled disbelief. Gretchen knew Mrs. Crane had recognized that stealthy visitor, but she'd made up her mind never to tell.

Mrs. Crane reached for the pitcher of tea, refilled the glasses. "Anyway, nobody needs to hear any more about that. Faye was such a good mother. . . ." Her voice fell away.

Gretchen placed her napkin beside her

plate. "The *Gazette*'s going to do a story about people's memories of Mrs. Tatum. Would you . . ."

The smell of apple pie scented the house with cinnamon and nutmeg. Gretchen smiled as she hurried toward the kitchen. "Grandmother?"

Grandmother turned, her face lighting with love, "*Mein Schatz*. Oh, you should not have called Cousin Hilda, but I am glad you did. I have rested and cleaned and cooked and everything is ready for your mama to come home on Saturday. I have cut roses and put them in my cut-glass vase to be so pretty for her. I wish they could stay longer but we will have a beautiful day. And for dinner we will have fried chicken and mashed potatoes and gravy and peas and" — she pointed at the pie cooling on the drainboard — "your mama's favorite."

And Gretchen's favorite. But the prospect of pie and seeing her mother couldn't erase the hard lump in her stomach. Mama's friend. Why did she have to bring someone home with her? They always had so little time and now that time wouldn't be theirs to enjoy.

Grandmother's smile slipped away. "Gretchen, what is it? What have I said? What is wrong?"

Gretchen felt the burn of tears prompted by fatigue and worry and uncertainty. And jealousy. She didn't want to admit the cold core of her unhappiness. Especially not to Grandmother. But why would Mother bring a man here? Gretchen blinked, forced a smile. Instead of answering, she tossed the *Gazette* on the table and moved past her grandmother to the sink. Over the rush of water, she washed her hands, bent over, tossed water on her face, spoke fast, "Grandmother, I stopped by the café and helped clean up and get everything ready for tomorrow. I told Cousin Hilda Mother was coming and Cousin Hilda said she would take care of the café Saturday too. She said Cousin Ernst will help. When I left, she was already planning the menu." Because of the shortages, they offered only two lunch choices. "She's already decided to fix liver and onions with stewed tomatoes and okra and ham patties with macaroni and cheese." Gretchen smiled. "She enjoyed herself today." Cousin Hilda liked being in charge. The only person who didn't have fun was Mrs. Perkins.

"Oh," Grandmother's blue eyes widened, "I can't let Hilda do that."

Gretchen's grin was quick. "Grandmother, not even General Patton could order Cousin Hilda around."

Grandmother smiled. "Oh, to have the

whole day with Lorraine. What a gift from God. We will do something very special for Cousin Hilda. I will have to think. . . ." She walked to the stove, lifted the lid. "Hmm, do you smell the bratwurst, Gretchen? Supper is almost ready."

Gretchen hurried to her room and changed into a white cotton blouse and seersucker shorts. When she came back, she set the table, thinking, as she always did, how bare the table looked with only two plates. There used to be her mom and Jimmy and often they'd have friends over, too. But now . . .

"Mein Gott." Grandmother's voice was low and strained.

Gretchen jerked around. Grandmother was bent over the counter, looking at the front page of the *Gazette*. Gretchen dropped the silverware, moved to stand close. She touched her Grandmother's rigid arm.

Grandmother turned away, walked slowly to her chair, slumped into it.

"Grandmother . . ." Gretchen didn't know what to say. She couldn't let Grandmother know that she'd followed her to the cabin where Clyde Tatum was hiding.

"Our supper . . ." Grandmother's voice was vague. Her face crinkled with worry.

Gretchen served the bratwurst and sauerkraut along with rye bread and spicy mustard. It was one of her favorite meals, but they never served this food at the café anymore.

Grandmother forced a smile. "What did you do today?"

"Oh, I was here and there." The bratwurst was delicious. Gretchen ate fast. "Mostly I talked to people about Mrs. Tatum." Her face furrowed. "I hope I can write a good story. I learned a lot about her. Nice things, Grandmother."

Grandmother put down her fork. "There are wonderful things to remember about Faye. I'm glad you are going to tell people about her. They should remember something besides the sadness."

But even as she told Grandmother bits and pieces about Faye Tatum, Gretchen worried. It was up to her to make people see a woman's life and not her death. Could she do it?

Gretchen stared at the bar of moonlight flaring across her room. She felt hot and uncomfortable lying in bed wearing her blouse and shorts. But she knew Grandmother would go to the cabin tonight to ask Clyde Tatum about the gun. Gretchen's eyes ached with tiredness. She listened for

Grandmother's step in the hall. Maybe she should tell Grandmother she knew about the cabin. Was it dangerous for Grandmother to go there, to ask about the gun? Gretchen had a sharp, clear memory of Clyde Tatum bent forward, his big hands against his face, the light shining on his muscular arms. He'd sworn he hadn't killed his wife, but why had he come back to his house for a gun? Did he know who Faye had been seeing? Did he get the gun to go after somebody? That's what Grandmother would ask him. Surely he wouldn't hurt Grandmother. Not if he was innocent. . . .

Gretchen fought to remain awake. What was it Grandmother sometimes said? Bone tired. Now Gretchen understood how it felt to have the night press against her, closing her mind, weighting her bones and muscles, pushing her down, down, down into darkness.

Gretchen woke. Grandmother . . . where was she? Fear swept Gretchen. She pushed out of her bed, not bothering to be quiet. Gretchen knew she was alone. The house had that unmistakable feel of emptiness. Was this how it felt to be stranded on an island? She was certain no one was near. There was no one to call to, no one to reach out and hold.

Gretchen slipped on her loafers. She knelt, reached under her bed, and pulled out Jimmy's .22 pistol and a flashlight that she'd hidden there earlier. She ran to the window. How long ago had Grandmother left? Gretchen dropped to the ground, ran through the night, the pistol in her hand, the flashlight tucked under her arm. The bright moonlight coated the trees and road with cream. She didn't need the flashlight until she reached the overgrown path to the cabin. In the thick darkness of the woods, she flicked the light on and off, in short quick bursts, and all the while she listened. How could she have fallen asleep? What if he had the gun? God, please don't let him hurt Grandmother.

At the clearing, she hesitated, trying to catch her breath in deep, heaving gulps. The moonlight silvered the old wood. No light shone from the front window. But there had been a blanket tacked there. Gretchen eased up the steps, crept across the floor, stopped once as a board creaked. She tiptoed the remaining steps, reached out, felt the roughness of wool and heard the low murmur of voices, almost lost in the rasp of the cicadas.

The relief was so sharp and sudden, it almost made Gretchen dizzy. Grandmother's voice! She was all right. Gretchen knelt, bent close to the window, cautiously pulled the edge of the blanket away from the frame, saw the flickering golden glow, smelled the rankness of kerosene. She stiffened. Clyde Tatum and Grandmother stood by the front door, only a few feet from her, so near Gretchen saw the thick black bristles on Tatum's unshaven face and the soiled patches and stains on his khaki uniform and the taut muscles in his powerful arms, his hands clenched into bulging fists. Gretchen's fingers tightened on the butt of Jimmy's gun. Her eyes scoured Clyde. The gun . . . But his hands, the fingers tight against the palms, held nothing. His uniform crumpled against his body, the pockets empty. Gretchen's gaze swept the counter and the stove and the rickety wooden table, two pans, the remnants of a meal, the lantern, Grandmother's picnic basket, a child's Big Chief tablet with ruled pages, a couple of pencils, a beer bottle, a rusted pie tin overflowing with cigarette butts, a package of Lucky Strikes, a copy of the *Gazette*. No gun. No gun anywhere. Her tight muscles relaxed.

". . . when I find out who killed her . . ." His voice grated.

"Oh, Clyde." Grandmother reached up,

touched his grimy cheek. "I beg of you. Give this up. Come with me. We shall tell the police —"

"Tell the police!" The words exploded like shotgun pellets. "Yeah, I tell them somebody else killed Faye and they'll throw me in jail. No, I've got to find out more. There's some guys I know who were at the Blue Light. I called 'em today and they didn't want to talk to me, but I was asking if they saw anybody paying special attention to Faye Tuesday night." He took a deep breath. His face glistened with sweat. It was hot on the porch but Gretchen knew the cabin sweltered, the windows swathed for darkness, no air to stir the fug of the lamp, no breeze to lessen the oppressive weight of the heat. He lifted his clenched hands, looked at them, slowly let go, his shoulders sagging, his hands falling limp to his sides. "I've made a start" — he gestured toward the open tablet on the scarred table — "I only need a little more time. I was out last night. I tried to catch Ed Newton, but" — he heaved a tired sigh — "there was always somebody around. I kept watching his house and I've got it figured out. I'm going to talk to him — just him and me — and he's going to tell me where he heard this stuff about Faye. Maybe some guy had been bothering her and she told him to get lost and he came after her." His voice trailed away, words he didn't believe, wanted to believe. "Anyway, I've got to find out more."

A June bug buzzed near Gretchen. She flicked away the beetle. How odd that she was almost close enough to Clyde Tatum to reach out and touch him and she held within her the knowledge he sought, knowledge he was willing to risk arrest to discover. What good would it do if he spoke to Ed Newton? Even if Clyde learned about Mrs. Crane, Gretchen knew she would never tell him the name of the man she had seen entering the Tatum house. She wouldn't tell the police and she wouldn't tell Clyde. She was grieved and sorrowful that she'd ever told anybody.

". . . I can talk to whoever it was. And if he hurt Faye . . ."

"Then it will be time to go to the police." Grandmother clasped her hands together. "Chief Fraser is a good man, Clyde. He will listen."

Clyde rubbed at his face. "As soon as I find out, I'll tell him. Now, you better get home. I didn't want you to come here again."

Grandmother's hand plucked at the collar

of her dress. "I had to come. That gun . . . who could have taken it, Clyde?"

He rubbed his cheek, frowned. "I don't know. It doesn't make any sense. Faye ran to the closet and got it. God, she was mad at me." He put his hands together, stared at them, cracked his knuckles. "She said she was going to shoot me and then she threw the gun across the room. It banged on the sofa and fell on the floor. That's when she screamed at me to get out. And I went. I was mad, too, so mad everything was in a red haze and I was shaking. It said in the paper that Mrs. Crane called the police. Maybe somebody was on the party line and heard about the gun. But I promise, it wasn't me who got it. Maybe a kid broke in, just for the hell of it. Maybe Faye left the gun on the floor and whoever broke in found it there."

"They think you have the gun. That story in the paper" — Grandmother shook her head — "it makes you sound as if you would hurt people. The police and the men hunting for you will have guns. Clyde, we should go now and tell them it wasn't you." Grandmother clasped his strong, tanned arm.

"Not yet." His face hardened. "I got to talk to Ed Newton. But I can do that tomorrow. Or tomorrow night at the latest.

Then I'll go to the police. I promise." He gave her a quick, gentle hug. "You go home now. It will be all right."

Grandmother turned toward the door.

Gretchen ran to the edge of the porch, jumped. She reached the fringe of the woods and plunged into darkness.

. . . That's when I started drinking at night — I took a bottle of bourbon from the house and hid it in the woods. I chewed Sen-Sen the day Mama was buried. God, what an awful day. Aunt Darla was a bitch, telling me she'd always known Mama would come to a bad end, that the family warned Mama not to be an artist. That very morning I started thinking about having a drink so I could forget. That's what I tried to do — forget. But I never, ever could. Whisky and men, starting that summer . . .

Chapter

7

. . . in mother's eyes and the way she'd hugged me, held me so tight. I remembered the scent of her perfume and the feel of her thin arms and the sweet sweep of her breath against my cheek. I smiled and felt warm despite the cold eddy of the March wind, rustling the bare limbs of the cottonwoods, swirling leaves across the graves. We shared so much laughter, Mother and I, and she was always so proud of me. Through my life, I wore that pride like a shield, deflecting envy, jealousy, uncharitableness, indifference, hatred. Her grave wasn't in this winter-browned cemetery, but she was here with me now, her gamine face radiating delight, her peal of laughter ringing in my heart. Perhaps it is only the old who know that the unseen is as real as the seen. I knew that. I knew, too, that nothing could alter the past, but it was important to know truth. I was still seeking truth. . . .

"It's going to be a hell of a dog and pony show." Ralph Cooley snickered, his thin lips drawn back, his nicotine-stained teeth dingy yellow like the bared fangs of the stray dogs slinking away from the butcher shop when Mr. Heinrich yelled at them. "Everybody's mad as hell, the mayor, the chief, the sheriff, the county attorney, the bluenoses who think anybody who'd go inside the Blue Light's tainted by hell. . . ."

Gretchen rolled in a fresh sheet of copy paper, tried to ignore Cooley's cough-punctuated chatter as he typed, smoked, relished the coming city council meeting. In her wastebasket, wadded-up sheets puffed like cheerleaders' pom-poms. She tried another beginning:

Five friends remembered Faye Tatum . . .

She ripped out the sheet, squeezed it, added another crumpled ball. Mrs. Hopper couldn't be called a friend. There had been no warmth in her rough voice. Her observations were unemotional, brusque, her tone remote.

". . . going to bring back the dogs, see if they can pick up a trail from the Tatum house. Everybody seems pretty clear that Clyde ran into the woods after he got the gun. Durwood says the chief's a day late and a dollar short, he should've . . ."

Gretchen pressed her fingers against her cheeks, stared at the typewriter.

The wooden floor creaked. Mr. Dennis ambled toward her desk. He carried a chipped blue pottery plate. He stopped beside Gretchen, stood with his back to Ralph Cooley. "Glazed and cake and some long johns with caramel icing."

Gretchen took a long john. Her mug was half full of coffee. Mr. Dennis made the coffee fresh every morning from a mixture of coffee and chicory. She'd puckered her mouth when she first tasted the strong brew. Now she loved it. She hadn't told Grandmother she'd started drinking coffee.

The minute hand on the old wall clock made a distinct click when it reached the hour. She heard it now and looked up, her face taut. She'd been working all morning and she didn't have anything. "Mr. Dennis, I don't have the story on Mrs. Tatum."

Cooley gave a rattly cough. ". . . and Durwood's showing the strain, too. He's got to get this one solved or he might as well forget about running for the legislature. . . ."

Mr. Dennis poked at a cinnamon-sugared doughnut. "This looks good." He took a bite. Pink sugar wavered in a thin line above his lips. He gave her a casual smile, like he was talking about the weather. "You'll do fine. Keep it simple. Tell it the way it happened."

Gretchen picked up her mug. The bitter coffee jolted her. Keep it simple. . . . She put down the mug. Keep it simple. . . . She lifted her hands, began to type, a word, another, more, then faster and faster:

Who was Faye Tatum?

Five people described her for the *Gazette*. Each knew her in a different way. Lucille Winters worked with Faye at Jessop's Five and Dime. Jim Dan Pulliam is an aspiring artist whom Faye encouraged. Betty Steele took classes from Faye. Lou Hopper owns the Blue Light where

Faye loved to dance. Martha Crane lived next door to Faye.

Mrs. Winters has big dark eyes and a smooth pompadour. She talks fast and has a quick laugh, but sometimes as she remembered she held a handkerchief to her eyes. She has worked at Jessop's since she graduated from high school in 1930. "Faye loved to sell jewelry. I never knew anybody who liked pretty things better than Faye. She always dressed to the nines, even when she had to redo clothes from before the war. She'd add a crocheted collar or new piping. And hats! She made one with red felt and spangles for our Christmas party. Most of all, she loved to dance. People ought to know that's why she went to the Blue Light. Whenever she told me about somebody she met there, she talked about how they could dance. That was all. She didn't take anybody home with her. I know that's so because she would have told me. She told me a lot of things that were private, not things you'd tell just anybody. She told me how much she loved Clyde, that he was the only man she'd ever cared about and how she prayed for him, that he'd come home safe and not have to go overseas. When she got word he was going to be home on furlough before his unit shipped out, she cried. She was so afraid he'd get killed. She said having him home was like heaven. There's been all this talk about Faye, that somebody said they'd seen a man going to her house late at night, well, I want to tell everybody that's a lie. Faye never thought about any man but Clyde. All she wanted was for the war to end and him to come home."

Jim Dan Pulliam works at Purdy's Garage. Tall, slender, quick moving, he speaks softly. His hands are stained with grease and dirt. He is seventeen and he is an artist. "In the ninth grade, I got in a fight with these guys who made fun of me because I liked art class. I broke this one guy's arm. Barb Tatum told her mom. She came to my house." His smoky blue eyes moved away to gaze at the head-high sunflowers pushing against the wire fence near the garage. "Not a house really. A trailer over in Burn's Flat." His eyes were defiant. "But she came and you would have thought I lived on Hickory Hill. She looked at my drawings. Some of them were charcoal on grocery sacks. She told me people don't understand about capturing light and color. She said an artist sees the pulse of life. That's what she called it, the pulse of life. That was the first time I understood what I was doing and why it made me feel right." He smoothed his fingers on a shiny wrench. "Sometimes I feel right. Lots of times I get mad and throw the painting away. Because it's not good enough. Mrs. Tatum told me I had to keep on painting, no matter if people laughed. I must never quit, not even if they hated me. If I gave up, I'd shrivel away like corn left in the field. I've got a painting I've been working on this summer. I was going to show it to her. The sun on the water at Hunter Lake . . ."

Water beaded the bright, green ferns on Betty Steele's screened-in porch. Despite the Oklahoma wind, there was no dust on the freshly painted swing. The cushions on the wicker chairs have been recently re-covered. Mrs. Fletcher is a Home Economics teacher. Her brown pageboy glistened in the afternoon sunlight. She clapped her hands together, her face eager. "Faye loved painting. I know I'm not any good, but I always wanted to paint and she had classes at the store on Saturdays for people like me who work. I learned a lot about teaching from her even though she never even went to college. But when she looked, she really saw what was there. People. Beauty. She'd be halfway through a class and all of a sudden, she'd dart across the room and point at somebody and she'd cry, 'Look at the way the sun's coming through the window. If we could paint Mrs. Harris in the sunlight, wouldn't that be beautiful, class?' And Mrs. Harris, now I'm just using a name because I don't want to embarrass anybody, but she might be a plain woman with thick glasses and a tired face, but Faye would make us see the beauty, the glow in her eyes, the delicate line of her jaw, the life. Oh, I tell you, Faye was a teacher who had magic. You ask people who took her classes, they'll tell you. Most of them never heard of Rembrandt and couldn't draw a lick, but if they opened their hearts even a little, they took something from Faye's class that they never forgot. I was so sorry when she had to give up most of those classes to work full time at Jessop's. It was a loss to everybody in town who loved art. I know she kept on teaching a few, like Jim Dan. . . ."

Lou Hopper said she doesn't put up with any nonsense at the Blue Light. A tall red-head, she doesn't smile and her voice is gruff. "Lots of people in town don't like beer joints, but I run a clean place and there's no trouble here. People can drink beer, dance, eat ribs or a hamburger when we've got meat, cheese and rye and chips when we don't. Since the war started, we're full every night. Music helps people forget their troubles. I hardly ever spoke to Faye Tatum, but I knew her because she was a regular. She was the best dancer I ever saw. She'd dance with anybody, old, young, as long as they kept their hands to themselves and danced like there was nothing left in the world but the music. You could take one look at her on the dance floor — and that's where she spent the whole evening, never sitting in a booth or at the bar — and know she was here for the music, the beat, the sound, the rhythm. God, she could dance. There was a soldier boy from Louisiana — he's gone now, shipped out to the Pacific — and he and Faye used to jitterbug. Everybody else would stop and make a big circle and when the music ended, they'd shout and clap. And I can tell you, she came by herself and she left by herself. She was never off in a corner with a man." Mrs. Hopper raised a thick dark eyebrow. "A lot of people who come here are lonely. They're looking for love. You can always tell. But not Faye. All she wanted to do was dance. Now, I hardly ever spoke to her but I remember once she said, 'When I dance, I'm not afraid.' " Mrs. Hopper lit a cigarette, drew a deep lungful. "I told her,

'Honey, I don't know what you're afraid of, but I'm glad you got the music.' "

Martha Crane has lived on Archer Street for thirty-three years. Her husband, William, managed the Hamilton paint store for forty years until his death in 1935. Mrs. Crane's house shines with care, the window curtains crisp, the floor bright with polish, the slipcovers freshly laundered and ironed. Family pictures are everywhere, on the mantel, the bookcases, the tables. A portrait of her son, George, in his captain's uniform, is in a place of honor on the mantel. "My husband liked Clyde. Clyde helped William when we had trouble with the car. Clyde could almost always get a car to start, but he wasn't much to keep things up around the house and Faye was too busy with Barb and her painting to keep after him. She didn't spend time cooking or cleaning, but she loved to play with Barb. I remember when Barb was about five, she and Faye used to laugh and giggle and make mud pies, and they'd poke sprigs of grass on top and Faye would say, 'Pass the parsley,' and she and Barb would just die laughing. I never could see what was so funny, but they laughed and laughed. I guess Faye really didn't much care how the house looked or the yard. She was crazy about the wildflowers, always said God made the prettiest flowers so why not just enjoy them. There was Indian paintbrush in the field behind their house. But for a woman who always had daubs of paint on her face and her clothes, you'd think she would have wanted their house to look nice. It needed painting a long time before Clyde got drafted. And that broken-down clothesline was just a disgrace. Sometimes she strung the wash on my fence and if that didn't look tacky! But I'm glad now I never said a thing about it. Sometimes she'd set up an easel underneath the oak tree, the big one that spreads shade so far there isn't a scrap of grass beneath it. I used to go hang out my wash on those days and take my time about it so I could watch her paint. There was something — oh, I don't know how to say it, but it was exciting to see her, her hair swept up behind a bandana and splashes of paint on her old blue smock and her face streaked like an Indian on the warpath. It was like she was more alive than anybody. You know how you can see a crow in the sunlight, eyes bright as a new penny, feathers shiny as polished coal? That crow — just for a minute you look and you see him living, just like you are, and the whole world seems bursting with life, you and the crow and a big old sunflower and the cicadas. That's what it was like to watch Faye paint."

Faye Tatum still loves and laughs and paints and dances in the memories of those who knew her.

Gretchen read over the copy, corrected typos, put her name and a slug — *Memories* — in the upper left-hand corner. She marked the page numbers in the upper right. She pasted the sheets together. When she was done, she sat at her desk, holding the story. The story ran twenty-eight inches, the longest she'd ever written. Was it stupid? Would Mr. Dennis wonder why he'd ever hired her? Maybe she should crumple up the copy paper, throw the story in the wastebasket, walk out into the oven-hot noon, go over to the café, and scrub and clean and forget about —

The floor creaked. A shadow fell across her desk. "Let me see, Gretchen." Mr. Dennis reached down, took the copy.

He always read fast. Yet the minutes — it couldn't have taken more than two or three — seemed never to end. When he was done, he nodded and turned away, carrying the pages. He walked back toward his desk, then said over his shoulder, as if it weren't a matter of importance, "Yeah, Gretchen. I'm sending it out on the wire. With your by-line."

She sat very still. . . . On the wire . . . her story would go out on the wire. . . .

Gretchen slipped on her dull blue wool crepe dress. It was her best winter dress and the pleated skirt felt heavy as a blanket. She'd be hot as blazes, but none of her summer church clothes were dark. She had one pair of pumps for summer, white, and one for winter, dark blue. Should she wear the winter shoes? She shrugged, stepped into the dark shoes. She popped on a navy straw hat. She'd carefully taken off a cluster of yellow feathers. Why did people wear dark clothes to a funeral? To show they were unhappy? Gretchen wasn't sure. But that's what everybody did. Funny. Just like ants swarming around an anthill. Was she like an ant? Doing what everybody else did because that was all she knew? She tucked the question in her mind to think about.

Grandmother was waiting in the living room, wearing her best navy silk dress and a blue straw hat. Her white-blond hair was freshly braided in a coronet. Usually, when they were on their way to church, her blue eyes would be shining with eagerness, her plump cheeks pink in anticipation. Today she looked old, her face drawn and pale, her shoulders bent. She held a blue pottery bowl covered with wax paper. "I have made a fruit salad. Barb and her aunt are at the house so I thought we'd take it there." Her round face creased. "I don't know if people will come to the house after the funeral. . . ." Her purse and gloves lay on the table by the front door.

Gretchen reached out for the bowl. Murder changed everything. Murder had turned Faye Tatum from a woman eyed with suspicion because she was an artist into a bad person. At least that seemed to be how Reverend Byars saw Faye. How many people in town felt the same way? Grandmother had made the salad because that was what she always did when someone died. She fixed food and took it to a bereaved family and after the funeral everyone gathered at the house and ate and talked and laughed and cried. But today, nothing was familiar, not even sun-baked Archer Street with two unfamiliar cars parked in the rutted drive of the Tatum house. A mud-streaked green coupe was nosed in close to a pile of logs. Behind it, a shiny black sedan gleamed with fresh wax.

Blazing heat pressed against them. Every patch of shadow from the thick-leafed oaks was a welcome respite, a fractional lessening of the heat's burden. Gretchen held the bowl in one hand, braced Grandmother's elbow with the other. Grandmother moved slowly, as if each step took effort. When they left the Tatum house, it would be three blocks more to the funeral home. Could Grandmother walk all that way? The thought wiggled in Gretchen's mind, dark and ugly as a cottonmouth slithering through red-tinted lake water. Fear for Grandmother made Gretchen feel cold, despite the waves of baked air that rolled against her like hot drafts pulsing from a grass fire. Grandmother had always stepped with dignity, but she had been able to walk anywhere she wanted, even the two miles to Cousin Hilda's farm. Today, her gait was leaden, like an old, old woman's.

The Tatums' rusted gate still hung from its hinge. The unkempt yard seemed weedier than ever, the house shabbier. The front door was open. Gretchen moved ahead of Grandmother, lifted one hand. Before she could knock, the screen door swung out.

Barb, her face white as a clown's grease-paint, held the screen. She, too, wore a dark dress and hat, held gloves tightly in one hand. She didn't say a word. Red-rimmed eyes, glazed with misery, stared emptily. Her features looked like they'd been chopped from pond ice, hard, gray, rigid.

Gretchen stepped inside even though she wanted to turn and run, leave behind Barb's pain, flee from this square room with its awful freight of memory.

Grandmother climbed the steps, breathing heavily. She came inside, folded Barb in her arms, held her tight.

Footsteps clipped on the hardwood floor. "Come in. I'm Darla Murray, Faye's sister. Barb, mind your manners, introduce our guests." Darla Murray's voice was sharp. Her face was a heavier version of Faye's, the artist's elegant bone structure blurred by age. She, too, might have been beautiful, but her green eyes were hard and cold. Tiny, deep, dissatisfied lines fissured her face, bracketed tight lips.

Grandmother patted Barb once more. "Mrs. Murray, we are neighbors to Faye and Clyde." She spoke his name with a trace of defiance. "This is my granddaughter, Gretchen. She has brought the salad."

Mrs. Murray waved a thick hand, the nails a bright red. "Oh, you can put it in the kitchen. It's very nice of you." There was no thanks in her tone. "I don't know whether we'll need anything. Some people brought dishes, but I've got to get on the road as soon as the burial's done." She glared at Barb. "And you have to get your things ready to go to the preacher's house. I can't stay more than a few minutes after everything's done so if you don't want to be here" — she waved her hand at the living room — "by yourself, you're going to have to move fast. One of us has to lock this place up." Her cold eyes scanned the living room. It was neat, no magazines or Coke bottle or crackers scattered about. Someone had cleaned and straightened, the rug smooth without a ripple. There was nothing left to remind of the careless easy lives spent here or the painful death.

Barb's stricken face turned toward Gretchen. "I'll take the salad." She reached out, grabbed the bowl, limped toward the kitchen.

Mrs. Steele, her sweet face solemn, bent past Lucille Winters's big dark pompadour, to flutter her fingers in greeting. "Lotte, Gretchen." There was an old man Gretchen didn't know in one corner talking to Mrs. Crane, who held a handkerchief tight in her hands and dabbed at her eyes, but the living room didn't hold the usual big gathering of family and friends after a death.

Grandmother moved past Mrs. Murray.

Gretchen sped toward the kitchen. She didn't want to think that Grandmother was standing right now where Faye Tatum's body had lain.

Barb stood in the doorway to the back porch, slumped against the door frame, facing the welter of canvases and the easel with the unfinished painting.

"Barb," Gretchen called softly.

Barb turned as if her body ached. She looked at Gretchen dully, her face heavy with sadness and despair. "Daddy didn't come home. They're going to bury Mama and he isn't here. Aunt Darla said" — she took a deep breath and now her shoulders shook — "what could Mama expect, no man would put up —" She buried her face in her hands. "Oh, God, I wish I was dead. That's what Daddy thought. That's what he thought and . . ."

Gretchen fought tears as she hurried toward Barb.

A crisp hand clap sounded from the doorway.

Barb's head jerked up. Her eyes blazed.

"Time to go." Barb's aunt adjusted her hat, dropped down a short veil. "Have you got your gloves? Come on, girl."

Barb started across the kitchen, then whirled and limped back to the porch.

Mrs. Murray clapped her hands on her broad hips. "What do you think —"

Barb came through the door, clutching a paintbrush. She held it tight to her body.

"You can't take that —"

"I'm going to take it. I am." She moved across the floor, her face set and hard, stopped by Gretchen. "You and your grandmother will sit with us, won't you? And come in the car? There's room. There's so much room." Her voice was uneven. "There's only me and Aunt Darla. Please, Gretchen, say you'll come."

Mrs. Peck taught music at her house. When a student played, she turned on the metronome. Gretchen remembered trying hard to keep up and always falling behind, the heavy tick sounding louder and louder. When Mrs. Peck played hymns for funerals, she wore a black hat and black dress and her thick arms moved like pistons, mechanical and lifeless. Now she pounded out "Onward, Christian Soldiers."

They sat — the four of them, Barb's aunt and Barb and Grandmother and Gretchen — in the family room that overlooked the pews. The heat was suffocating, thick and heavy as the dusty purple velvet curtains at each end of the opening into the chapel. In the chapel, only a handful of mourners sat in wooden pews, their faces waxy in the dim gloom beneath yellowish lights. Of those, only two were young, Jim Dan Pulliam and a soldier. Gretchen was puzzled. Where were Barb's friends? Barb was popular though a lot of the girls were jealous of the way the boys flocked around her. She'd always had plenty of friends. But murder changed everything.

Gretchen's gaze moved from face to face, in part to avoid looking at the white casket. The casket was closed. Gretchen was glad. She'd not attended many funerals, but she remembered the slow, shuffling lines that inched past and the awful empty grayness of a dead face. She didn't understand looking at a dead person. Why remember anyone that way? She sat in the hot, fetid room and was glad she didn't remember her father's funeral, not really. She remembered the smell of flowers and her Mother's icy stillness, but not the casket or a dead man. She remembered her father striding toward her, picking her up, swinging her in the air, his face alight with love. And with life. Maybe someday she would blot out the ugliness of Faye sprawled broken on her living room floor and remember Faye's laughter on a summer evening as she played jacks with

Barb and Gretchen, her narrow face alive and eager, her artist's eyes seeing more than anyone ever realized.

Reverend Byars, his face flushed, was waving a manicured hand and shouting, "... our sister, if her heart is repentant, will find forgiveness and peace. And someday, brothers and sisters, we too ..." Gretchen blocked out his words, refused to listen. She was intensely aware of Grandmother's soft sobs, a handkerchief pressed to her face, and the rigidity of Mrs. Murray, her bulky body still as stone, though tears slipped down her hard face, and, most of all, Barb, who trembled like a brown leaf swept by a November wind.

Gretchen refused to hear even though Reverend Byars's voice rose higher and higher. She stared through into the chapel, her gaze moving from person to person among those whom she knew. . . .

Martha Crane plucked at the strand of pearls at her throat. She stared at the casket, her expression forlorn.

Lucille Winters opened and shut the clasp of her purse. She looked older in her Sunday dress than she had at Jessop's Five and Dime. She kept shaking her head and frowning.

Betty Steele's head was bent, perhaps in

thought, perhaps in prayer. She held a rosary in one hand.

Mr. Dennis's suit coat was bunched up around his thick neck. His arms were folded across his front. His wrinkled skin was more pronounced when he frowned. He looked irritable and impatient, his grizzled eyebrows a thick straight line, his lips pursed. As clearly as if he'd shouted, Gretchen knew his thoughts. If he'd had a copy pencil, he would have marked through Reverend Byars.

A strand of chestnut hair fell across Jim Dan Pulliam's face. His worn white shirt was mended but he wore a tie. Occasionally, he lifted a graceful hand to smooth back his hair and then his expression for an instant was clearly visible. His eyes were lifted to the sunlight streaming in a cascade of color through a stained-glass window. The brilliant shaft poured over one end of the wooden casket, making the white paint glisten bright as dime-store pearls.

A chunky young soldier, his khaki uniform crisp, sat next to Jim Dan. The soldier's brown hair was cut short, his freckled face sunburned. Every so often, his eyes slipped toward the family room. He held his uniform cap in big-knuckled hands, nervously turned the cap over and over.

Behind them, Ralph Cooley sprawled in a

pew, arms widespread, legs outthrust. He wore his hat on the back of his head. His flaccid face, worn by years of too little sleep, wrinkled in a sardonic sneer as Reverend Byars concluded, smacking his Bible on the podium, ". . . know that hell awaits us if we pursue the path of damnation."

The last rumble of his voice still hung in the air when Mrs. Peck began to hammer out the first stanza of "The Old Rugged Cross."

In the last pew, Chief Fraser lifted a big hand to rub his rough-skinned cheeks. His imposing bulk made the bench look small, the space confined. He looked like an old crow waiting to scavenge, bright cold eyes darting about the room.

At the other end of the last row, as far from the chief as possible, sat Sheriff Moore and County Attorney Donny Durwood. Moore's watchful face, the bones jutting at odd angles, turned toward Durwood as he bent his head to whisper. The county attorney looked tired, his cheeks sagging with fatigue. But he blinked his eyes and listened intently, finally nodding.

The door to the family room opened and the funeral home director, pink face solemn, natty blue suit tight across his chest, stepped inside. "Mrs. Murray, Barb, if you wish to go by the casket now . . ."

Barb reached out, grabbed Gretchen's arm, clung so tight it hurt. "I can't. . . ." It was a thick deep whisper.

Mrs. Murray stood, started forward.

Barb still sat in the cushiony chair, her fingers digging into Gretchen's skin.

Grandmother held out her hands. "Come, girls." She made a soft sighing sound. "I will be with you both. And please to remember that our lovely Faye is not here. She is in heaven with Jesus. 'And God shall wipe away all tears from their eyes; there shall be no more death, neither sorrow, nor crying; neither shall there be any more pain.' " She took Barb's hand.

Mrs. Murray waited in the hallway. "Come on. Let's get this over."

Barb clutched Grandmother's arm and ignored her aunt as they walked slowly through the door into the chapel and toward her mother's casket. It wasn't until they stopped beside the casket with its single spray of white flowers that Gretchen saw the paintbrush in Barb's hand. She reached out, pressed the brush against the wood, held it there for an instant. "Mama . . ."

Cottonwood leaves rustled. Splotches of shade from an oak splashed across the graves. Squirrels fled the mourners and blue jays quarreled. Dirt clods mounded beside the new grave site. The dank smell of disturbed earth mingled with the summer scent of new-mown grass. The rasp of cicadas rose and fell.

The small circle of listeners, sweltering in the heat, was held captive by the red-faced minister. Barb's aunt glanced furtively at her wristwatch. Mrs. Crane's worn violet dress sagged against her, making her appear small and defeated. Lucille Winters tugged at an earring as if it were too tight, moved restively on her high heels. Mrs. Steele patted at her face with a lace handkerchief but her expression was as serene as if she were in her class kitchen, watching the girls mix and measure and cook. Jim Dan Pulliam and the young soldier stood a little separate. The sun burnished Jim Dan's hair. He wasn't like the others. Not to Gretchen. Was it because he was young? Or was it the way he stood, so easy and graceful, his beautiful hands hanging loose in the summer sun? Did she think he was different because he was an artist? Or because she found him attractive, wished she knew him better? The soldier was young, too, but there was nothing remarkable about him. He hunched his stocky shoulders, his cap tight in his hand, and watched Barb, his eyes squinting against the sunlight, his lips folded tight. Donny Durwood's face glistened with sweat. He mopped his cheek with a crumpled handkerchief. His wrist poked from the sleeve of his navy blue suit coat and sunlight danced on a gold cuff link. Sheriff Moore stood unmoving beside the county attorney. The sheriff's khaki shirt was short-sleeve but he, too, looked hot. His dark-skinned drooping face was unreadable, but his eyes darted from person to person, probed the thick grove of trees. Of the officials, only Chief Fraser stared at the casket poised above the grave. Deep lines scored the chief's heavy face. He looked exhausted. And sad. Ralph Cooley's wrinkled hat was tilted down onto his face. He scrawled rapidly on a handful of copy paper. Mr. Dennis's suit coat hung open. He fingered his heavy watch chain impatiently.

Not even the shrill bursts of the cicadas could overcome the impassioned rhetoric of Reverend Byars. Gretchen tried to block away his words but they battered against her, harsh and discordant as a dropped pot lid bouncing on the kitchen floor.

". . . hellfire awaits sinners. We have to thrust away from us the desire that wrecks lives. And can lead to death." He clapped his hands together.

Gretchen wished she knew what Mr. Dennis was thinking. He stood almost opposite her, across the yawning darkness of the grave, his bristly eyebrows in a tight line, his cheeks puffed, his lips pursed. Was he thinking, as she was, that the clap of Reverend Byars's hands wasn't scary or impressive or imposing as the preacher probably believed? No, the plop, scarcely heard above the volume of the cicadas, was squishy, like a dishcloth slapped on a tabletop.

". . . this poor sinner must now regret the path that led to her destruction. Had she fulfilled her solemn promises made before God and man, she would be here today, a wife and mother. But she chose to flout the laws of God —"

"No, no, no!" Barb's deep cry exploded.

Reverend Byars's thick lips hung apart, like the flaccid mouth of a gaffed fish. For an instant, no one moved or spoke. The cicadas' rasp burred into Gretchen's mind, like steel shrieking against concrete.

Wild-eyed, trembling, Barb backed away from the grave. "Mama didn't. I tell you, it's a lie. I won't stand here and listen. I won't."

"Barb, shut your mouth." Darla Murray's face twisted in fury. "Get yourself over here. Don't disgrace us even more. Faye's done that already."

Barb hunched her thin shoulders, clenched her hands tight. Suddenly, she whirled and ran unevenly toward the woods, favoring her hurt foot.

"Barb, come back." Darla Murray's shout was sharp and ugly.

The young soldier bolted after Barb, caught her at the edge of the woods. He pointed to the road where a half dozen cars were parked.

"The wrath of God follows those who defy him!" Reverend Byars shouted. "There is a place in hell for those who will not hear. Let us bow our heads in prayer. Dear Lord, forgive those who . . ."

The sound of a car motor drowned out the words. Dust roiled on the cemetery road.

The funeral home car pulled onto the rough Tatum drive.

As Gretchen reached for the door handle, Darla Murray snapped, "The car can take you home." She stared at the house. "No sign of Barb." She sniffed. "Well, it's her lookout. If the girl won't behave, there's nothing I can do. The preacher said he'd take her in. Well, he's welcome. Not that I wouldn't have her if I could. But I can't. Ted and I are squeezed in a tiny apartment near the base and I don't have any room at all. And it looks like he's going to be shipping out soon. I'll stay there 'cause I've got a good job on the base. So tell her —" A heavy sigh. "I'm afraid it's too late to tell her anything." She clambered awkwardly out of the backseat.

Grandmother leaned forward. "Barb can stay with us."

Mrs. Murray lifted her shoulders in a shrug. "She has to stay somewhere. And the preacher may not take her now." She closed the door. As the car began to move, she brushed back a tangle of damp hair. "Tell her I'll write."

The black car backed out, turned, took them to their house. Gretchen settled her grandmother in her bedroom, insisted she rest. "I'll fix supper." She was standing at the kitchen sink when the dusty green coupe backed out of the Tatum drive. Gretchen made tuna fish salad with plenty of pickles and onion and celery and Miracle Whip. She sliced tomatoes, washed lettuce, spread the tuna fish on thick white crusty bread, dished up the fruit salad, poured fresh iced tea.

They sat at the white kitchen table. Gretchen was suddenly ravenous. Grandmother sipped her tea and ate slowly, her face weary and abstracted.

Gretchen speared a dill pickle, put potato chips on her plate. "I don't blame Barb for running away. I would have, too." If somebody talked about her mother that way . . . Gretchen had a sudden sick feeling. Her mother was alive and eager and coming home tomorrow. Faye Tatum would never come home and Clyde was hiding. Oh, poor Barb. "Reverend Byars was saying awful things. I talked to Lucille Winters for my story. She said it couldn't be true about Mrs. Tatum, that she was seeing another man."

Grandmother's face lightened. "And that is in your story?"

"Yes, it's in tonight's paper." How could she have forgotten to tell Grandmother? "I'll go get it." She dashed outside, found the paper next to the steps, opened it, and there was her story across the bottom of the page, a 36-point head:

FRIENDS REMEMBER FAYE TATUM,
WIFE, ARTIST, FRIEND, TEACHER

Grandmother pushed aside her plate. She held the page close to her eyes. When she put the paper down, her face glowed. Her lips curved into a wondering smile. "Oh, Gretchen, this whole long day I have struggled to remember Faye the way she was. You have made her live again. God will bless you." She picked up the *Gazette,* touched the story with her fingertips. After supper she took the newspaper with her to her old cane rocker and sat beside the radio listening to the news with Edward Kaltenborn.

Gretchen was almost finished with the dishes when the phone rang. "I'll get it." She hurried, wiping her hands on a tea towel. "Hello." Surely Mother wasn't calling to say they weren't coming. . . .

"Gretchen. Hi. Listen, I had to call you." A saxophone wailed in the background.

Gretchen frowned. "Wilma?" It sounded like Wilma, but not quite. Her voice was stiff, like she was talking to the principal. Wilma Fuller was the most popular girl in their class. The third floor of the Fullers' huge old Victorian house had once been a ballroom. Sometimes as many as fifteen girls spread out their sleeping bags on a Friday night after the movies. They had a record player and they'd stay up most of the night and drink Cokes and talk about boys and practice different hairdos.

"Yeah. Anyway, I've got to rush. There's not going to be a slumber party tonight. I just wanted you to know so you wouldn't come over." She spoke fast, still in that odd, stiff manner. "Sorry, Gretchen, I have to go. See you."

Gretchen slowly replaced the receiver.

The radio switched off. "Gretchen?"

Gretchen walked to the living room. She made her voice brisk. "It's okay, Grandmother." But that wasn't true. "It was Wilma Fuller."

Grandmother relaxed against the cushions. "Oh, yes. It's Friday night." She tried to smile. "And you will go to Thompson's and —"

Gretchen interrupted before she would have to tell Grandmother what Wilma said. "Not tonight. Mr. Dennis wants me to come to the city council meeting. Mr. Cooley will write the news story but Mr. Dennis wants me to write about the crowd and what people are saying. I'll go in early tomorrow and write the story and I'll get home before Mother comes." There was no paper on Saturdays but they usually worked until two on Saturday afternoons for the Sunday paper.

Grandmother's face furrowed. "The council is meeting at city hall tonight?" She fingered a gold tassel on the fringe of the cushion. "Why?"

"Because . . ." Gretchen paused. Ralph Cooley said there would be fireworks for sure, the mayor wanting to know why Clyde

256

Tatum wasn't in jail, and the police chief butting heads with the sheriff and the county attorney. Grandmother must not realize that people were frightened, especially after the story saying Clyde Tatum was considered to be armed and dangerous. "The mayor wants to know why they haven't arrested Mr. Tatum."

"Oh." Grandmother sighed. "I wish . . ." She didn't finish.

Gretchen wondered if she wished for tomorrow. Clyde Tatum had promised he would finish his search by tonight. That meant he would turn himself in tomorrow. If he didn't, what would Grandmother do? She'd been frightened after the gun was taken, frightened that Clyde had the gun and worried what he might do with it. He'd promised her he didn't have the gun. But if he didn't have it, who did? Maybe Chief Fraser would make an announcement at the council meeting.

Gretchen stopped beside the rocker. "Will you go to bed early? I'll lock up when I get back from the meeting."

Grandmother sagged back against the cushions, her face drained, her hands limp in her lap. "Yes. I will do that. But tomorrow" — her voice was soft — "we will celebrate to have your mother home."

Gretchen bent down, kissed Grandmother's cheek. She moved fast, finishing her last check of the kitchen, hurrying to her room to change from pedal pushers to a skirt, grabbing a pencil and copy paper. She heard the rush of water, the rattle of the pipes. Grandmother was taking a bath. Gretchen stopped at the telephone, picked up the receiver. She gave the operator Tonya Harris's number. Tonya's mother answered. Gretchen said quickly, "Is Tonya there? It's about the slumber party at the Fuller house." She stood by the phone, already hot even though her blouse and skirt were fresh. As she waited, she heard the chirps of birds settling in the trees and the rasp of cicadas.

"Hello?" Tonya's voice was high and sweet.

"Tonya, this is Gretchen. About the slumber party —"

A gasp. "Oh. Didn't Wilma call you?"

"Yes. But I just wanted to know. There is a slumber party, isn't there?" She rolled the thick copy pencil in her fingers, around and around.

"Oh, Gretchen." It was a wail. "I'm sorry. Reverend Byars is mad about that story on Mrs. Tatum. He told everybody it was just like consorting with the devil, to write things that make her sound like she was a good person. Wilma's dad — you know he's a deacon — he said she couldn't have you over again and she had to call and tell you. Oh, Gretchen, I'm sorry." Tonya hung up.

Gretchen replaced the receiver. Last year everybody said Jolene Carter had spent the night in the barn with Will Toomey. After that, nobody had anything to do with Jolene and she walked through the halls by herself, sat alone in the cafeteria. One day she didn't come to school anymore. A man fishing at Placid Lake found her body. Everybody said it was an accident.

The lot behind the courthouse was full and every parking place was taken on both sides of Cimarron Street. People milled around outside city hall. Lights burned in all the ground-floor windows of the long red brick building.

Gretchen, trying to squeeze past a clot of men near the shallow front steps, caught bits of their conversations. " . . . can't get in . . . packed . . . sheriff said no progress . . . carry out a table . . ."

"Excuse me, please," she said. "Excuse me . . ."

Mr. Kraft, the banker, shook his head, his thick silver mustache quivering. "You can't get through." His silvery brows drew down

259

over his pale green eyes. "Why are you here, Gretchen? This isn't a place for girls."

She lifted her voice to be heard over the crowd, a deep rumble like cows mooing in a feedlot. "I'm here for the *Gazette*, Mr. Kraft."

His face was unsmiling. "Gilman . . ." He tugged at his mustache. "I saw the paper tonight. You wrote that story about Faye Tatum, didn't you?" His lips poked out like a man who'd tasted vinegar.

Gretchen lifted her chin, met his sharp gaze. "I did." It was a good story. Mr. Dennis put it on the wire. She wanted to tell Mr. Kraft, but she didn't dare.

"You shouldn't be talking to people like Lou Hopper." The banker's voice made the name sound ugly. "I can tell you my daughter wouldn't go near a place like the Blue Light."

Gretchen's hands balled into fists. "Mrs. Hopper said —"

His face pinched like he was looking at shiftless Mort Baker who never could hold a job. "Girl, I don't care what Mrs. Hopper said." He turned away.

"Make way!" The deep shout parted the crowd jammed on the walk in front of city hall. Mayor Burkett bustled importantly down the steps, his plump face flushed and excited. He was followed by Sheriff Moore, who swept the onlookers with a sardonic gaze. County Attorney Durwood, his face beaded with sweat, shook hands in passing, slapped friends on the shoulder. Behind them, Chief Fraser and Sergeant Holliman carried a rectangular oak table. Chief Fraser's face bulged in a grim frown. A lumpy white bandage swathed the left side of Sergeant Holliman's head. His uniform cap was perched on the back of his head.

Mayor Burkett gestured toward the gazebo in the city square. "There will be plenty of room for everybody on the square. We'll set up in the gazebo."

Those who had come early and squeezed inside city hall came streaming out. A knot of men fanned out to make way for Sheila Durwood, slim and elegant in a white shantung dress with turquoise sleeves. Her hat was a froth of white feathers on her dark hair. She smiled graciously and walked with easy confidence across the street. There was always space for her. She was a Winslow. Gretchen spotted Mr. Dennis and Ralph Cooley and hurried to join them. They wormed their way right up to the steps of the gazebo. The crowd pressed close. Gretchen made notes as a Boy Scout troop put chairs behind the table. The four council members took their places.

Gretchen knew all the council members:

Mr. Thompson, the druggist; Mr. Evans, the town's richest lawyer; Mr. Wilkins, who owned Wilkins Plumbing; and Mr. Randall, Best Department Store. Mr. Thompson's suit was too large. Since Mike and Millard were killed in action, he'd lost weight and his face was always grooved in sadness. Mr. Evans wore pince-nez perched on a thin nose above pursed lips. A few strands of lank gray hair lay over a balding crown. Burly Mr. Wilkins loved baseball and coached a semipro team. He knew everybody in town and spoke in a booming shout. Mr. Randall's white summer suit didn't have a wrinkle and his panama hat sported a feather in the band. He sat stiffly, as if he wished he were somewhere else.

Mr. Dennis bent down, whispered, "Keep your ears open for comments from the crowd, Gretchen."

Ralph Cooley rubbed his nose. "Durwood's brought out the heavy artillery."

Gretchen looked up at him. "Artillery?"

"The little woman. Or in his case, maybe he's the little man." Cooley's voice was derisive. "Everybody says she runs him pretty good. Wants to be the governor's wife — and he damn sure better make the grade."

The police chief and his sergeant stood to the left of the council members. The chief looked as grim and tired as he had the night Gretchen and Barb found Faye Tatum's body. Sergeant Holliman occasionally touched his bandage as if his head hurt.

Sheriff Moore and County Attorney Durwood were on the other side of the gazebo. Sheriff Moore, his expression impassive, leaned against a pillar, as tall and thin and somber as a white-faced Abe Lincoln in a daguerreotype. Donald Durwood lifted a hand in greeting, nodded hellos, managing to appear both serious and friendly, determined yet relaxed. Occasionally he glanced toward his wife, who looked as comfortable as though she were pouring tea at a women's club meeting. But Durwood lacked his usual sheen; his face was sweaty, his blue suit wrinkled. Every so often, he wiped the sweat from his face, jammed the handkerchief back into his coat pocket.

The mayor bustled importantly to the front of the gazebo.

Ralph Cooley muttered, "Don't hold your breath waiting for somebody else to get a word in." But he folded copy paper over his hand, held his pencil ready.

Gretchen thought about the man in the dirty khaki uniform hiding in the ramshackle cabin. These people wanted him run down and caught.

Mayor Burkett boomed, "Fellow citizens, welcome. As your mayor, I am determined that public concerns shall always be promptly addressed. My fellow council members" — he waved a plump hand at the men sitting behind the table — "share that commitment. The safety of our families —"

A shout came from the back of the crowd. "How come you ain't caught Tatum yet?" Gretchen turned, stood on tiptoe. A rangy farmer's leathery face twisted in a scowl. He shifted a wad of chewing tobacco in his cheek.

A skinny man in a seersucker suit and white boater waved a copy of the *Gazette*. "Yeah. Where's he got to? The paper says he's got a gun. I don't want to leave my wife and kids home alone. But she's ready for him. I got the shotgun waiting."

"Stupid," Mr. Dennis muttered. "Do they think Clyde's gone nuts?"

Voices rose. The crowd moved toward the gazebo. Mayor Burkett cried, "Wait a minute here. We're here to —"

Chief Fraser strode forward. He snatched off his big tan cowboy hat, thrust it out in front, like he was at a victory rally and everybody was pledging to buy war bonds. He glared at the crowd, stern as the Purdys' bulldog, all bulging eyes and cheeks and blunt chin. "If Clyde Tatum's out there, we're going to find him. Nobody's seen him since he left the Blue Light Tuesday night just after seven o'clock. Faye Tatum left at midnight. Clyde's car is still in the Blue Light parking lot. We got dogs out there Wednesday morning. They ran around the lot, to and from the door, and then they sat on their butts. Now what does that tell us?" He jammed his hat on his head and his pugnacious gaze swept the crowd. Nobody spoke. Nobody stirred. "Clyde left in a car. We don't know who took him. We don't know where he went. We've checked the buses and the trains, got word out on the Teletype. Search parties have been all over the county." Chief Fraser turned his big, callused hands palms up. "Not a trace. Nobody saw him near Archer Street. Nobody saw him with Faye. And Faye didn't have a car to come and get him. Yet all of you" — he swept that big hand toward the crowd, swung to look at the mayor and county attorney and each council member — "are positive that Clyde strangled Faye."

Sheriff Moore shrugged, but his face was cold and hard, determined. Mayor Burkett's eyes fell away. Mr. Thompson tugged on an earlobe. Mr. Evans's thin nose wriggled. Mr.

Wilkins shifted uncomfortably in the too small chair. Mr. Randall smoothed the lapels of his white suit. The county attorney jammed his handkerchief in his pocket. He glanced at his wife. Her head tilted in an almost imperceptible nod. Durwood took a step forward.

The chief spit out the words. "There's no evidence. Sure, Faye and Clyde quarreled, but nobody saw him with her when she left the Blue Light. We've been checking out everybody who was there Tuesday night —"

"Wait a minute, wait a minute." Durwood's voice was mellifluous and it flowed out into the evening cool and certain as a river. The county attorney moved to the center of the platform, shaking his head a little. He suddenly seemed in his element, his smile deprecating, patient. "Let's look at the facts." Durwood sounded as though he were in court, addressing a jury, a man sure of his ground. Judge Miller once described him as a modern-day Wyatt Earp. "Donny always gets his man." On that gazebo platform, he was in command even though his face was still sweaty.

"Got his hands stuck in his pockets." Ralph Cooley's raspy whisper was amused. He cocked a cynical eyebrow. "Bet they're shaking. Durwood knows he better sound

266

good tonight or forget politics. He's scared shitless this case is going to wreck him."

Durwood rocked forward on his feet. His voice dropped. "Faye Tatum and her husband quarreled Tuesday afternoon. They quarreled again at the Blue Light. Faye was strangled in her living room just after midnight. The police were on the scene within minutes." Durwood walked to the edge of the steps, looked out at the crowd. "Did the police find Clyde Tatum there? No." His hands came out of his pockets. "Did Clyde Tatum return to his home that night? No." Each question and answer was louder. "What would an innocent man do if his wife was murdered? I'll tell you." Now it was a shout and he pounded a fist into his palm. "An innocent man would rush to the police, demand they find his wife's killer. Instead, Tatum goes to earth, like a fox. Tatum didn't come to the police or to the sheriff or to me. But Wednesday night, he goes to his house and even though there are officers there, he gets inside, gets his gun. And he gets away." Durwood swung toward the chief. "Where's Clyde Tatum?"

The crowd roared. "Where is he? Where is he?"

"That's what we all want to know." Mayor Burkett frowned and his pink face looked like a querulous Kewpie doll. He waggled a plump finger at Chief Fraser. "How come you let him slip through your fingers Wednesday night?"

Chief Fraser said sharply, "The man who broke in wasn't seen —"

"Broke in?" The county attorney sounded shocked. He flung his arms wide. "There was no evidence of a break-in when Sheriff Moore and I examined the house on Thursday. Maybe you found something we didn't." He folded his arms, bent his head in a listening attitude. Sheriff Moore slowly nodded.

Chief Fraser's rough skin flushed a dull red.

Ralph Cooley smothered a cough. "Durwood's got him on the ropes."

The chief walked slowly across the planks, stood face-to-face with the county attorney, too close for comfort, but Durwood didn't give an inch. Fraser was a much bigger man. Massive hands clenched, the chief leaned toward Durwood. "We don't know how the intruder got in. The house was locked up but —"

"So it looks like he had a key. Right?" Durwood's voice was silky.

"Maybe. But you know what, Donny?" The chief's voice was hard. "Clyde Tatum left his keys — including the key to the front door — in his car." Fraser reached in his pocket, pulled out a big shiny metal key ring with a half dozen keys dangling from it. "Here they are. Clyde Tatum didn't have a key to his house."

Durwood frowned. "He could have had another key."

"Sure he could. So could somebody else. But you want to talk about facts." The chief glared at Durwood. "The fact is we don't know who got in the house or how he did it."

A chair scraped. Mr. Evans stood. "Gentlemen, please."

Cooley poked a cigarette in his mouth, lit it. "Oh, God, another lawyer. We'll be here all night." He heaved a sigh.

Gretchen thought the lawyer looked as cool and gray as a dead fish belly up in the water.

Councilman Evans cleared his throat. His voice was high, precise, and sharp, his narrow face sour. "Chief Fraser, what is the status of the investigation?"

"The search for Clyde Tatum continues. We are seeking leads to Faye Tatum's actions the night she died. We know she used the pay phone at the Blue Light. Who did she talk to? Did she make plans to meet somebody? Or did somebody follow her home from the Blue Light? We know she was surprised by the person who killed her. Her daughter overheard Faye say, 'You've got a nerve coming here —' "

Sheriff Moore ambled forward, his cowboy boots clumping on the wooden planks. "Many a husband's heard his wife yell something like that when he comes home after they've had trouble. For my money, Clyde Tatum killed his wife and there's only two possible reasons he's not in jail."

Everybody quieted down. It was like the thick heavy quiet of a summer night when a storm was coming.

Sheriff Moore's cold gaze swung slowly over the crowd, his face somber. "Tatum's dead — or somebody's hiding him. Because we've hunted." He jerked his big head toward Chief Fraser. "The chief and his men, me and my men. We've looked. So if Clyde's not dead, he's still hiding and the only way he can hide" — the sheriff's voice rose — "is with help. I'm telling you people that when we find him, we're going to find out who helped him. Make no mistake, whoever helped Clyde is going to rot in jail. That's a promise."

. . . You remember Buddy Wilson? He wasn't much to look at but he sure could dance. He was crazy about me. He was so kind to me the day they buried Mama. I almost told Buddy when I finally figured out what happened to Mama. But I don't think even Buddy would have believed me. I knew nobody else would believe me. They'd have thought I was making it up. I was scared, so scared. I had to get away. Buddy wanted to marry me and his leave was almost up. We ran away to Tulsa and got married by a justice of the peace. Nobody looked too hard at how old you were in those days, not when the guy had on a uniform. I was sixteen. I went out to the coast with him. He shipped out in September. . . .

Chapter
8

. . . about that summer. All these years, I'd refused to remember that Saturday. But age is a

271

merciless companion. There is something within us when we are old that accepts reality. It's like climbing up a rugged gorge, every foot a desperate scramble, fending off debris from above, knocking loose rocks that rain down upon others. Reaching the precipice, clinging with bloodied, bruised hands, we look back at the tortuous path, gazing in wonder at occasional moments in the sun but seeing the darkness and shadows, understanding how near we came to destruction, counting the missed opportunities, the botched efforts, the unintended consequences of our struggles. The unintended consequences . . .

Cimarron Street blazed with light and movement. People greeted neighbors as they walked toward their cars. Some people stood in clumps, talking, looking over their shoulders as the chief and the sheriff and the county attorney strode past. Mr. Dennis nodded toward her. "I'll give you a ride home. I'm parked in the alley behind the *Gazette*."

"Thank you." Her voice could scarcely be heard over the rumble of the crowd, almost as loud as people streaming away from a high school football game after a victory. But this crowd's mutter was harsh and angry, worried and fearful.

The farther they walked from the town square, the quieter it was. When Gretchen climbed into the editor's dusty black coupe and the engine rumbled, they drove away from the ugly murmurs, but over and over Gretchen remembered the sheriff's bleak voice: . . . *rot in jail . . . rot in jail . . .* If the sheriff found out about Grandmother, what would happen? Would he put Grandmother in jail? Make her go into one of those concrete cells and slam shut the iron bars? She'd seen the cells when she went to the sheriff's office. The words ballooned in her mind, pressing until she felt her head would burst.

". . . Gretchen?" In the light from the dashboard, Mr. Dennis looked gray and tired.

She jerked toward him. "Yes?"

"Are you all right?" His face furrowed in concern as he braked in front of her house.

"Yes, sir." But she wasn't. She could scarcely keep from flinging open the door and running to the Purdy cabin. She had to hurry. . . .

"You're tired. You worked all day. And there was the funeral." He pulled his pipe from his pocket, poked it in his tobacco pouch. "Don't come in tomorrow. Enjoy your mom's visit. I'll do the story on the crowd."

As she opened the door, Gretchen held tight to her sheaf of copy paper. She had good notes: Reverend Byars jostling his way through the crowd with a petition calling for the padlocking of the Blue Light; the grocer, Mr. Hudson, telling about Clyde working for him when he was in high school and how Clyde found a bald eagle chick whose mother had been shot and Clyde raised the chick with scraps of fish and how he set the eagle free when it was able to fly; Mr. Salk, who lived eight miles out of town, claiming he saw Clyde in the early morning mist Friday near Hunter Lake; Mrs. Gordon saying somebody broke into her barn and took fishing tackle; the Whittle sisters on Colson Road demanding police protection, saying old women living alone shouldn't be at the mercy of fugitives; the high school football players volunteering to make up a search party. . . .

Gretchen shut the car door, leaned in the open window. "I'm okay." She could write a good story. The lead was coming clear in her mind:

Sergeant Clyde Tatum wasn't at the city council meeting Friday night but nobody talked about anyone else.

"I'll come in early. I know where the key is. I'll get the story done before Mother and

— before she comes." Before Mother and the man arrived. Maybe she didn't even care if she got home before her mother arrived.

The porch light was on. Mr. Dennis didn't drive away until she opened the front door and turned and waved. She stepped inside, closed the door, carefully placed her notes on the stand below the mirror. The notes would be there in the morning.

Tomorrow. It seemed far away. Because tonight there was much she must do. She tiptoed down the hall, trying to be quiet, but the wooden floor creaked. Grandmother's bedside light flashed on.

Gretchen stopped at her bedroom door. "I'm home," she called softly.

Grandmother struggled to sit up.

Gretchen hurried across the floor. "It's all right. Go back to sleep."

"The meeting . . ." Grandmother's voice was dull and very faint.

"I'll tell you about it tomorrow. Nothing really happened" (. . . *rot in jail . . . rot in jail . . . rot in jail . . .*) "But people are frightened." Gretchen looked at Grandmother's lined face, so gray, so quiet on the pillow. "Don't worry. Everything will be all right." She patted a heavily veined hand, reached up, clicked off the lamp. "Good night."

As she stepped into the hall, Gretchen

drew Grandmother's door almost shut. Once in her room, alert for any sound from the hall, Gretchen changed into shorts and a top and loafers, grabbed Jimmy's gun and the flashlight from their hiding place beneath a stack of underwear in her top dresser drawer, quietly eased open the screen of her window, and dropped softly to the ground.

Heavy clouds obscured the moon. The night was hot and still. Faraway lightning crackled. In the brief flicker of gold, the sky looked like ridges of black lava tinged with pearl. Gretchen walked fast to Maguire Road. She kept to the edge of the narrow road, but there wasn't any traffic. The Turner dogs yelped as she passed by. Gretchen reached the faint path that angled into the woods. The woods loomed ahead of her, dark and forbidding. When she edged onto the trail, darkness pressed against her like a black blanket. Tucking Jimmy's .22 under one arm, she cupped her hand over the flashlight lens, using just enough light to find her way. Occasionally, she stopped, her breath shallow, and listened to the crackle of leaves, the movement of branches, the shriek of cicadas. Gnats and mosquitos swarmed around her and she wished she'd worn a long-sleeve blouse and jeans despite the heat. Once she jerked the full beam of the flash to her right, stared into a mass of shrubbery and vines and ferns. She knew coyotes and bobcats moved soft-footed through the night. She glimpsed — or did she? — a patch of tawny fur. She pointed the pistol, waited, her heart thudding. The woods were alive with sound, the shadows with movement. Finally, she forced her leaden legs to move. She crept through the night, burdened by fear. She'd not felt this way before when she'd come to the cabin. Maybe she was tired. Maybe it was the terrible worry that Grandmother might be found out. If the sheriff knocked on their door, his rock-hard face in a glower, Grandmother would be frightened to death.

Death . . . Gretchen pushed away her memory of Faye Tatum, sprawled on the floor of a room where she'd laughed and cried, a room where she'd lived and died.

Gretchen was shaking when she reached the overgrown clearing and the dark cabin. She flicked off the flashlight and stared, seeking even the barest hint of light from the gloom-shrouded shanty.

Nothing. No light. No sense of life or occupancy, simply darkness and an overwhelming sense of danger. She wanted to turn and run. Slowly, every step an effort of will, she walked across the humpy ground, flicking aside the tendrils of waist-high grass, hating the buzz of insects, the pricks against her skin, and the darkness, the terrible, heavy, inimical darkness. The steps creaked as she climbed. She froze, head bent forward. Behind her grasses rustled.

Gretchen whirled. The circle of woods was darker than the overgrown clearing. Anything might be hidden in the trees. She had a feeling of a watchful presence, malevolent, hurtful, malignant. She couldn't bear it. She snapped on the flashlight, swung it back and forth, the beam sliding across the trees and wild grasses and tangled ferns. Nothing moved and now there were only sounds of the night, the whirr and rasp of insects, the chitter of disturbed squirrels, the eerie moan of owls.

She yanked the flash toward the cabin. The spear of light swept past the closed door — the unmoving door — and illuminated the open window, the sash raised halfway. The door remained shut. Her quick breaths slowed. Clyde Tatum surely would have seen her light if he were here. She walked across the porch. She held the flashlight in her left hand, the .22 in her right.

"Mr. Tatum? It's Gretchen Gilman." Her words fell into silence. Awkwardly, gripping the flashlight in her thumb and forefinger, she curved the rest of her hand around the door handle, turned it. She pushed and the door swung in. She stepped slowly into the cabin, the tongue of light flicking in every direction, picking out the gilt of the discarded harp, the stacked boxes and broken furniture, the scarred wooden table, the dingy green of the lantern. Her nose wrinkled. The smell of kerosene cloyed the air. An old wooden crate, the splintered top agape, served as a garbage pail. Ants crawled in a thin dark line over a sodden lump of newspaper.

She didn't close the door behind her. She glanced toward the window. The blanket used to hide light from outside lay in a crumpled heap on the floor. She wondered if he rigged up the blanket only when he used the lantern. That made sense. The window was open, ready if a breeze came.

Thunder rumbled in the distance. It might storm or it might not, but the thunder urged her to hurry. She was half glad Clyde Tatum was gone, half sorry. She'd intended to tell him what the sheriff said and beg him to protect Grandmother. He'd promised Grandmother he wouldn't tell anyone she'd helped him, but he needed to know how much his silence mattered. She didn't have any paper with her, but it didn't matter. She didn't dare leave a note behind. What if the police chief or sheriff came here? No, she couldn't leave a note. She had to hope Clyde would keep his promise.

Lightning flashed, pouring blue light across the jumbled mass of junk. Gretchen turned her light to the kitchen counter, the top of the range, across the uneven, worn wooden tabletop. She moved the beam slowly and stopped. There's where the picnic basket — Grandmother's picnic basket with her fingerprints on it and her name, Pfizer, burned in clear black letters into the wooden handle — had sat when Gretchen last saw it. Clyde Tatum's big hand had flipped open the lid. He'd grabbed a chicken leg and eaten and talked. Now there was only the tabletop with scraps of brown paper on it.

She came closer. The paper was torn from crumpled old grocery sacks. Had Clyde Tatum found the sacks in someone's garbage, brought them here to record his search for his wife's murderer? A big, thick leaded pencil lay near the pieces of paper. There were names printed, five or six, on one piece. Gretchen scarcely glanced at the scraps. She had to find the picnic basket.

The room was stifling, not a breath of

breeze through the open window. No wonder he'd let the blanket drop. Sweat beaded her face, slid down her back and legs, sucked her clothes against her skin. She forced herself to move slowly. She stood on tiptoe, bent low, looked up and down and around, on the counters, behind boxes, beneath tables. She was on her hands and knees, poking at a lopsided bucket, when she found the basket, wedged beneath a rickety table. Gretchen grabbed the wooden handles, tugged it free. She opened the basket. Yes, there was the plate and napkin, cutlery, everything. She felt relief so overwhelming, she was almost dizzy. She dropped the gun inside and closed the lid. Would he notice that the basket was gone? It didn't matter. Nothing mattered but protecting Grandmother. She hurried through the door, pulled it shut behind her. Lightning flickered over the trees to the south.

She was at the steps, the light from the flash dancing across the grass-choked clearing, when fear washed over her again. She held tight to the basket, looked out at the dark mass of trees. Was he coming? There was someone near. There was danger — evil — close to her.

Panic swept her. She flicked off the flashlight and jumped from the porch. She ran lightly to a big shrub, waited, darted from one shadow to another. When she reached the woods, she slipped onto the path, trusting to her night vision, quiet as a fox. She eased open the picnic basket, dropped the flashlight inside. She yanked out the gun, held it tightly in her hand.

One stealthy step, another and another, she crept on and on through the sultry hot night with the occasional burst of lightning high in the sky, the gun hard in her hand, fear searing her soul. Once beyond the woods, she clung to the dark edge of the road, walked fast, glancing behind, startled by every crackle and rustle. She reached Archer Street. She was almost home. She began to run, pounding as if hounds yipped at her heels. She made no effort to be quiet but the midnight street lay empty and no one heard her feet crunch against the gravel.

At the house, she leaned against the wall and struggled for breath, staring back the way she had come. Chief Fraser . . . she had to call . . . something bad . . . something awful . . . a sense of incipient doom pressed against her. But first, the basket. She gulped air into her burning lungs and darted toward the back steps. On her flight away from the dark cabin, she'd held so tight to the wooden handles that her hand ached. She put the basket on the steps. She took out the flashlight. Grandmother would find the basket in the morning. She would be puzzled, but she would believe Clyde Tatum had left it. Whatever happened, Grandmother was safe now. There was nothing to link her to the cabin, that dreadful, silent place.

Thunder crashed nearby. Gretchen ran to her bedroom window. She eased open the screen, held the pistol carefully, and climbed inside. For the first moment since she'd fled the clearing, she felt safe. She walked to the dresser, placed the gun and flashlight in the top drawer. She didn't want to think about the fear that had blazed within her on the uneven, worn porch of the cabin, hot and destructive and terrifying as flames leaping out of control in a tinder-dry forest. No matter how hard she tried, the memory clung to her even though nothing scary had occurred at the cabin or on the path. Nonetheless, deep inside, the fear remained. In Sunday school several years ago, Mrs. Burris, who was thin and diffident and easily confused, spoke very firmly, telling them that you didn't have to prove God existed, that there were truths your soul knew without question or doubt if only you listened. Was evil as clear? Gretchen knew she'd come close to something unutterably dark and dangerous. She couldn't prove this, but she knew. She should call Chief Fraser. . . . Could she tell him about the cabin without endangering Grandmother?

Gretchen sat on the edge of her bed, her hands clasped tightly together. Slowly the peace of her room eased her tight muscles and the dreadful fear began to seep away. Her eyes ached with fatigue. Her legs felt heavy as logs. What had frightened her? That's what she needed to know. She hadn't seen anyone, but she had felt that someone watched her. Who? Clyde Tatum? Who else? No one knew Clyde was hiding in the cabin except Gretchen and Grandmother — oh, wait — the woman who called to tell Grandmother that he was at the Purdy cabin. She could have told someone else Clyde was there. Maybe somebody had come looking for him and then Gretchen arrived. Maybe the watcher was scared. Maybe that fear triggered her fear. Or the silent observer could have been Clyde Tatum. He surely would be frightened if anyone approached the cabin. The more she thought about it, the more certain she was that Clyde had heard her coming and fled to the woods. She'd been silly, thinking she was in danger. Nothing bad had happened. Maybe a fox had watched her, cold yellow eyes alert and inimical. Relief buoyed Gretchen like a fluffy, soft cloud.

A huge bolt of lightning illuminated her room, bathing the world beyond her window with milky luminescence for a wavering instant. As the bluish light faded, rain whooshed over the house, slapping on the roof, pelting the window. Gretchen undressed, put on her gown, and fell on her bed.

Gretchen glanced at the tiger-striped cat sitting atop the big garbage pail near the back door of the *Gazette*. The cat held one paw near its face, rough pink tongue extended, and watched Gretchen, hoping for food.

She leaned forward, searched, found the back door key. The cat jumped down, twined around her ankles. She let him come inside with her, pad across the backshop to the newsroom. There was an old icebox in a little closet off the newsroom. Gretchen found a bottle of cream — Mr. Dennis liked his chicory-laden coffee a soft tan — and poured a little into a saucer, placed the dish on a folded newspaper.

As she settled at her desk, the early morning sun spilling pink and gold through the front windows, the cat's purr, the hard feel of the slight depression on the round metal buttons of the typewriter keys, the familiar smells of cigarette and pipe smoke and lead and ink combined to reassure her. She would not think of those moments in the woods. Not now. Not ever. She unfolded her notes from the city council meeting and began to write, one word after another, and each one was like a brick sealing away fear and worry and uncertainty.

She was almost finished when Mr. Dennis arrived. His seersucker suit, the same one he'd worn last night, was wrinkled. His eyes were doleful in his seamed face, but he tried to sound jolly. "Hey, Gretchen, long john?" He held up the white cardboard box from Lyon's Bakery.

"Yes, sir. Thank you."

He brought the long john on a cracked yellow saucer. The long john was still warm. Gretchen took a bite, swiped sticky fingers on a piece of copy paper.

In a moment, the editor placed a white pottery mug on her desk. "Watch out. It's hot." The smell of strong coffee and chicory wafted toward her.

She typed -30- at the bottom of the page, pasted the sheets together, handed him the story.

He stood beside her. Mr. Dennis scanned copy faster than anyone she'd ever known. He nodded, said "Good," and turned away, carrying her story.

That was all he said, but Gretchen cupped the word in her mind, smooth and shiny as the buckeye that sat on the nightstand by her bed. Jimmy had given it to her before he left on the bus to go to the induction center. Buckeyes were good luck. Sometimes, she'd hold the big nut tight and wish Jimmy had it with him. It was Jimmy who needed luck.

If only buckeyes really brought luck. Then Grandmother would be safe. The sheriff must never find out that Grandmother had helped Clyde Tatum. Gretchen took the last bite of the long john but the still warm cake and delectable brown sugar icing had no taste. She pushed back her chair, looked toward the editor's desk. He wore his green eyeshade now. Cherry sweet smoke rose from the pipe balanced in his ashtray. His stubby fingers flew over the keys, the staccato rattle certain and sure.

Gretchen hesitated, then moved determinedly to his desk. She waited until he paused, glanced at her, his eyes blank in concentration. His gaze slowly sharpened. "You're done, Gretchen. Go home and enjoy your mama. Give her my best."

"I will, Mr. Dennis. But" — she needed to be careful what she said — "I wondered what it meant last night when the sheriff said somebody must have been helping Mr. Tatum. What did he mean?"

Mr. Dennis's light green eyes seemed to look through her, all the way into her mind and heart. She shouldn't have asked. She stood, scarcely breathing.

"He means somebody's going to be in big trouble." Mr. Dennis picked up his pipe, poked it in his mouth. He drew deeply, gave a puff. His tone was thoughtful. "Sheriff Moore's nobody's fool. Clyde's been missing since Tuesday night. Now it's Saturday. Where's Clyde been staying? How has he got food? Oh, it's pretty clear Clyde's had help." His bristly gray eyebrows bunched. "Listen, girl, if you know anybody — like Barb, maybe — who knows where Clyde is, for God's sake, tell them to warn him. People are scared. They've got their guns out. Clyde better turn himself in pronto." He pointed his pipe at the typewriter. "I'm writing an editorial and I'm going to put it on the front page. This is no time for a bunch of vigilantes to shoot first and ask questions later. Clyde Tatum deserves his day in court."

Gretchen backed away, shaking her head.

"Barb doesn't know where her dad is. I just wanted to be able to tell her what happened last night and I didn't understand what the sheriff meant."

The editor's lips turned down in a sour grin. "Just what he said, girl. Somebody's going to rot in jail, right along with Clyde."

The Tatum house had a look of abandonment. Gone-to-seed grass wavered in the breeze. Yellowing newspapers, soggy from last night's brief storm, were strewn near the worn front steps. The windows were closed, the shades drawn. Gretchen stopped by the mailbox. The broken cover still hung askew. Rain had smeared the ink on one envelope. There was no sign that Barb had returned to the house after her mother's funeral. Gretchen hadn't seen Barb since yesterday afternoon when she bolted from the cemetery, running away from her anger and hurt with that young soldier, the strident voice of Reverend Byars following them. Where had they gone? Last night Gretchen had looked for Barb at the town square. Gretchen wondered if Barb knew what had happened, what had been said. Mr. Dennis was afraid for Barb's father. Barb needed to know. . . .

Gretchen started up the cracked sidewalk. A flash of brightness startled her. She looked to her left, squinting against the glitter of sunlight on metal near the overgrown honey-suckle bush at the end of the Tatum drive-way. She crossed the yard, gnats rising in a cloud, and walked up the rutted drive. A battered coupe, missing the right front fender, was parked behind the sweet-scented shrub. Gretchen didn't recognize the car. It was quite well hidden from the street and the bush, grown wild and tall and out of control, hid the car from Mrs. Crane's watchful gaze.

Gretchen swung toward the Tatum house. The screen door of the back porch banged open. Barb stood on the top step, her pink halter and blue shorts perfect for the thick heat promised by the burnished sheen of the morning sky, strangely shocking in contrast with the dark dress she'd worn at the ceme-tery.

Gretchen walked slowly toward the porch, not wanting to talk to Barb, certain that she should, wondering about the car and the house and where Barb had been since yesterday afternoon.

Barb waited, standing stiff and still. Her long auburn hair shone in the summer sun, the kind of hair that should have framed beauty, not an old-young face with misery-filled eyes. When Gretchen was a few feet away, Barb plucked at a strap of the halter.

"I saw you coming from town." She paused, swallowed. "Have they found my dad?"

Gretchen shook her head. "No."

Barb let go a little breath. "Daddy . . ." She wasn't speaking to Gretchen, didn't look at her. Barb's voice was high, like a little girl calling out in the night.

Gretchen wrapped her arms tight across her front, as much to keep herself there, facing Barb, as to hold back the words she wished she could speak. Barb wanted her father and Gretchen knew where he was.

. . . rot in jail . . . rot in jail . . .

Gretchen burst out, talking fast, "Were you at the town square last night? I didn't see you."

"No." Barb looked at Gretchen sharply. "Why?"

"They had a meeting of the town council. About your dad." Gretchen took a deep breath. "Everybody's pretty upset."

Barb's dark, despairing eyes demanded more.

Reluctantly, her voice uneven, Gretchen said, "People are talking about getting out their guns. The police chief and the sheriff and county attorney are mad at each other, and the whole town's mad at them since nobody's found your dad. The sheriff said somebody's going to jail for helping your

dad hide out. And Mr. Dennis is afraid —"
She stopped.

Barb limped down the steps, grabbed
Gretchen's arm, dug sharp nails into her
skin. "Afraid of what?"

"That somebody's going to shoot your
dad. Mr. Dennis says if anybody knows
where he is, they need to tell him to give
himself up. Quick." Each word hurt deep inside Gretchen. She knew where Clyde
Tatum was. She knew and she had to do
something about it.

"Why should they shoot Daddy? He
wouldn't hurt anyone. That's crazy! He'd
never hurt —" Barb broke off, as if hearing
her own words. Her fingers loosened their
grip. Her hand fell away. She stood in the
steely heat, the sun already blazing even
though it wasn't nine o'clock in the morning
yet, the bright hot weight of summer pressing
down against the dusty yard, and seemed to
grow smaller in front of Gretchen's eyes.
Barb's head sagged, her shoulders slumped,
her hands hung limp. "Oh, Daddy." Her
voice quivered. "Oh, God, he loved Mama.
He loved her."

And he killed her. Barb didn't say it, but
the realization was there in her pain and
sorrow. Barb turned, stumbled blindly toward the steps.

The back door banged open. "Barb, honey, don't cry." The stocky young soldier jumped to the ground, took her in his arms. Barb clung to him, sobbing. He bent his blunt head to hers, murmured softly, then looked defiantly at Gretchen. He had a kind face, freckled and open, and his big hand was gentle as he stroked her long reddish brown hair.

Gretchen backed away. When she reached the side of the house, not looking back, the screen door banged again, and she knew Barb and the soldier were once again in the house. That's why Barb had been able to stay there. She wasn't alone with death and despair. Gretchen knew what people would say if they found out, but she would never tell. Barb needed him. She didn't have anyone else.

Gretchen hurried toward the street. She would go to the cabin now, calling out in the bright sunlight to let Mr. Tatum know who she was, and warn him of his danger. And she would tell him how important it was never to let anyone know that Grandmother had helped him.

She paused in the street. Grandmother mustn't see her. Gretchen retraced her steps, not even glancing toward the Tatum house. She hurried to the alley, moving fast.

The Crane house was closed, too, the windows down, the shades drawn. A note was pinned to the back screen door. Gretchen hesitated, ran up the neat graveled path. The note read:

Willis — No milk until next week. Out of town. Martha

A bumblebee in the wisteria looped near Gretchen's head. She jumped off the steps, backed away. Mrs. Crane had left town. Gretchen knew as surely as if Mrs. Crane were there, obstinate eyes in a determined face, that she'd gone to see her daughter to avoid telling the chief about the man she'd seen coming late at night to the Tatum house. But maybe the chief had found out some other way. Gretchen shook her head impatiently. It didn't really matter. What mattered was getting to the Purdy cabin and warning Clyde Tatum.

It didn't seem to take nearly as long in the bright morning sunlight to reach the path into the woods. Gretchen was fine until she stepped onto the path, the dim, snaking path. She went five feet, ten, pushing through the thickets of honey locust and gooseberry and wild blackberry.

The fear caught at her with a suddenness

that left her breathless. She stood rock still and listened. Birds chittered and cawed and trilled. The wind rustled the leaves in the pin oaks and river birch and black walnuts. She tried to take another step, then whirled, clawing and scrambling up the path and out into the road. She broke into a frantic run. She didn't slow until she was in sight of home. She stopped in the shade of a sycamore, leaned against the scaly trunk, struggled for breath.

She felt a hot curl of shame. What was wrong with her? Bright daylight and nobody around and she ran away. There was nothing to be scared of. It wasn't like she'd seen a rattlesnake. All she had to do was walk through the woods and reach the clearing and call out Mr. Tatum's name. He would be nice to her. She was Barb's friend. She could tell him how upset Barb was and how he needed to come home.

But she couldn't tell him that Barb knew he'd killed her mother.

Gretchen walked slowly to her front yard. The door was open. Grandmother would be in the kitchen, making sure everything was ready for their wonderful lunch. She'd tell Grandmother what Mr. Dennis said and then admit she'd followed Grandmother to the cabin. When Grandmother understood that Clyde Tatum might be in danger, they could go to the cabin together. That was all Gretchen needed, someone to walk through the woods with her. Already she felt silly that she'd started down the path, then turned and run away. Maybe they could persuade Mr. Tatum to come back with them. That would keep him safe. They could bring him home and call Chief Fraser.

She hurried up the steps. She stepped into the hall and smelled the sweet musky scent of roses. On the letter stand, Grandmother's best cut-glass bowl overflowed with roses from the backyard, pink and red, cream and white. Lying in front of the bowl, arranged in the order they'd arrived, were the latest letters from Jimmy. The living room was neat as a pin and the dining room table was already set with china and crystal and silver. A dozen long-stem red roses, so deep a color they were almost maroon, gleamed in a tall cut-glass vase.

Peace washed over Gretchen. Grandmother would know what to do. "Grandmother?"

"Gretchen." It was Grandmother's voice, the cadence sweetly familiar but the sound so slight it might have been a dream.

Gretchen plunged toward the kitchen.

Grandmother sat slumped in a wooden chair, her face pale, tiny beads of sweat glistening on her forehead, making a shiny trail above her mouth. Her blue eyes were huge and staring. Her buttercup yellow apron was bunched against her blue silk dress.

"Grandmother!" Gretchen darted across the room, picked up limp hands that were cold and clammy to the touch.

"Ach, I will be fine. Please to get me some coffee." Grandmother took a deep breath.

"Dr. Jamison." Gretchen's heart thudded as though she'd run a desperate race. "I'll call him." She let loose her grip, whirled toward the phone.

"Gretchen." Grandmother's tone was louder, sharp, imperative. "No. I will be fine." She placed one hand on the kitchen table, pushed herself straighter in the chair. "It is the heat. I have worked too fast. But I want everything perfect for my Lorraine. Now, you must help me. I will sit here and you will see to everything. But please, bring me some coffee."

Gretchen glanced over her shoulder as she moved to the stove. The percolator was on the back burner on low, the gas flame scarcely visible, just high enough to keep the coffee hot, hot and strong. Gretchen poured the pungent black brew into a thick white china cup, added two teaspoons of sugar and a quarter inch of cream.

Grandmother managed a smile as she took the cup. "You are such a good girl, Gretchen. And we shall have a perfect day." She drank almost greedily and sighed and some color touched her plump cheeks. "Now, if you will please to check the potatoes. They should be done."

Gretchen used a crocheted pink and white hot pad to lift the lid and a long-handled fork to spear the potatoes in the bubbling water. They were perfect. She set the big pan in the middle of the stove. The potatoes would still be hot when they were drained and mashed. She turned toward the table. Grandmother looked better, though she sat in the chair as if rooted there. She beckoned to Gretchen.

"Your mama will be here soon and I want you to ask her to go to the lake." She paused, drew in a breath and another and another as though it was hard to find air for her words. She gave a little shake of her head. "It is so hot today. I shall urge her to go, too, say that I want her — and her friend — to have a real holiday and we shall have our visit later this afternoon. I will tell her" — Grandmother's voice was growing fainter — "that I have worked too hard this week and I wish to stay here and rest and then when you come back from your swim, we shall have our special dinner. You will do this for me, *mein Schatz?*"

"Grandmother," Gretchen begged, "please let me call Dr. Jamison. He will come —"

A car turned into their drive, the sound of the motor a loud rumble.

"They are here." Grandmother tried to rise, fell back in the chair. She waved her hands at Gretchen. "Go see. Hurry. I shall come."

Gretchen ran to the front door. The dark blue Buick was dusty, the windshield bug spattered. Sunlight reflected off the shiny chrome grille. Gretchen shielded her eyes. The driver's door opened. Gretchen didn't care about the man getting out of the car. The passenger door swung out. Wiry blond curls poked from beneath a saucer of a hat with a bright pink feather.

"Mother! Mother!" Gretchen jumped down the steps, ran. Her mother ran, too, despite her high heels and short tight skirt. They came together and Gretchen felt her mother's thin firm body, her warmth, the loving pressure of her arms.

"Oh, baby, baby, it's so good to see you." Another hug, tight and warm, and Lorraine stood back, holding Gretchen at arm's length. "You're so grown up. G. G. Gilman."

There was a new tone in her voice, almost as if she and Gretchen were grown-ups together. She reached out, gently touched Gretchen's cheek. "I feel like I haven't seen you in a long time." She shook her head, laughed. "Come on, G.G., I want you to meet Sam. I hope —" She broke off.

He was standing beside them. Gretchen didn't want to look at him. His shadow fell between them. She stared at the elongated streak.

"Hi, Gretchen. Lorraine's told me a lot about you." He had an easy voice, warm and friendly. "You read faster than Clark Kent changes into Superman and you write better than Lois Lane."

Gretchen slowly turned. He was a big man, taller than her daddy had been. Beneath his white cap, his blunt face was burned coppery red. Sandy eyebrows bunched over deep-set dark eyes and a beaked nose. He had deep grooves in his cheeks like he laughed a lot. His uniform was crisp, all white with dark shoulder boards.

She stared at him unsmiling.

Abruptly, his face looked older, heavier.

"Lorraine." Grandmother stood on the top step. She'd taken off her apron. She looked as if she were on her way to church, her hair in regal coronet braids, her round face smiling, her best dress a vivid blue, honoring her guests. But she was so pale.

"Mother." Lorraine whirled and in an instant she was up the steps, her arms around Grandmother. "Mother, here's Sam." Lorraine's voice was eager, her gaze clinging to Sam's face. "Sam Hoyt. He's a petty officer and he's been on leave and he's going back to California next week. I met him last week at Crystal City. I went on Friday night with a bunch of the gals from the plant. I can't believe I could be such a kid. I was riding the Ferris wheel and he was in the car behind ours. We got stopped at the top and Jenny rocked it and I was so scared. When we got down to the ground, Sam called out that I had a nice scream. I thought he wanted to know where to get ice cream and the first thing you know we were all on our way to Hawk's —" She paused, breathless.

"Mrs. Pfizer," he said solemnly though there was laughter in his deep voice, "I didn't used to eat ice cream, but now it's my favorite food. And Hawk's is my favorite ice cream shop."

"We have homemade ice cream for today. And apple pie so fine." Grandmother beamed. "Come in now, out of the hot sun."

They walked into the living room.

Gretchen came last. Her mother took Sam by the hand. "I want you to see this picture of Jimmy." Sam stood close to her, so close, as they looked at the framed photographs on the mantel.

Gretchen looked at the pictures: Grandmother and Grandpa on their thirtieth wedding anniversary, her mother and father on their wedding day, Jimmy in his cap and gown from his high school graduation, Gretchen on her eleventh birthday.

Sam picked up the picture of Jimmy, carried it with him. He and her mother sat on the sofa. Lorraine bent forward, her chin cupped in one hand, her gamine face eager and happy, talking a mile a minute about Jimmy.

Sam Hoyt's dark eyes met Gretchen's.

Gretchen looked away.

"I have saved for you our letters from Jimmy." Grandmother sat in her easy chair. "We have so much pride now, Mr. Hoyt. Our brave Jimmy. And Gretchen works so hard. She helps me at the café every day and then she goes to the newspaper office and her stories are in the paper every night. Last night she had to work late and so I hope you and Lorraine will make this a special day for her. Lorraine, will you and Mr. Hoyt take Gretchen to the lake? It will be so much fun for all of you, a summer day like we used to have. I will find a suit of Jimmy's for Mr. Hoyt to wear." She smiled but her face was gray white like dirty ice and she braced herself on one elbow against the armrest of the chair.

Lorraine clapped her hands. "Oh, Sam, that does sound like fun. I haven't been swimming in forever. And then, we'll have Mother's wonderful food." She looked hesitantly at her mother. "We have to leave right after lunch. Sam promised his folks we'd come by this afternoon. They live in Tahlequah."

"You're leaving that soon?" Gretchen stared at her mother.

Lorraine reached out her hands.

Gretchen backed away. "I better get my suit," she said and turned to hurry down the hall.

As the car backed into Archer Street, Gretchen sat gingerly on the edge of the seat, her swimsuit no protection against the hot leather. She reached down, picked up her shorts and blouse, tucked them under her on the seat.

"Oh, Gretchen" — Lorraine's face shone with happiness — "isn't this fun!" She adjusted the strap on her swimsuit, a pretty two piece Catalina with bright red hibiscus against a yellow background. "I haven't been out to the lake in so long." She turned toward the driver, eager and happy. "Hunter Lake's beautiful, pine trees and real sand."

Gretchen loved the lake, loved the sticky feel of the heat and the shock of plunging into cool water. But the lake seemed remote, unreal. She looked out at the road. They'd go right by the path to the Purdy cabin and she couldn't do a thing about it. When they got home, it would be time for lunch and no way for her to slip away long enough to get to the cabin. Gretchen had a sense of time racing away from her, like coins spilling out of a purse.

Lorraine twisted to look out the rear window. "Look back, Sam." She pointed. "That's the Tatum house, where the grass is grown up and the papers piled by the front steps. Oh, poor Faye. Poor Clyde. Poor Barb." She turned and hung over the seat, her face drooping. "Oh, baby, it's awful that you had to see such a terrible thing. And they haven't found Clyde yet, have they?"

"No. The sheriff thinks somebody's helped him hide." Gretchen wished she could snatch the words back. Mother had a way of knowing when words meant more than they seemed to.

Sure enough, a little frown creased Lorraine's face. "Hide . . . He'd need food. I hadn't thought about it."

Gretchen reached up, held tight to the hand grip. "Anyway, Mr. Dennis . . ."

Lorraine murmured to Sam, "Walt Dennis owns the *Gazette*. His daughter June was one of my best friends. She got polio and died when we were in high school."

". . . is afraid someone will shoot Mr. Tatum."

Lorraine gasped. "Shoot Clyde? Oh, Gretchen, why?"

"People are scared. There was a meeting last night at the town square." As they drove, the dirt road twisting and turning, uphill and down, the trees pressing close, Gretchen described how the chief stood up for Clyde Tatum and the sharp mutters from the crowd and the county attorney's sarcasm. Gretchen didn't glance toward the almost hidden break in the trees that marked the path to the Purdy cabin.

When they came over a rise and saw the lake and cars and swimmers and picnickers, it seemed odd to her that the noise and excitement and summer fun wasn't even a mile from the cabin in the overgrown clearing. Nobody here was scared about Clyde Tatum. The big dusty parking area was jammed with cars. Sam hunted for a parking place, finally squeezing the car in on a slant near a cedar.

Lorraine grabbed their towels. As they piled out, Lorraine called over her shoulder, "Last one in's a monkey," just as she always had with Jimmy and Gretchen, and she began to run.

When they reached the man-made beach, golden sand curving around an inlet, Lorraine tossed the towels on a log. Gretchen burst ahead and splashed into the cool murky water, shallow here and cleared of reeds. Lorraine was right behind her.

They kept going until the water was up to their chins. Sam joined them. Gretchen knew he was there, so near, but she had eyes only for her mother. Lorraine ducked beneath the water, came up sputtering, her hair in ringlets. "Oh, baby, I wish we could do this forever."

It was almost the way it had been before the war, a summer day at the lake with her mom and Jimmy. Sometimes Grandmother and Grandpa came. Grandpa liked to fish and there was a pier off to the side of the swimming area. He'd bring a bucket of bait and spend the afternoon, his lure bobbing on the water, and when it was time to go home he'd have a mess of catfish for dinner.

They'd have fried catfish and hush puppies and cole slaw and watermelon. Gretchen could almost taste the crisp sweet fish. The feel of the water was the same and the shouts of the big boys as they jumped from a tower into deep water, folding into balls to see who could make the biggest splash, and the high squeals of the little kids as they made sand castles and played toss. Teenage girls stretched out on towels and blankets, their hair dry, their mahogany-shaded skin glistening with a mixture of baby oil and iodine. The jukebox blared "Besame Mucho." A chunky red-haired boy strummed a mandolin. The smell of hot dogs and popcorn mingled with the scents of honeysuckle and suntan lotion and car exhaust and water. Hunter Lake was just as it had always been. It was Gretchen who was different, remembering the Purdy cabin and the dark, deep woods.

"Gretchen, honey, tell Sam what it's like to work for the *Gazette*. I'm so proud of you." Lorraine reached out, took Sam's hand, drew him near.

They stood so close, the water lapping against the three of them. Lorraine moved until her shoulders touched Sam's. Her glance toward him was eager — and something more. It was as though a strand of light linked the two of them, creating a bridge only they could cross.

Gretchen felt cold. And alone. Separate. Burdened.

A shout rose on the beach. "Tommy, don't you dare!" Shrill squeals drowned out the caw of hungry crows.

Gretchen looked past Sam, her gaze sweeping the crowded beach. Wilma Fuller shouted, "Help, help!," and ran toward the wooden lifeguard stand where Bo Hudson, tanned dark as brown shoe polish, lounged. Bo was king of the beach, every girl's dream. Tommy Krueger, his bony face alight with mischief, the muscles standing out in his thin arms, stalked Wilma, carrying an old fish bucket with water slopping over the top. Wilma danced back and forth, trying to elude him. Tommy gave a triumphant roar, jumped forward, and sloshed the water over her. She screamed and he turned and ran toward the water.

"Gretchen . . ." Lorraine frowned.

"I see some friends." Gretchen pointed toward the shore. "I need to talk to somebody for a minute. I'll be right back."

"But Gretchen, Sam's come all this way. . . ."

Gretchen ducked into the water, began to swim, hating the look of disappointment on her mother's thin face. But Tommy would help her. . . .

Tommy was climbing the ladder to the diving boards. He went to the very top. From the shore, Wilma shouted, "I'll get you, Tommy Krueger, you wait and see." Gretchen ducked under the rope separating the diving area. The water was deep here, maybe twenty feet. She treaded water, shaded her eyes against the sun. Tommy came out to the end of the high dive, stood with his toes at the edge. He bounced and curved into a smooth dive. The water scarcely rippled as he entered.

As his head bobbed to the surface, his hair tight and slick against his head, Gretchen swam fast. She came up beside him. "Tommy." He would help her.

His head turned toward her.

She looked at a stranger, blue eyes that slid away, lips pressed together, no trace of a smile, no warmth. It seemed impossible that her lips had touched his, that she'd felt the beat of his heart, the long hard line of his body.

"Tommy? What's wrong?" The sun blazed down, spilling hot golden light, but she felt cold as winter. "Is it last night? I didn't come to the movie because I had to work."

"No." It was a mumble, scarcely heard.

"Then what's wrong?" If Tommy wouldn't help her . . .

He stared at her with those stranger's eyes as they treaded water. "I saw your story on Mrs. Tatum. You made her sound like she was somebody wonderful — instead of a cheating whore."

She knew the word. She'd only heard it in whispers before. She'd never heard anyone she knew called that. "Tommy, Barb said she just wanted to dance. That's all."

"Oh, sure." His voice was ugly with sarcasm. "Some guy was sneaking in their house late at night just to talk about dancing, I guess." He threw out his hands like he was pushing away garbage and the water rippled away. "She was a whore. No wonder he killed her. He ought to get a medal. Just like I'd kill the guy who took my mom away. If I could. She ran away with a guy." His face squeezed with pain, he ducked down, and all that was left was a flurry of movement in the dark water.

Gretchen turned and swam away from the deep, didn't stop until she was in the middle of a group of little kids and then she hunkered down, well hidden from shore, the mud of the lake bottom squishy against her knees.

The big clock over the concession stand read 10:07.

Gretchen pressed her hands into the cold mud. Tommy hated her. And all because of what she wrote. But couldn't he understand? The answer was clear and cold. No, he didn't want to understand. He wanted to hate. Hate . . . that's what the mutter of the crowd had meant last night. Hatred and fear. She'd hoped Tommy would help her, go with her to save Clyde Tatum. But she couldn't count on Tommy. Not now. Not ever. And Clyde Tatum was still in danger. But he was safe as long as he stayed at the cabin. Surely he wouldn't go out during daylight. He'd told Grandmother he would turn himself in to the chief after Friday night. At least, he'd said he hoped to see everyone he wanted to see by then. Those lists on the old wooden table — were those people he hadn't yet talked to? If so, his time was running out. If he skulked around town, looking worn and rumpled and dirty and dangerous, some people were ready with their guns.

Gretchen pushed up. She swished her hands, and mud swirled into the dark water. She shaded her eyes. Mother would help. Maybe Gretchen could make up a story, say Tommy had heard that Barb had run away and might be at the Purdy cabin. . . .

Gretchen's gaze darted across the water. There they were! Mother and Sam swimming side by side on their way out to the wooden float. It was a long way out. Not many people swam out to the float, the older boys sometimes, but usually only if a pretty girl had gone there first. Gretchen dived, swam fast. She didn't pause until she reached the square wooden raft bobbing in the water. She came up beside it, held on to the warm wood. The float rocked gently, pulling her up and down. She looked around, seeing no one. She pushed away, swam completely around the float. Mother and Sam had come out here but nearby she saw only the Jenkins twins, squabbling over an inner tube. Mother and Sam must have dived down and come up underneath the float in the gauzy, brownish green, two-foot space between the platform and the water. Gretchen took a deep breath, curled down. She kicked and rose in the water, a hand outstretched to grip the rough edge of one of the barrels supporting the platform. Her head came out of the water. She blinked the water from her eyes. Her mouth opened but no sound came. In the wavering moss green light, Lorraine and Sam embraced, their bodies melded into a single form, her hand, the fingernails a glossy red, tight against his neck, drawing down his face to her uplifted lips.

The water closed over Gretchen's head as she dived down, down and away.

. . . Maybe Buddy and I could have made a go of it if he hadn't been killed in the war. But I don't know. I couldn't stay off the bottle. When you're all shriveled up inside, you have to do something to get warm, to feel good. Buddy's folks came out to California. I was living in Long Beach. Funny, I never knew you were there at the same time. Anyway, they came out and found me drunk and Rod dirty and hungry. Rodney James Wilson, Jr. I named him after Buddy. I loved Rod, yet every time I looked at him it all came back to me, that summer. . . . But he was just a baby and none of it was his fault. That's the problem. Everything was my fault. . . .

Chapter
9

Was it jealousy that caused me to run away from the lake that day? Of course. Jealousy and fear. I didn't want to lose Mother. I didn't want to share her. I knew — I needed no one to tell me though I was yet to experience passion — that the embrace beneath the float signaled a connection I didn't want to accept. I never had a chance later to ask her if she knew why I left the lake. There was so much I never told her, never told anyone. Perhaps it was only now that I understood what that summer cost me. I felt abandoned by my mother and by my friends and by Tommy, the first boy I'd kissed. Years later as we sat on the terrace of a hotel in La Jolla, my husband of a few weeks — Edward, whom I'd married after years as a divorced single mother — looked at me with brooding, puzzled eyes when I deftly deflected a gentle question about my past. "Don't you trust me, G.G.?" My response was quick. "Of course, Edward. But it's too lovely a morning to be solemn. And all of that was so many years ago." I'd flung down my napkin and jumped to my feet, pointing out to sea. "Look, there's a whale. Look out beyond the headland."

Look away, look away. . . .

Gretchen stopped running. She gasped for breath. Her lungs ached. Her heart pounded. Tears mixed with sweat, stinging her flushed face. Mother only met him a week ago. How could she kiss him like that?

But he was going to go away soon. Everything would be all right when he left.

She moved forward, her swimsuit uncomfortable beneath her blouse and shorts. She'd grabbed her clothes from the backseat of the car, pulled them on, slipped her feet into her sandals, used a borrowed pencil to scrawl a note on a napkin from the concession stand, placed the message on the front seat: *Gone home. Gretchen.* All she thought about was escape, escape from her mother and from the girls she'd thought were her friends and from Tommy. But every step on the road took her nearer the trail to the Purdy cabin.

She hesitated, almost turned back to the lake. She didn't want to go into the woods. But someone had to warn Clyde Tatum. Only three people knew where he was, Gretchen and Grandmother and the woman who'd called Grandmother to ask for help for Clyde.

Gretchen forced herself forward, one reluctant step after another. Soon the sweat didn't matter. She didn't think about her mother and Sam or the lake or the girls or Tommy. There was nothing in the world but the hot, dusty road and the inner coldness of fear.

She came around the bend and stopped, staring at the faint gap, almost indistinguishable in the tangled undergrowth of the woods. Birds chittered. Cicadas whirred. Leaves sighed in the breeze. Alone. She was all alone. There was no one to walk with her.

She had to go down that trail.

The thought glittered bright as the sun. No matter what happened, no matter how terrible it was to walk in the dim, silent woods, she had to warn Clyde Tatum.

Abruptly, she hurried across the road, plunged into the murky half-light, moving fast before she could change her mind. She didn't try to be quiet. She slapped away at the branches of the honey locust, broke twigs, scuffed against the dirt. If she let the silence of the woods slip over her, fear would balloon inside until she dropped to the ground and hid.

She brushed against wild hydrangea. Bracken ferns clutched at her. Vines and branches whipped against her bare arms and legs. She plunged into the overgrown clearing. The cabin almost seemed a part of the woods, heavy branches of a post oak crowding against the roof, eight-foot-tall gooseberry shrubs banked against the walls. Waist-high grasses wavered in the breeze. Ivy masked one end of the porch. The rotten steps sagged. The dirt-grimed window-panes were as blank as dead eyes.

"Mr. Tatum!" Her voice wavered, high and shrill. "Mr. Tatum, Mr. Tatum . . ." He wouldn't be afraid of a girl's voice. "It's Gretchen Gilman, Barb's friend. Mr. Tatum . . ."

Despite the sounds of summer and the rustle of the woods, silence flowed over her thick and quiet as fog rising from a pond. Gretchen's breathing slowed. She reached down, rubbed one ankle. She was eaten up by chiggers. "Mr. Tatum . . ." She broke off. He wasn't here. She'd come all this way, been scared to pieces, and he wasn't here. Gretchen ducked her head, used the collar of her blouse to mop sweat from her face. She stared at the cabin, the silence thick and heavy in the clearing. Maybe he'd already gone to turn himself in. The thought lifted her for an instant. But if he hadn't, if he was coming back here . . .

She took a deep breath, remembering the dirty rough table and the scraps of paper from grocery sacks. He'd written down names with a thick-leaded pencil. She would have to leave a note, warning that people were looking for him and they had guns. She'd print in block letters and be careful not to leave any fingerprints.

Gretchen made no effort to be quiet. She strode briskly through the tall rippling grass, silencing the rasp of the cicadas for an instant, and climbed the shade-dappled steps. The old wood planks on the porch creaked under her weight. The door was open. She was in a hurry now, eager to leave a message and be gone.

She reached the doorway, stopped.

"Oh . . ." The voice, scarcely audible over the renewed crescendo of the cicadas, was hers, a faint moan of sound. "Oh . . . oh . . ." She backed away. She carried with her an indelible memory of the dim, crowded, junk-filled cabin and the body of Clyde Tatum slumped over the table.

She jerked about, clattered down the steps, thrashed through the grass, flailed into the woods, tearing through creepers and vines. She stumbled over a log, fell, scrambled to get up, and knew she was lost. Trembling, she stared around the forest. She needed to retrace her steps, find the path to the road. She had to get help somewhere. She felt sick with horror. Barb's dad was dead, dead, dead. . . .

"You are surrounded." The deep heavy voice boomed through the woods. "Come out with your hands up. We are armed. Come out . . ."

Gretchen ducked behind a white ash, pressed against the thick trunk. The

319

shouted commands continued, loud and menacing. Cautiously, she slipped back the way she'd come, wormed her way among the low-slung branches of a magnolia, dropped to her knees behind a branch with huge glossy leaves, the scent of the flower sickeningly sweet, and peered into the clearing.

Sheriff Moore stood at the bottom of the cabin steps, a bullhorn in one hand, his big black service pistol in the other. A shaft of sunlight pierced the canopy of the trees. The brim of his cowboy hat shadowed the upper part of his face, but the harsh summer light exposed the taut muscles of his cheeks, the jut of his chin, the ridged cords in his neck. The gun in his hand moved back and forth, slowly, gently, like the head of a swaying cobra.

Gretchen scarcely breathed. She'd never seen a man poised to kill. There was threat in every line of the sheriff's tall, angular body. Fanned in a semicircle behind him were Chief Fraser, Sergeant Holliman, Sergeant Petty, and Donald Durwood.

Chief Fraser stood a few paces in front of his officers. The chief's bulbous, seamed face was alert, his rheumy eyes mournful. He leaned forward, head to one side, big shoulders bunched as if straining to hear. Sergeant Holliman's hat was tilted over his bandage. He crouched like a linebacker ready to bull across the line. Sergeant Petty, bright red lips pressed together, legs braced, held her gun in both hands like she stood on a firing range. Sweat beaded Donald Durwood's face. He was empty handed.

Durwood watched the doorway, eyes wide, staring, puzzled. "Maybe the note's a hoax. This place doesn't look like anybody's been here in years."

"Quiet." The sheriff thrust down the hand with the bullhorn, as imperative as the finish flag at the racetrack. The sheriff cocked his head, listening. He took a slow step forward. "Come out of there, Tatum." Another careful step. "Or I'm coming in to get you."

"Wait a minute." Chief Fraser strode forward.

Sheriff Moore remained rigid as a lamppost. He didn't turn his head. His eyes never left the gray oblong of the open doorway. "I'm going to count to five. And then I'm going to start shooting. One —"

The chief gripped Moore's elbow. "Christ, man, he could have gunned us all down by now. Give me a chance. Let me go up there." He took a deep breath. "Let me try."

"And have him grab you? Use you as a

hostage? I'm telling you, Buck," the sheriff said, dropping the words like dirt clods on a coffin, "the man's got a gun."

"Nobody's shot anybody, Paul." The chief started forward.

The sheriff lifted his hand. The gun, big and black, pointed at the door. And at the chief's back.

"Clyde, Buck here." The steps creaked as the chief climbed. He stopped on the porch. "Listen, it's time to come out. We need to talk." One step, another. He reached the doorway. "Clyde . . ." The chief's big shoulders slumped. Slowly, he poked the gun in its holster. He reached out, held to the door frame. "Oh, God." The chief's voice was low and deep.

The sheriff shouted, "Careful, Buck, careful!" The county attorney's handsome face creased in a tight frown. Sergeant Holliman ran toward the porch. Sergeant Petty lowered her gun, took a tentative step, her eyes fearful.

Chief Fraser looked at them, big face drooping. "It's over. Put your guns up. Clyde's dead." His voice was ragged. "He's blown his head to hell and gone." He kneaded his cheek with his fist. "I thought he was innocent." He took a deep breath. "I was wrong."

Donald Durwood stretched out his hands. The lion head cuff links in his starched white shirt glistened in the sunlight. He looked out of place in the weed-choked clearing, natty in his slacks and shirt. "If we'd found the note earlier, we might have got here in time."

Sergeant Petty's face crumpled. "God, I'm sorry I was late. My bike had a flat tire. That's why I was late to work. If I'd been on time, I'd have found the note first thing this morning."

"It doesn't matter, Rosa." Chief Fraser walked heavily across the porch. "It wouldn't have made any difference if you'd got to work on time. Clyde's been dead for hours. The blood's all dried. Now" — his big shoulders lifted, fell — "if we'd found the note last night, maybe we would have got here in time. We'll never know. But whoever stuck it under the wiper of the cruiser must have put it there after the rain. Somebody knew Clyde was here." He nodded his head toward the sheriff. "It's just like Paul said last night. I expect that person was at the town square and went home and thought about it and decided to turn him in. But Clyde was already dead by then."

Gretchen leaned against the magnolia branch. Last night, before the rain, that's when she was here in the woods and she'd felt surrounded by danger. Was it death she'd sensed? Had Clyde Tatum hidden in the trees, watched her, holding the gun that was going to end his life, waiting for her to leave so that he could return to that cramped cabin and greet death?

Sheriff Moore thumped up the steps. "Think he's been hiding out here ever since he killed Faye?"

The chief massaged the side of his face. "Probably. I don't guess it matters now. Clyde killed Faye and he couldn't live with it. All right" — the chief's voice was tired — "let's wrap it up. Rosa, get back to town. I want you to call Doc Jamison."

Gretchen eased toward the path. She hurried up the trail. When she reached the road, she stopped and stared. So many cars . . . the chief's old Packard, a police cruiser, a black Ford, a black Cadillac. If she'd come along here, walking home from the lake, a few minutes ago, she would have seen the cars and recognized the Packard and the police car.

She heard the rumble of a car coming. She could walk on home. No, she couldn't. She couldn't go inside her house and see Grandmother and Mother and pretend that she didn't know. All right, if she'd been walking home from the lake and seen the cars, she would have gone down the path to see what was happening. She plunged back into the woods. She was halfway to the clearing when she came face-to-face with Sergeant Petty.

The police officer jolted to a stop, her long face startled. She held out her hands. "Mercy, girl, what are you doing here?"

"I saw the cars in the road and I wondered why. I came to see." She tried to look past the sergeant.

"This is no place for you. Go home." The sergeant's voice was sharp.

Gretchen stood her ground. "Have you found Mr. Tatum?"

"What makes you think that?" Sergeant Petty's eyes narrowed.

"The cars." Gretchen waved her hand back toward the road. "Why else would everybody be here?" She tried to peer down the path. "Isn't the Purdy cabin around here?"

Rosa Petty's face hardened. "Police business, Gretchen. This is off limits for now. Move along now."

Gretchen didn't budge. "I'm here for the *Gazette*."

Twigs snapped. Chief Fraser loomed up behind Sergeant Petty. "Go on, Sergeant. I'll deal with this."

The police sergeant brushed past Gretchen, leaving a sweet scent of perfume, an odd counterpoint to the blistered dry smell of the woods.

Gretchen forced herself to look straight at the chief, hoping he wouldn't see her guilt and fear. If she'd told someone sooner, if she and Grandmother had gone to the chief and told him about the Purdy cabin, Clyde Tatum might now be in jail — and alive.

Chief Fraser's eyes were remote.

Gretchen's stiff face muscles relaxed. He looked at her, but he wasn't seeing. "I was walking home from the lake —"

He didn't care. "You know where Barb Tatum is?"

"I'm not sure." It wouldn't do for the chief to know — for anyone to know — that Barb was staying at the house with the soldier. "I can find her. Is it" — she couldn't keep the wobble out of her voice — "about her dad?" Gretchen had only briefly glimpsed the slumped figure before she'd bolted from the porch. But now — she shuddered, remembering that still body, the huddled shoulders in wrinkled khaki, that stiff arm, the smooth skin gray, dangling beside the chair.

The chief's face creased. He took a deep breath. "Clyde's dead. Shot himself. See if you can find Barb. Take her to your house. I'll come there" — he glanced at his watch — "about two o'clock."

Gretchen folded her arms across her front, hard and tight, felt the uncomfortable ridge of her swimsuit. "What do I tell her?"

Chief Fraser slammed a fist into one hand. "God almighty, tell her the truth." His voice trembled with anger and hurt. "I never believed Clyde killed Faye, but he did. And now he's gone off and left his girl. Tell her" — he rubbed his cheek hard — "that sometimes people we love do bad things. Maybe he had too much to drink. Maybe he got mad and his mind was roaring and he didn't realize what he'd done to Faye until it was too late. Tell her he was a good man at heart and he loved her and she should remember him that way." His defiant voice cracked. "Tell her that her daddy's dead and he's past suffering now. And he's sorry."

A cardinal cut through the air, bright as the evening sun. "Sorry?" How did the chief know?

"He wrote a note. I'll bring it with me when I come." The big man turned away, walked heavily up the trail toward the cabin.

The screen door slammed open. Lorraine's eyes flashed. Her thin face twisted in a scowl.

327

She stood on the top step, hands planted on her hips, a pink cotton blouse loose over her swimsuit, teetering a little on high wedge sandals. "Gretchen, where have you been? You scared us to death. We couldn't find you anywhere. I didn't know what to think. And then we ran to the car and found that note. I don't know when I've been so upset. And we came home and you weren't here. We were just getting ready to go back to the lake. We've waited dinner and you've made Mother sick —"

Gretchen pressed her hand against her lips. She wanted to cry or shout. She wanted to run away, but there was no place to go. She was hot and cold, her stomach a hard knot, her chest and legs sweaty, and she had to find Barb. She had to tell Barb. . . . Beneath the thoughts that squirmed through her mind like eels sliding in dark places was the memory, that slumped figure resting immovable on the scarred table.

Her mother's face changed. She plunged down the steps, took Gretchen in her arms. "Gretchen, baby, what's wrong? What happened?" There was no anger in Lorraine's voice now, but there was fear.

Gretchen clung to her mother. "I was on the lake road. . . ." It hurt to talk. "I was coming home to help Grandmother" — the first lie — "and I saw the chief's car and I went into the woods. They found Clyde Tatum." This was the second lie that she must forever keep. No one must know she'd walked that path first, seen him dead. "He killed himself."

"Gretchen!" Grandmother's voice was high and faint from the doorway. "What is it that you say?" She leaned against the door frame, her plump face ashen, one hand pressed against her chest.

Gretchen pulled free, hurried to her grandmother. "It's over." Chief Fraser's words gave her strength. "Please, Grandmother, no one can do anything now for Mr. Tatum. The chief said he's past suffering now."

"Clyde . . ." Grandmother's face crumpled.

"Come inside, Mother." Lorraine's voice quivered. She jerked her head toward Sam. Together they helped Grandmother, who sagged against them.

Gretchen followed, but she stopped just inside the door. "Mother, I've got to find Barb. I promised Chief Fraser."

Her mother knelt by Grandmother's chair, tightly holding one limp hand. Lorraine turned toward Gretchen. "No. You shouldn't have to do that. The chief should tell her."

"He has to see to things." Gretchen clasped her hands tightly together. "In the woods." She looked at the grandfather clock. Almost noon. They should be sitting at the table with crisp fried chicken and mashed potatoes and green peas and Grandmother's perfect cream gravy. Almost noon. The *Gazette* went to press early on Saturday afternoons for the Sunday paper. The *Gazette* . . ."Excuse me." She turned toward the kitchen.

Her mother looked startled.

"I have to call Mr. Dennis." She brushed past Sam as she entered the kitchen. He was carrying a cup of steaming tea, almost as dark as strong coffee.

Gretchen grabbed the receiver. She gave the operator the *Gazette* number. She looked away from her mother's questioning face. Sam held out the cup to Grandmother.

"Here you are, Mrs. Pfizer. Please drink it. You've had a shock . . . try to breathe deeply. . . ."

Mr. Dennis answered on the first ring, brusque, quick, intent. "City desk."

"Mr. Dennis, this is Gretchen. They've found Clyde Tatum dead at the old Purdy cabin. He shot himself." And he's all stiff and still, like a starched shirt hanging on a line at the laundry.

In the living room, her mother said sharply, "Who's Gretchen talking to?"

Grandmother's voice was faint. "Her editor at the newspaper."

"The newspaper." Lorraine sounded strange.

"Oh, but she must." Grandmother's defense was swift. "It is her job, you see. Mr. Dennis has to know. For tomorrow's paper."

On the phone line, there was a perceptible pause. Mr. Dennis cleared his throat. "When?"

"They think sometime last night." In the deep darkness of the frightening woods. "A little while ago I was on my way home from the lake and I saw the cars on the road. I went to see."

"The Purdy cabin." His tone was thoughtful. "How'd they find him?"

"Somebody left a note on one of the police cars saying he was there. Sergeant Petty didn't find it until this morning. And she almost cried because she thought her being late made a difference. But the chief said it didn't. The chief said he died last night."

"Clyde's gun?" Mr. Dennis barked.

Gretchen pictured the editor at his desk, green eyeshade with tufts of hair curling beneath, his round face creased in thought, light eyes intent, smoke wreathing up from the pipe in his teeth.

"I don't know." She hadn't seen a gun.

"Ralph'll get all that. Who's there?" He half covered the receiver, shouted out, "Jewell, get on the phone. Find Ralph. Pronto." The staccato words mixed with the background clatter of a typewriter.

Five people and a dead man. She was precise. "The chief, Sergeant Holliman, Sergeant Petty, the sheriff, Mr. Durwood." In the hot, still clearing, the grasses waist high, they'd looked at the old cabin and the sheriff moved his gun back and forth, ready to kill. But he didn't have to.

"Good work, kid." Mr. Dennis's voice was crisp. "Look, you don't have to go to the cabin, but go to that spot in the road and wait for Ralph and show him the way."

"I can't go back now. The chief asked me to find Barb." Nobody must know about Barb alone in her house with the soldier. "Mr. Cooley won't have any trouble finding the place. The cars are parked every which way. The path's overgrown but it's pretty beaten down now."

"Sure, Gretchen. I understand." A door slammed and a distant voice called out: "Ralph's on his way, Walt. Want me to get over to the hospital?" Mr. Dennis said quickly, "Yeah, do that." Then sharp in her ear, "Gretchen, you okay?"

"Yes." Another lie.

There was a pause. "I'm sorry, girl. Try not to think about it."

"Yes, sir." She hung up the receiver and wished she could stay where she was, safe in Grandmother's kitchen. The ruffled curtains at the kitchen window were shiny white in the sunlight. Waxed paper covered the platter full of fried chicken. The house smelled like Sunday dinner, familiar and comforting as church bells. A fly buzzed near the sliced watermelon. She ought to get the swatter —

A gentle hand touched her arm. "Gretchen."

She looked at her mother. Their eyes met, held, Lorraine's uncertain, worried, sad.

"Baby . . ."

Gretchen wanted to fling herself into her mother's arms and cry.

Footsteps sounded. Sam came up behind Lorraine, slipped his arm around her shoulders. "Don't be scared, Lorry."

Gretchen stared at him. Lorry, that was the special name Grandmother had for Lorraine.

Sam's voice was reassuring. "Your mom's going to be all right. She's had a shock. Nobody expects something like this to happen to neighbors."

"More than neighbors." Tears rolled down Lorraine's cheeks. "I grew up playing with Clyde. He spent a lot of time at our house. His mom died when he was eight and Mother always made him a part of our family."

Sam bent, spoke softly. "We need to get your mom to eat, then lie down. And, Lorry, I can call my folks, tell them we can't come this afternoon."

Lorraine straightened, used her hands to wipe her cheeks. "No. We're going to your folks."

There was a determination in her voice that Gretchen didn't understand.

Lorraine held out her hands toward Gretchen. "You'll take care of Mother, won't you?" She reached up, touched Gretchen's cheek. "Oh, baby, I know it's hard. But everything's hard now." Her voice was bleak. "I'm afraid every time someone knocks on the door that Jimmy's dead. People come to work and you know what's happened, their eyes are red and they walk like they don't care where they're going or if they ever get there. And now Faye and Clyde and poor little Barb. And here you are in the middle of something you don't even understand and there's nobody here to help you. Gretchen, if I could make it better, I would. But there's nothing I can do. And Sam and I have to leave right after lunch. Please, will you understand if I don't stay?"

Gretchen would have understood if Mother had to get back for her shift. Like Grandmother said, everybody had to do their part and they talked about it on the radio, how important it was for plant workers not to miss work. But that wasn't why Mother was going to leave after lunch. It was more important to her to go to Tahlequah to see Sam Hoyt's family than to stay here with Gretchen and Grandmother, even though Grandmother was sick and upset. "Sure." Gretchen ducked her head, squeezed past them.

Sam called out, "Gretchen, if you'll tell me where the girl is, I'll find her, talk to her."

Gretchen didn't want any help from Sam, no matter what. "I have to find Barb. I promised the chief."

Gretchen went straight to the back door of the Tatum house. She knocked on the screen door. The door to the kitchen was open. Gretchen rattled the door, lifted her voice. "Barb. Barb!"

The soldier came to the kitchen doorway.

"Barb doesn't want to see anybody."

Gretchen pulled open the screen. "I have to talk to her." Gretchen wasn't thinking now of what she had to say, only that she had to say it. "I've got bad news."

"Bad news . . ." He clenched his big hands into fists, turned away. He stood, head bent for an instant, then walked stolidly into the house.

Gretchen stepped onto the porch. Faye's painting — the one she'd been working on — was close enough to touch. The canvas was spotted. Gretchen took a step, reached out. Her fingers came away damp. The rain had blown through the porch. A tarp lay in a crumpled heap near her foot. No one had bothered to cover the painting before the storm. Once the porch had seemed exotic, jumbles of canvases, the palette with brilliant smudges of color, a wicker table next to the easel with a bottle of beer and an overflowing brass ashtray shaped like an elephant, a matchbox tucked in the curve of its trunk. Now the little screened-in enclosure was simply frowsy, like a catchall room in an old house. On impulse, Gretchen bent, grabbed the tarp, draped it over the painting.

"What difference does it make now?" Barb's voice was dull.

Gretchen whirled toward the kitchen.

Barb walked heavily onto the porch. Her sunken eyes were red rimmed. Her chalk white face was bare of makeup. Her reddish brown hair hung in tangles. Her body sagged as if every muscle and bone ached. "I kept hoping we'd have a tornado and blow the house away. And me with it. But it just rained. Do you think rain is like God crying?" She caught a tendril of hair, curled it around one finger.

"Barb, honey." The soldier grabbed her arm. "I'm here. I'll take care of you."

Barb looked at him, her eyes empty. Her lips quivered. "Buddy . . . Buddy, I don't deserve you."

His hand slid down her arm, caught her hand. His face lighted. "All I want is to make you happy."

"Happy." Barb repeated the word as if she'd never heard it. "Happy."

His big face drooped. "I'm sorry. God, Barb, I'll do everything I can for you. You know that, don't you?"

"Yes." She lifted her head, stared at Gretchen. "You didn't come about Mama's painting. It's Daddy, isn't it?"

"I'm sorry." Gretchen felt a bond with the young soldier. He wanted to help Barb, but nobody could, not he, not she. "Your dad's dead."

Barb didn't move, her face was still as the stone angel on my daddy's grave.

Gretchen spoke fast. "He shot himself last night. At the Purdy cabin. They found him a little while ago. I promised Chief Fraser I'd come and get you."

"Get me?" Brooding eyes focused on Gretchen.

Gretchen felt as if Barb was as distant as a faint star in the night sky, leaving Gretchen and the soldier behind on the hot, still porch. Gretchen lifted her voice. "I told the chief I'd bring you to my house. He's coming at two o'clock. Your dad left a note."

The door banged as Gretchen came inside. The hot living room was empty and dim, the shades drawn, a fan whirring in one corner. Gretchen looked into the dining room. They always ate at the dining room table on Sundays and special days. The lace tablecloth was draped in a diamond shape. Two place settings remained.

Steps sounded in the kitchen. Sam Hoyt, holding a dish towel in one hand and a filled china plate in the other, walked toward the table. "We saved your lunch, Gretchen." He was once again in his crisp white uniform, military as could be except for the bright yellow apron tied around his middle.

She stood in the archway. "Where's Mother?" Who was he to take over their kitchen, offer her food, use Grandmother's apron?

"She's with your grandmother." He placed the plate on the table. "Did you find the girl?"

"Yes." Gretchen almost turned to go down the hall to Grandmother's room, but what good would it do? Mother was getting ready to leave, going away with this stranger. Gretchen slipped into the chair. Fried chicken and mashed potatoes and cream gravy and peas, her favorite dinner. She picked up a chicken leg, began to eat, ignored Sam.

He looked toward the front door. "I thought you were bringing her here. I've got another plate ready. Is she all right?"

"No." Her tone was scornful. Barb all right? Her mother dead and now her father. What kind of fool was he? "She didn't want to come now." Was Barb still standing on the porch with Buddy, standing there but not there, her mind and soul far away? "She'll be here at two when the police chief comes." Maybe Barb would feel about her daddy's note the way she felt about the spoiled painting. What difference did it make now?

Sam returned to the kitchen, came back

with a tall glass of tea. "Would you like sugar?"

Grandmother always sweetened the tea as she made it. He didn't know. "No, thank you." The food had no taste, but she ate, one mouthful after another.

He stood just a foot or so away. Gretchen could see him from the corner of her eye.

He cleared his throat. "Gretchen . . ."

She didn't answer, but she watched him without turning her head. He looked tired and sad and his eyes had a faraway gaze as if he was looking at something she couldn't see.

"Gretchen, the war has changed everything. It used to be we had time to get to know people. But now, first thing you know, people are here or there and we can't count on tomorrow coming." He spoke quietly.

Gretchen put down her fork, twisted to face him.

"I just want you to know that I think your mother is . . ." His eyes were soft. "Well . . ." It was almost a laugh. "I don't have to tell you how special your mother is."

"Sam?" High heels clattered on the wooden floor. Lorraine burst into the dining room. "Oh, baby, did Sam take care of you? I knew he would." She looked around. "Is Barb here?"

"Not yet." Sam took off the apron, folded it. "She's coming in a little while."

"Oh." Lorraine sighed. "I wish we could stay." She took a deep breath. "But we can't."

Gretchen pushed back her plate, the drumstick half eaten, the potatoes and peas untouched.

Lorraine came close. Her hand touched stiff shoulders. "I love you, baby."

Gretchen managed a whisper. "Love you, too."

Lorraine lifted her hand. Her fingers smoothed a dark curl at the side of Gretchen's face.

Gretchen looked up.

Lorraine's smile was tremulous. "You're going to do all right, honey. Today. Tomorrow. Whatever happens, you can handle it. Even something as awful as Faye and Clyde. Gretchen, as dreadful as it is — Clyde killing himself — it may be better for Barb this way . . ."

Gretchen pushed away the memory of Clyde Tatum slumped over the table.

". . . because even though it's terrible for her that Clyde killed Faye and then himself, it would have been worse if they arrested him and Barb had to hear the dreadful things they would have said in court. Clyde would have been convicted and gone to prison — or worse, they might have sent him to the electric chair. The chief said Clyde left a note?"

Gretchen nodded.

"You know, I've been thinking and thinking." Lorraine clasped her hands together, almost like saying a prayer. "Clyde loved Faye. I know that. Now, that may sound strange since he killed her. But I don't think he ever in a million years meant to hurt her. He cared too much and he was angry and hurt. That's why he ran away. He couldn't live with what he'd done. He never even thought of trying to brazen it out, pretend he was innocent . . ."

Gretchen wanted to say that he had told Grandmother, sworn to her, that he didn't kill Faye. Gretchen heard him. But she couldn't tell her mother. Or anyone. And neither could Grandmother.

". . . and he hid out and then he knew what he'd done and he knew what it would do to Barb if they caught him. I think he thought it all out. And maybe he couldn't go on living without Faye. But it's better for Barb though she may never be able to think that's true. Poor Barb, poor Barb." Lorraine bent down, pressed her cheek against the top of Gretchen's head. And then she moved away.

The loss of her touch was like a cold draft

when the door opened in the winter. Gretchen pushed up from the table, followed them to the front door. Lorraine looked very pretty, once again in her polka-dot blouse with the soft tie and her short pink pleated skirt that swirled when she walked. Her high heels wobbled on the graveled drive. Her hair, still damp from the swim, was brushed in a mass of ringlets, shiny as polished wood. The saucer-style hat pitched forward, gay as a sailboat on the lake, the feather rippling like a sail in the wind. Her makeup was perfect, her eyebrows arched thin and dark.

Sam held open the car door, touched her arm as he helped her in, a lingering, gentle, holding-on kind of touch.

Her mother leaned out of the open window, waving. "Take care of Mother. Good-bye, honey, good-bye."

Sam got behind the wheel. The motor coughed, rumbled.

Gretchen stood on the front steps and watched the blue Buick back into Archer Street, head for downtown. She waved until the car reached the end of the block, turned, and was gone.

Gretchen put the cup with hot tea on the bedside table. Grandmother lay unmoving in the big double bed, her head turned toward the door, her golden braids resting on the pillow. She slept, one hand tucked beneath her chin. Her face, moist with perspiration, looked old and heavy, pale and worn.

Gretchen tiptoed out of the room. Did Grandmother sleep because she was sick? Or was sleep a way to escape the morning's sad news? Whichever, the rest would be good for her. Gretchen eased the bedroom door closed.

She wandered into the living room, pausing to straighten a crocheted arm cover on the sofa. Despite the fan, the room was heavy with heat. And so quiet. It didn't seem real that her mother had been there for awhile. Her mother and Sam Hoyt.

Gretchen sank onto the sofa. She almost turned on the radio. But the sound might wake Grandmother. She fingered the lace arm cover. The grandfather clock chimed twice. A car turned into the drive.

Gretchen went to the front door. Heat poured down from the sun like syrup spreading over pancakes, thick and heavy. She shaded her eyes.

The motor sputtered as Chief Fraser's old green Packard rocked to a stop. He opened the door, got out, then ducked his head to

reach inside for his hat and a manila envelope. As he walked across the yard, dust
scuffing beneath his cowboy boots, he
craned his head. "Miss Barb here?"

Gretchen held open the door. "She's
coming. She said she would."

In the living room, he settled in the biggest chair, planted his boots on the floor,
placed his hat and the envelope on a side
table, next to the lamp.

"Would you like some iced tea, Chief?"
Gretchen spoke softly.

"Sure would." Chief Fraser looked
around. "Nobody here?"

"Grandmother's resting. She doesn't feel
very well. And Mother had to leave." But
she didn't have to go.

He rubbed at his tired red face. "Hope
your grandma's all right."

"It's probably the hot weather." Gretchen
forced a smile. "I'll get —"

The screen door opened. Barb had
changed from the halter and shorts. Her
white blouse was crisp and ironed and she
wore a peasant skirt with a scalloped hem
and green embroidery, and sandals with
thick crepe soles, but her hair still looked
unkempt and her face was the dull white of a
soft winter snow.

She stood just inside the door. "My

dad . . ." One hand plucked at the trim on a big patch pocket.

The chief pushed up from the chair, moved heavily across the room. He stood, looking down at Barb, his big head poked forward, his chin almost to his chest, like an oversize, too ripe tomato sagging against the vine. His massive shoulders slumped. "Barb, your daddy shot himself sometime last night. At the Purdy cabin. Looks like he'd been staying there since the night your mama died. We traced the gun. It's his. One bullet gone. His fingerprints on the stock. He left a note." The words came steadily like a bugler hitting one note. Then he heaved a sigh, turned away. He walked to the end table, picked up the manila envelope, faced Barb. The chief stared down at the envelope, his lips pressed tight.

"A note to me?" Barb's voice was dry and stiff like a burned-up stalk of corn in a neglected garden.

Chief Fraser lifted his big head. He looked like an old bulldog, massive forehead, bulging cheeks, sagging pouches beneath rheumy eyes set in deep sockets. "This here's evidence, I guess. That's what the county attorney said. He told me I didn't ought to take it with me. I should put it at the courthouse in some vault. But I told him we didn't have a murder investigation any longer. All we got is heartbreak, a man who couldn't bear it when his wife cheated on him —"

"Mama never did!" Barb's cry was high and shrill.

The chief held up a callused hand. "Hear me out, Miss Barb. It don't help now to say it was any way other than what happened. Your mama was lonely. Lots of people are lonely now, their menfolks gone. People do the best they can. Your mama did her best, but I want you to understand that your daddy did his best, too. In my heart I know nobody grieved for your mama more than Clyde. That's why he wrote this note." The chief rattled the envelope. "He wanted everybody to know and he 'specially wanted you to know." A gnarled finger poked open the envelope. He slowly pulled out an irregular piece of heavy brown paper.

Gretchen recognized the paper, torn from a grocery sack just like the pieces she'd seen on the table in the cabin. Would the chief say anything about those other pieces? Gretchen wished she'd taken the time to look at those pieces of paper. Probably they contained the list of people Clyde hoped could tell him the name of the man who came in the darkness to his house to see

Faye. But the chief would no longer search for that visitor. Faye's late-night visitor was safe.

A trembling hand outstretched, Barb slowly walked toward the chief, took the scrap of paper from him. She held it in both hands. She looked down. Her lips moved soundlessly. "Oh, God . . ." The cry came from deep within Barb. Her head jerked up, she stared wildly from the chief to Gretchen and began to shake, her entire body rippling like a flag in a high wind. "Oh, Daddy . . . Daddy." She gasped for breath then swung around and ran blindly across the room, bumping into the door, yanking it open, plunging out into the hot afternoon.

The chief took a step toward the door, then stopped. "Guess she's got to face it her own way." He pulled a handkerchief from his hip pocket, wiped his face. "But she had a right to see that note." His cheeks puffed out. "I don't care what anybody says. There's no case to build, no matter how much Donny Durwood complains. It's all finished and done with. Durwood be damned. Barb can keep that scrap of paper. It's all she's got left from her daddy, hard as it is, little as it is."

Gretchen hurried to the door, looked out. The graveled street lay quiet and empty. To be out of sight so quickly, Barb must have run all the way home, flung herself inside the Tatum house. If Buddy was there, he would hold her tight, make it better. Or no, not better. It would never be better. . . .

". . . have to see to things."

Gretchen turned. "What did you say?"

"I was wondering if you know what family might be left. I don't feel like I can leave it this way." He folded his handkerchief, stuck it back in his pocket. "I mean, Miss Barb's just a girl. Somebody's got to take charge, decide on the funeral. All of that. Well, I'll call around. Thanks, Miss Gretchen."

It wasn't until the green Packard had pulled into the street that Gretchen realized she'd never asked Chief Fraser what the note said.

There wasn't a parking place on all of Main Street. Everybody came to town on Saturday, to shop or see a movie or eat at Victory Café. Gretchen knew she should go to the café, help Cousin Hilda. Gretchen ducked her head and pedaled faster, turned the corner and swung into the alley. She propped her bike next to the trash cans.

Despite the steady whirr of overhead fans, the backshop sweltered. Gretchen shouted hello over the clatter of the Linotypes. It was almost time for the press run. Soon the Sunday papers would be stacked, ready for the paperboys to deliver in the morning.

Gretchen pushed through the door to the newsroom. Mrs. Taylor's desk was immaculate; a dark hood covered her typewriter. She always turned her weekend copy in early and never came to the office on Saturdays. Ralph Cooley leaned back in his chair, crossed feet up on his desk. His hat was tilted to the back of his head. Smoke drifted lazily from the cigarette dangling from a corner of his mouth. Mr. Dennis, pencil gripped in his fingers, hunched over yellow copy paper. His pipe smouldered in a big brass ashtray.

The reporter took a final drag, stubbed out his cigarette, slouched to his feet. "Look who's here! Maybe Gretchen knows." He ambled toward her, fingers tucked behind red suspenders. "You'd think I was trying to interview Charles de Gaulle." His raspy voice curled in disgust. "I mean, what's the big deal? Fraser better watch himself or he's going to come a cropper."

Gretchen kept her face blank, but she couldn't forget how tired Chief Fraser looked when he got out of the car at her house. She didn't answer Ralph. She turned away from him, walked toward Mr. Dennis's desk.

The editor tapped the sheets of yellow copy paper. "We got the story, Gretchen. Thanks to you."

Ralph sauntered after her, stood on the opposite side of the editor's desk. "Not all the story." He lit another cigarette, smothered a cough. "According to Durwood, the chief took the prime piece of evidence with him, like he'd picked some cherries at the side of the road. Sergeant Petty admitted the chief was going to Gretchen's house this afternoon, then she clammed up. What I want to know is this — where's the note Clyde Tatum wrote? I want to see it. How do we know he wrote it?"

"He wrote it." Gretchen laced her fingers together. "The chief gave it to Barb." Gretchen swallowed. "Barb cried."

Ralph rocked back on his heels. "Oh. She recognized his handwriting." He heaved a dissatisfied sigh. "I guess that wraps it up. The show's over."

"I told you to drop it, Ralph." Mr. Dennis's voice was sharp. "Chief Fraser's no fool. And the sheriff told us what Clyde's note said."

Gretchen stepped past the reporter, looked at the editor. "What did the note say?"

Mr. Dennis picked up his pipe, poked at the embers. "Not a lot, Gretchen. Enough."

His face wrinkled and he said carefully, repeating what he'd heard, " 'I didn't mean to kill Faye. Tell Barbie I love her —' "

Tell Barbie I love her —

Gretchen felt the sting of tears. No wonder Barb cried and ran away.

The sweet refrain of "Do, Lord" hung in the evening sky like the settling cry of birds. Youthful voices rose in the dusk, competing with the twilight rasp of the cicadas. They sat on folding chairs on a grassy lawn beside the church, holding hands, the circle unbroken. The girls all wore pretty summer dresses, the pinks and yellows and creams indistinct in the deepening evening. Gretchen tried to ignore the flat sound of Tommy Krueger's voice. He was always off key. She'd taken her accustomed place in the circle — it was funny how everyone always sat in the same chair — but she felt as if she were all alone. It was as if she were invisible. The girls spoke past her or over her or around her. Yet it was so much the same, the girls taking eager sidelong glances at the boys — Tommy and Joe and Carl and Hal — and laughing in that special self-conscious way girls do when they want boys to notice them. Gretchen had always been a part of this group and now, though she still sat among them, she was not.

She wondered if this was how gawky Al and shy Melissa and dull Howard felt at the Sunday evening youth group. And there were the others her friends casually ignored, Judith and Roger and Harry.

As the last refrain sounded, the youth director said, "Let's close with a prayer." Everyone stood, still holding hands. The director, Mr. Haskell, had a drowsy voice that rose and fell like little waves lapping at the edge of the lake. He prayed for them and their parents and for brave servicemen and -women around the world, fighting to keep them free and —

". . . please hold in your hearts a special prayer for Barbara Tatum and her parents, Faye and Clyde . . ."

Wilma's hand jerked in Gretchen's. All around the circle, there was movement. It was as though someone had poked them with a sharp stick.

". . . and help all of us to support Barbara in her hour of need. Thank you, God, for hearing our prayer. Amen." Mr. Haskell wiped his perspiring face. "Good night, everyone, good night."

Gretchen hung behind, watched her friends leave. They were on their way to the town square. Tonight a barbershop quartet was going to perform at the gazebo.

At the edge of the field, Cynthia Reeves looked back. She lagged behind the others for a moment, her eyes locked with Gretchen's. Then she looked away, turned, and hurried to catch up.

Gretchen felt hot and cold as she walked home. It was still close to a hundred even though it was dark now, the far-apart street lamps spots of gold against the night sky. But deep inside, she was cold. She didn't have any friends. Not now. Not since she'd written the story about Faye Tatum. Would people — would Wilma and her dad and Tommy and the others — forget as time went on? Maybe. But Gretchen knew she'd never forget. Of course, if she stopped working at the *Gazette*, told them she'd only written the story because Mr. Dennis asked her to, they might be her friends again.

"I'd rather die." Gretchen said it aloud. She wouldn't quit. She would write the best stories she could write. No matter what. Deeper than the sense of loss and loneliness was pride. Her story was good. Mr. Dennis sent it out on the wire. In other cities, places she would never be, people she would never know had read that story and for a moment they pictured Faye Tatum and she became a part of them. Faye lived and breathed and moved in other minds because of Gretchen.

She reached Archer Street. Her street. The street she'd grown up on, every inch of it familiar. Always before, she'd felt a quiet serenity when she reached Archer Street. But now . . . She stopped to stare at the Tatum house. Gretchen knew the house was empty. Not a glimmer of light shone. In the silver of the moonlight, the house looked shrunken, drawn in upon itself, like a body with the soul departed. No wonder Barb wasn't there tonight. How could she bear ever to return?

The Crane house was dark, too, but it wore the darkness like a well-dressed woman with a soft shawl, proud and confident.

Light spilled from the living room of her house. Gretchen walked slowly toward the steps. Would Grandmother notice she was home early? She paused just inside the door, heard Grandmother's voice.

". . . oh, so happy I am for you. If only Gretchen were here . . ."

Gretchen ran across the living room.

Grandmother stood by the telephone. Her blue eyes, softened by tears, widened as Gretchen burst into the kitchen. Her lips curved in a happy smile. "Lorraine, Lorraine, here she is. Our Gretchen has come home just in time to speak with you.

Oh, it is a gift from God that we have." And she held out the receiver.

Gretchen scarcely took in the words, her mother's voice almost lost in the crackle of the line and the roar of sounds behind her, voices and whistles and the rumble of train wheels. ". . . don't have much time . . . off the train at Albuquerque . . . on our way to California . . . Sam and I . . ." His leave was up . . . Oh, Gretchen, we got married last night. . . ."

Gretchen gripped the receiver with all her strength, holding on. "Married?" Her lips felt stiff.

"Oh, baby, I love him so. And I love you. I'll call when we get there. . . . Baby, I've got to go. . . ."

Gretchen stared at the shifting pattern on the wall, the moonlight shining through the wind-stirred branches of the elm tree. The tangled streaks of darkness kept changing. Even if the wind stopped, the moon would rise higher in the sky and the lines of darkness would thicken, thin, curve, merge, change.

California . . . She'd seen movies and read lots of movie magazines. Black-and-white images rose in her mind. Palm trees, tall and slender. Orange groves. Hollywood. Movie stars' footprints in cement. The ocean.

Against these sterile images was the sharp, bright picture of her mother and Sam Hoyt in the amber light beneath the float, their bodies melding together.

Gretchen lifted the edge of the sheet to wipe away her tears.

The feather — maybe from a peacock, it was so long and blue — on Mrs. Taylor's hat swooped perilously near Mr. Dennis's pipe as the society editor made a sweeping bow. "Your Highness," she proclaimed, slapping copy paper on his desk, "as a lowly serf with no rights or privileges, indeed as an abject figure accustomed to remaining mute in the face of slurs and slanders, I present myself as a sacrifice to the good name of the *Gazette*."

Mr. Dennis rescued his pipe. "So what's the problem, Jewell?" His gaze was wary.

The diminutive society editor perched on the edge of Mr. Dennis's desk, the upright feather quivering slightly in the downdraft from the overhead fan. "Actually, I did not remain mute. During the coffee hour at church yesterday, I talked until I was blue" — she patted pink cheeks — "in the face, so to speak. I proclaimed" — her voice rose and fell in a lilting falsetto — "I insisted loudly, I swore on the memory of my departed father, God rest his soul, the old blackguard, that the *Gazette* does not condone unfaithfulness on the part of wives . . ."

Gretchen rose from her desk, walked slowly toward Mr. Dennis and Mrs. Taylor.

Ralph Cooley clapped his hands together. "Everybody in favor of adultery, get in line for your scarlet letter."

Mrs. Taylor glanced at Gretchen then quickly away. ". . . that the *Gazette* upholds the sanctity of the family, that the *Gazette*—"

Mr. Dennis held up his hand. "I got it, Jewell. Did anybody listen to you?"

The society editor slowly shook her head, the feather dipping. She reached out, took Gretchen's hand. "Gretchen, it was a wonderful story. I told them that, too. So I may be joining you in purdah." She loosed her hold, pushed up from the desk. "Back to the trenches."

Gretchen remained by the editor's desk.

Mr. Dennis looked up at her, his eyes questioning, his face sober. "You getting a lot of flak?"

She had to tell him the truth. "Some."

He was silent for a moment. He pulled the tobacco canister near, carefully began to fill the bowl of his pipe. "Are you sorry you wrote about Faye?" There was no inflection in his voice.

"No." Her story. Out on the wire.

He squinted at her and slowly smiled. "You'll be all right."

On the way back to her typewriter, Gretchen stopped by the society editor's desk. "Thank you, Mrs. Taylor."

Mrs. Taylor had a Dresden china pretty face, but her eyes were sharp and bright. She wrinkled her nose. "Don't let the bastards get you down, kid. Not now. Not ever."

Gretchen sat in her hard chair, smoothed her fingers across the typewriter keys. She lifted her hands, and began to write about Billy Forrester who wanted to be a vet. She was almost finished when Mrs. Taylor slapped down her phone, flung out her hands, and exclaimed, "Marry in haste. Repent at leisure."

Ralph Cooley rested his elbows on his typewriter. "Sounds like soc's getting racy!"

Gretchen frowned. Marry in haste — that's what her mother had done. She'd run away to California with a man she'd only known for a week. She was on a train somewhere far away. It had been hard enough when she lived in Tulsa, sharing the apartment with other war workers, but now Gretchen didn't even know where her mother was. It was like her mother had disappeared.

". . . Rodney just disappeared without a

word and then she got a call." Mrs. Taylor picked up her notebook and pushed back her chair. "Walt, I don't know how to handle this." She paced to the editor's desk. "Jane Wilson's a fine woman and I'll tell you she was crying so hard I could barely understand her, but she wants the wedding story to be in the paper. But what will people think — Barb's parents dead — and the awful way they died — and then her running off and marrying Rodney Wilson . . . Do you think I should just write it the way I would any wedding story? I guess it would be Barbara Kay Tatum, daughter of the late — oh, I don't know how . . ."

Gretchen pulled the last sheet of paper from her typewriter, wrote -30-. So Barb had married her soldier.

". . . a justice of the peace. And certainly anyone would take Barb Tatum for a woman . . ."

Gretchen put her story in the incoming copy tray.

Mr. Dennis puffed on his pipe. "Go home, Gretchen. You deserve some time off." His telephone shrilled. He reached out, scooped up the receiver. "*Gazette*."

". . . and who won't marry a soldier these days?" Mrs. Taylor's feather quivered as she typed fast. "On their way to California . . ."

Gretchen was turning away when she saw the editor wince. He looked at her and there was all the sadness in the world in his eyes. "Heart attack? She's gone?"

Gretchen felt frozen. Her mouth curved into a soundless O. She wanted to cry or run, twist and turn, cover her ears, somehow escape the words that she knew were coming. Instead, she stood still, so still.

Mr. Dennis pushed up from his chair. He reached out, took her arm. "Gretchen, your grandmother . . ."

Her dark dress was hot. The straw hat chafed her forehead. Sweat slid down her back and legs. Her hands clenched and the gloves felt tight against her fingers. Beside her, Cousin Hilda sobbed. Cousin Ernst stood with his gray head bowed, heavy face solemn, hat clasped in his hands.

"Unto God's gracious mercy and protection we commit you. The Lord bless you and keep you. The Lord make his face to shine upon you, and be gracious unto you. The Lord lift up his countenance upon you, and give you peace, both now and evermore. Amen."

As the mourners walked slowly toward the cars that lined the gravel road, Gretchen shook free of Cousin Hilda. She twisted for one last stricken look at the casket with its blanket of white flowers and the gaping grave site. Grandmother . . .

The cars filled Archer Street and their drive and the lawn. Gretchen and Cousin Hilda and Cousin Ernst stood by the dining room table greeting Grandmother's friends. Gretchen shook hands and endured embraces and all the while she braced herself for what she knew would come.

There were only a few members of Grandmother's Sunday school class still working in the kitchen, pots clanging, water swishing, the hot water kettle keening, when Cousin Hilda brushed back a dank gray curl that had slipped loose from her tight bun. "Have you packed, Gretchen?"

Gretchen straightened the lace cloth on the walnut end table by Grandmother's chair. She'd never sit there again. Never, never . . . "I can't come out to the farm yet, Cousin Hilda. I have to stay here until Mother calls."

Cousin Hilda pressed her fingers against her temples. "Oh. Oh, yes. But if she didn't get an answer . . ." She trailed off, sighed. "Don't you have any idea where they are? Or how to get in touch with them?" Her lips thinned into a harsh line. Resentment boiled over. "I'll have to say, your mother certainly has acted irresponsibly, going off into the blue. I don't believe Lotte ever mentioned this man that Lorraine's married. The family doesn't know a thing about him."

"His leave was up." Gretchen glared at Cousin Hilda. "That's why they got married now. It's the war. She's gone to California with him. Sam's stationed there. She'll call soon. I know she will. Anyway, I've got to stay here. She doesn't know about Grandmother. I have to stay." And she wasn't going to go and live on the farm with Cousin Hilda and her taciturn husband, Ernst. Not now. Not ever.

Cousin Hilda patted her crumpled handkerchief against her face. Usually decisive and brusque, she simply shook her head back and forth. "Lorraine has to know. But I don't feel good about leaving you alone."

"I'll be all right." Abruptly, Gretchen reached out, gripped thin, muscular arms. "Thank you, Cousin Hilda."

The older woman's face crumpled. She stifled a sob with her handkerchief, whirled, walked toward the door.

Gretchen sagged against the cushions of the sofa. She'd slipped off her sandals, punched a cushion behind her head. There was no one now to tell her not to put her shoes on the sofa. Still, she remembered. Tired, so tired . . . The past few days she'd worked all day at the *Gazette*, gone to Victory Café early and late. Cousin Hilda had taken over the kitchen. Mrs. Perkins was threatening to quit. There was a For Sale sign in the corner of the plate glass window. Cousin Hilda said Mr. Whitby had been in to see her, explained that Cousin Hilda needed to get a power of attorney from Gretchen's mother and he'd talked about selling Grandmother's house or maybe renting it for the duration.

Gretchen fished an ice cube from her tea glass, crunched. She picked out another cube, wiped it on her face. She was so hot. Maybe she'd sleep outside tonight, set up a cot . . . No. She had to stay inside, where she'd hear the telephone.

Barb had slept on a cot in the woods, waiting for her father to come home. He hadn't come. Gretchen had known where he was. If she'd told Barb . . . what good would that have done? Nothing had done any good. She felt a bitter surge of anger at Clyde Tatum. If he hadn't hidden, if he'd given himself up as he should have, Grandmother might still be alive. Her heart had suffered from the strain of moving through darkness on the rough trail to the cabin and her heart had failed because she blamed herself for helping him hide, making it possible for him to shoot himself.

Gretchen pushed up, sat stiff and straight on the sofa. She stared at the rocking chair. "Grandmother" — her voice was harsh — "it was his fault. Not yours." She buried her face in her hands. She should have helped Grandmother. . . .

The phone rang.

For an instant, she didn't hear as demons flailed her mind, blame and fault and misery poking and tearing and rending.

Ring.

Gretchen's head jerked up. She bolted across the living room to the kitchen, grabbed the receiver. "Hello."

The operator's voice was high and thin. "I have a collect call from —"

"I accept. Mother? Oh, Mother, Grandmother . . ." She choked with sobs.

"Gretchen, oh, God, honey, tell me." Her mother's voice faded in and out.

". . . and the funeral was yesterday and Cousin Hilda wants me to come to the farm —"

"Oh, no. You'll come here. To me and Sam." Lorraine's voice was firm. "We're bunking with some of Sam's friends. Everybody's looking for a place to live. But it doesn't matter, baby, we'll manage if we have to sleep on the beach."

The thunderous clatter of steel on steel, a hiss of steam, an acrid smell of burning fuel, and the train roared into the station.

Cousin Hilda thrust a sack at Gretchen. "There's fried chicken and potato chips and a piece of pie. Then you can eat on the diner. . . ."

Gretchen gripped the sack, lifted her cosmetic case. Her heart thudded. She started toward the steps to the car. People jostled her, women with children, soldiers, sailors. California, California . . . She was almost to the steps. A porter with grizzled hair helped the elderly woman in front of Gretchen. "All aboard. All aboard."

"Gretchen, Gretchen!" The brusque bark sounded to her left.

A suitcase banged into her hip. "Hurry, kid."

Gretchen slipped to one side, passengers streaming past, tall, thin, short, fat, everyone in a hurry. She looked up at Mr. Dennis, his face flushed from exertion. He thrust an envelope toward her. "Almost didn't make it . . . just found out . . ." He paused, panting. ". . . old friend on the *Long Beach Press-*

Telegram . . . 604 Pine Avenue . . . take this to him . . ."

She grabbed the envelope and was caught up in the flow of travelers. She looked back from the vestibule and caught one last glimpse of Mr. Dennis, hat tilted to the back of his head, resting on the fringe of gray curls. His round face was creased like a bloodhound's. He looked envious, sad, admiring. His lips parted, but there was too much noise to hear. The train whistle shrieked. She stepped into the car. Clutching the envelope, she found a seat.

As the train pulled out of the station, Gretchen put her sack in the webbed pocket on the seat back in front of her, propped her feet on her overnight case. A child cried behind her. Beside her a sailor shuffled cards, began to lay out solitaire on the lowered tray. Cigarette smoke made a bluish haze the length of the car. The iron wheels clacked beneath her.

On the envelope, Mr. Dennis had scrawled in thick black pencil: *Harry.* The envelope wasn't sealed. She tipped out folded sheets. On three pages were the clips of her story on Faye Tatum. The cover letter read:

Harry — Read this. Hire her. Walt

. . . Do you know how many times I wanted to tell the truth? A thousand times a thousand. I never could. You see, there was Rod. You probably don't know about him. No reason you should. I'm so proud. He's a great artist. I don't say it because I'm his mother. Everybody in the Southwest knows him. He has a mural in the Gilcrease Museum and the Getty out in California commissioned him to do an acrylic painting and it's famous. Rod called it Left Behind *and it's a railroad track on the prairie. Buddy's folks raised Rod. They hardly ever let me see him. I understand why. I guess I felt so bad about everything, I never fought them. They're both gone now. I couldn't have said anything while they were alive. Or while Rod was alive. . . .*

Chapter

10

I turned away from Grandmother's grave. My last memory was of her flower-covered casket next to the open grave. I still felt that quick flare of anger, though now, old myself, I wondered whether I should blame Clyde Tatum for her death. Hearts can only pump for so long. The day comes when life must end. I knew that Grandmother had entered the gates of larger life with joy and in peace, more so perhaps than anyone I'd ever known.

A faraway peal of church bells marked the noon hour. I'd driven about the town when I arrived that morning. So much was the same and so little. The *Gazette* offices were gone. Even had they stood, I would not have entered. A tattered present can diminish a treasured past. I would remember always, for so long as I lived and breathed, the creak of the ceiling fans, the smell of ink and cigarette smoke and hot lead, Mr. Dennis's wrinkled, tired, hopeful face. The churches, the Methodist, the Baptist, the Church of Christ, the Catholic, were all on State Street. They'd added on to the Baptist Church but I could see where the old melded into the new. The same buildings still stood on Main Street, though there were no familiar names and some of the storefronts were boarded up. The Victory Café was an insurance agency. The movie marquees still jutted over the sidewalks, but the Bijou was a beauty shop, the Ritz an antique store. I'd been shocked at how small the courthouse seemed. Long ago I thought the building huge and I remembered running up the steps that hot June day, filled with excitement and energy. I was a reporter. . . .

The gazebo, which also seemed much smaller and rather shabby now, still stood on the slope of lawn to the south. The war memorials were new to me, World War II, Korea, Vietnam, lines of names carved in granite. I didn't remember the rosebushes on either side of the front steps. But I would never forget the antiseptic smell downstairs in the sheriff's office with the jail cells stretched behind. I knew my memories were erratic, perhaps not to be trusted. I remembered in patches and pieces, some bits of it clear and hard and bright as etched crystal, some murky and dim and impenetrable as lake water.

The letter — I reached in my pocket, touched the envelope — the letter from home had brought so many memories, bright, dark, happy, sad, sharp, blurred. I had not been able to resist the plea in the final paragraph:

I can tell the truth now. Will you come, Gretchen?

Barb

I pulled down the rim of my glove, looked at my watch. Almost time. I walked across the leaves, my cane poking the winter-hard ground.

Old oaks and elms and cottonwoods stood like sentinels among the graves. The cemetery flowed uphill and down. The Tatum graves were off to my left, not far from Grandmother's grave. I passed by with only a glance. My goal was over the hill, a family plot I'd never visited. I'd received clear directions when we spoke on the phone, both of us a little shocked at the difference in our voices after so many years.

I saw her when I reached the top of the hill. There was a hollow here, a little valley of graves, nestled between two low hills. She waited for me near the new grave, the one still heaped with flowers. The wind had picked up, that old familiar Oklahoma wind, rattling tree limbs, sending leaves and twigs twirling in a chill dance, jouncing the limbs of the cedar behind her. I turned up the collar of my coat. I was hatless, of course, and the wind tugged at my hair. I'd worn a straw hat to Grandmother's funeral. I walked down the slope.

When we faced each other, the mound of flowers between us, we were silent for a moment. Her face held remnants of beauty, despite the puffy pouches beneath her blue eyes, the crinkled skin that told of illness as well as age, the sagging mouth that revealed more clearly than words the loss of hope and joy. Her cloth coat, a rough tweed, was black speckled with gray. The hem dangled loose in front. Her black shoes, blunt and stubby, were fashionable but cheap.

Would I have recognized Barb Tatum? No. Never. Not the Barb who had enthralled our little world, moved with grace, face vibrant, eyes eager.

Barb took a deep breath, clasped her hands together. She had no gloves. Her hands were arthritic, the joints red and swollen. "You look good, Gretchen. Distinguished."

The words were at such a variance from my appraisal of her that I couldn't answer.

She gave a half laugh, half sigh. "Can't say the same about me, huh?"

I recognized the lilt of Southern California in her words.

I glanced down at the topmost funeral spray, jonquils, their bright yellow blossoms already faded. "I'm sorry, Barb."

"We have to stop meeting like this." Her tone was brittle. "Always standing beside a new grave." Her worn face crumpled. She stifled a sob behind a bunched, reddened hand.

I came around the end of the grave, pulling a Kleenex from my purse.

She took it, swiped at her eyes. "I know Rod's all right. He'd been so sick, Gretchen. Leukemia and they couldn't make it go away. He suffered so bad. He doesn't hurt now. I'm the one who hurts. Not Rod." She looked at me hopefully. "You being a reporter, I'll bet you checked him out after I wrote. He really is famous."

"Yes." Barb's son was famous indeed, known in the small, jealously restricted, snobbish art world for clean-lined acrylic paintings, for sculptures of jagged glass and twisted steel. I'd found a number of biographical sketches of Rodney James Wilson, Jr. There was a beginning, his birth in Long Beach, California, his death in Tulsa, Oklahoma. He'd grown up in our little town in northeastern Oklahoma, living with his grandparents, Buddy's mother and father. Always he'd drawn and painted and sculpted.

Barb leaned down, broke off a jonquil bloom, cradled the wilting blossom in her arms. "Rod asked me once about Mama and Daddy. I got up and left the room. I didn't want him to see my face. Later, there was a painting, a woman in black kneeling before two graves. She didn't have a face, just swirls of black and gray. He never asked again." Barb brushed loose a yellow petal. It floated lazily down to the leaf-strewn ground, a splash of color against the winter-dried leaves. "I expect Rod knows now. I expect Mama and Daddy were there to greet him along with Buddy and his folks." Her glance at me was sharp. "Do you think I'm silly?"

My voice was gentle. "Faith is never silly, Barb."

We looked at each other with sudden understanding, two old women in the autumn of their lives, knowing that those who believe can never explain to those who don't. Should golden radiance spill down over those who scoff, they would brush past, never see, arrogant, impervious, lost.

"Anyway" — Barb cleared her throat — "I know Rod's all right." She leaned forward, gently placed the flower on the tumbled mass of sprays. "Rod understands. My priest says everybody who dies has to forgive everyone who's hurt them." Her eyes glistened. "A lot of people had to forgive me, Gretchen. But that's not why I wrote you. See, the whole world thinks Daddy killed Mama and I got to tell the truth before I die. I'm the only one who knows. Oh, Gretchen, can I ever make you see?"

I had a sudden sharp sense of futility. Why

had I come? Why had I journeyed across the country, come to this sorrowful place? Barb was seeking an answer long lost in time. I clenched my hand on the knob of my cane. God knows I would help her if I could. But how could she or anyone else change the fact that Clyde Tatum killed his wife and shot himself?

She reached up, those painful fingers tugging at a thick flannel muffler as if it were hard to breathe. "You got to remember how awful it was, finding Mama dead, hearing that she and Daddy quarreled. I couldn't believe Daddy would hurt Mama like that, but finally, like everybody, I thought Daddy was guilty. What else could I think? He was a jealous man and he loved Mama. Maybe he loved her too much. When he heard that a man was coming to our house late at night, what else could he believe but that Mama was having an affair? That was the first awful blow, knowing that Daddy believed Mama was unfaithful. I couldn't sleep for grief. But the second was worse, when Chief Fraser gave me that note that Daddy wrote."

The note — Mr. Dennis had told us what Clyde wrote. I didn't remember the words now. It had been too many years.

"Then I knew." The eyes that moved to mine held an agony of pain.

I didn't say anything. What could I say that would help? But why did that note still hurt Barb so much?

"That's why I married Buddy. I had to get out of town. I was so scared. I wanted to tell Chief Fraser, but I knew he'd never believe me." Her voice was dull with hopelessness. "I couldn't prove a thing."

"Prove what?" I was impatient now. What was there to prove?

"Who killed Mama. And Daddy." She pulled her purse, the leather faded and worn, from under one arm, opened the clasp. She reached inside, carefully pulled out a plastic folder. She handed it to me.

I held it loosely in my gloved hands. The piece of paper — a scrap from a brown grocery sack — looked old and limp. I strained to read the faded scrawl:

I didn't mean to hurt Fay. Please tell Barbie I love her —

That was all. Two sentences, one unfinished, no signature.

I felt an icy prickle down my back. Chief Fraser saw this note, he took it from beneath the slumped body of Clyde Tatum. "Oh, God, Barb . . ." I breathed the words.

"You see. Oh, Gretchen, you see!" Triumph lifted her voice and she almost sounded young.

I willed my hands not to shake. It was as clear as though Clyde Tatum stood there beside us, ever young, his grieving face stubbly with beard, his uniform crumpled and dirty, his smooth muscular arms outstretched. *Fay* . . . Clyde would never have misspelled his wife's name, dropped the *e*. And Barbie . . . ? I'd played at her house so many times. His pet name for his daughter was Sugarbee, sometimes Sugar. Not Barbie. Never Barbie.

I smoothed a gloved finger over the plastic protecting the faded letters. "He wrote it."

She folded her arms tight across the bulky front of her old tweed coat. "He was telling us."

Clyde wrote those jerky letters because someone stood with a gun at his head. In his last, desperate seconds, trapped by the man who'd killed his wife, Clyde tried to tell those who would find his body, Chief Fraser and Sheriff Moore and County Attorney Durwood, that he wrote under duress, the gun stolen from his house held inches from his temple. Chief Fraser read right over the spelling of Faye's name. How many people in this world cannot spell, never notice when words are right or wrong? So many. So very many.

Barb shuddered. "He died thinking Mama made love with him. That's the worst part. That's what I can't forget. Or forgive. Daddy never knew it was me."

Her eyes met mine. It was as though I looked into her soul, weighted with the shackles of shame. "Yes. There was a man coming to our house. But Mama was gone dancing. He came for me, Gretchen, for me. I thought I was so sexy, that it was all so exciting, that he was so handsome. I never thought what could happen. Now it all seems stupid. Everybody screws around." Her voice was hard, bitter. "Grade school kids even. And Mama died and Daddy died because I was sleeping with Donny Durwood. Oh, God, what a waste."

I shook my head. "It would matter even now, Barb, a grown man sleeping with an underage girl. Especially a married man."

"Donny . . . I never saw him again. I wish I could stop hating him." Her tone was metallic, unyielding. "I doubt he meant to hurt Mama. She was yelling and he got scared. You know, I never thought of him. Not that night. Because Mama had pounded on my door. I locked it when she yelled for me to come out, that she knew what I'd been doing . . ."

Across the years, I remembered Mrs. Crane saying how she told Faye chapter and verse when she called from the Blue Light. . . .

". . . she was going to find out everything that had happened from me and that there was going to be hell to pay. I guess she called Donny from the Blue Light . . ."

Two calls that terrible night, not one.

". . . and he came over to try and talk her out of telling anyone. And when she yelled at him, he must have tried to make her be quiet. And he killed her. But Daddy — oh, God, he killed Daddy in cold blood."

"I saw him that Saturday." I understood now. Donny Durwood had been clever. Clever and desperate, guilty of murder, but seeing a way to safety, a terrible, agonizing way. Everyone thought Clyde Tatum was guilty. If Clyde committed suicide, leaving a note behind, Durwood was safe. The woman who helped Clyde reach the cabin had become frightened. Perhaps she decided Clyde was guilty, especially after the gun was stolen from the Tatum house. Did she go that sultry night to the town square, hear Donny Durwood's confident accusation? Whatever her motive, she tucked a note beneath the wiper of Donny Durwood's car. It was Durwood who slipped through the darkness of the woods, his scratched arms hidden beneath long sleeves, and awaited Clyde's return from another fruitless effort to find Faye's killer. After he killed Clyde, Durwood placed the note on the police cruiser. I remembered the sense of danger and evil in the darkness that hot summer night.

I spoke slowly. "That morning when they found your dad, Durwood looked sick." Sick and shaken, distraught, burdened forever. "Barb, there are killers and killers." I'd covered trials, seen murderers who were stupid or angry or scared or vicious. "Durwood had to care about justice. He would never have become a prosecuting attorney, not even for attention or political gain or power, unless he cared about right and wrong." What would it do to such a man to become as bad as the criminals he prosecuted?

"Donny drove his car into a tree a few years later." Barb's voice was cool. "Drunk." She lifted her chin. "I was glad. It made it better somehow that he was dead. That's when I could look at Rod and not see Donny."

"Rod?" I had printed out a good deal of material about the gifted artist. There was a studio portrait that hung in a gallery. A self-portrait. Blond hair, broad face, a hand-some man.

Barb's lips trembled. "I told you I was bad, didn't I? That everything was my fault? I had to get married. I was pregnant." Tears slid down her cheeks unchecked. "But maybe that was the only good I ever did. Having Rod. Letting Buddy's parents take him. They loved him, you know. Loved everything he did, everything he said. He was Buddy's boy and then when he became an artist, it was like they were farmyard chickens and there was a peacock among them. That's why I never could say anything. I couldn't do that to Rod. Or to Buddy's folks. But they're gone now. Whatever I say now can't hurt them. I guess I'm looking for peace, Gretchen. And I thought of you." Barb brushed back a tangle of dyed red hair. "I was afraid you wouldn't come. You didn't have to."

"No. I didn't have to come." There isn't much a woman my age has to do. It's easy to say no. But when the letter arrived, I'd just returned from a family holiday in Hawaii. We'd stayed on Kauai, splashed in the surf, played tennis, picnicked, run with the children across golden sand. My children and grandchildren came as my guests. I thrust my gloved hand into my coat pocket, felt the

letter and looked down at the spray of jonquils, their fading yellow blossoms a har-
binger of the spring yet to come. It was
simply a holiday, but a holiday made possible by my working years. I never forgot
how my career began. I still have the yel-
lowed clips of the story I wrote about Faye
Tatum, the story that I carried with me to
California and to the future.

". . . you're a writer. You could tell what
really happened. That Mama was faithful to
Daddy and that he never killed her, he never
did."

Yes. I was a writer. I could tell the story of
Faye and Clyde Tatum, and of their
daughter, Barb, and the little girl down the
street. . . .

-30-

About the Author

Carolyn Hart is the author of two bestselling mystery series — the Henrie O. mysteries and the Death on Demand series. She lives in Oklahoma City, Oklahoma.

The employees of Thorndike Press hope you have enjoyed this Large Print book. All our Thorndike and Wheeler Large Print titles are designed for easy reading, and all our books are made to last. Other Thorndike Press Large Print books are available at your library, through selected bookstores, or directly from us.

For information about titles, please call:

(800) 223-1244

or visit our Web site at:

www.gale.com/thorndike
www.gale.com/wheeler

To share your comments, please write:

Publisher
Thorndike Press
295 Kennedy Memorial Drive
Waterville, ME 04901

8/23/23: Water damage bottom
of book (binding side). WGRL-NL
SC